The
Merlinian
Legend

Merlyn Fuller

The Merlinian Legend written by

Merlyn Fuller.

© 2016 Merlyn Fuller

ISBN-13: 978-1519420664

ISBN-10: 1519420668

Table of Contents

Illustration Index

Anglesey

Cambrian Mountains

Bardsey Isle

Camelot

Demetae Dyfed

Carmarthen

Castell Coch

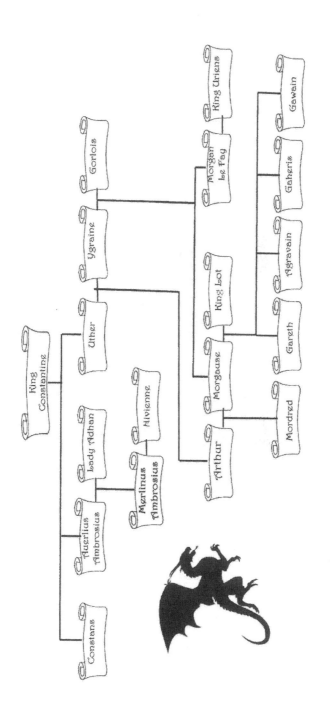

"I cannot list all the authorities I have followed. But I can hope, in all humility, that my Merlin trilogy may be, for some new enthusiast, a beginning."

Mary Stewart

"The Last Enchantment"

Introduction

The Blessed Bairn of Beltane

In days of old, when all things past had not since turned to dust nor had stories been turned into legend nor legend into whispered lore, there was a wee bairn son born to a noblewoman named Lady Adhan. She was both refined and knowledgeable and unfortunately for the babe's sake, not yet married.

Being a proud Lady, she would ne'er reveal the parentage of her fatherless son, although she loved and protected him and arranged for his tutoring in the ways of the magickal woods, much as her mother before her had given her similar lessons. The Sight had been given to her, and now, assuredly, to her baby as well. It has long been said that "A magician comes forth as such from his mother's womb," yet, it was a secret best kept to oneself...for now. The locals whispered that the new bastard was one of questionable parentage, mayhap, even sired by the Horned God, himself. The baby's conception happened thusly:

Lady Adhan, was daughter of Meurig ap Rhain, he who was King of the smaller kingdom of Dyved in Wales. She had fallen in love with a young man, who was also Prince Aurelius

Ambrosius. It was he, who was in line to rule High Britain, son of Emperor Constantine.

Yet tragedy had struck his lineage years earlier, when both King Constantine, and his first born son, Constans, had been assassinated. Constantine had a contingency plan in motion, should such things happen, what with the war against Vortigern waging nigh onto years long, and he had taken precautionary steps to vouchsafe his heirs apparent. Constantine had arranged for both his remaining sons, Ambrosius and his younger sibling, Uther, to be ushered away to safety. For years the boys were held in seclusion in the south of Wales. Constantine had ruled with a thoughtful hand and possessed a strong will. He had been a good leader in the days of darkness and the beginnings of the burgeoning new church of the crucified one called Jesus. This new religion was gaining ground and its leaders and its buildings spread inexorably across the land.

Yet, Constantine's reign after his death was besieged with avarice, which soon devolved into active malice. The young heirs to the throne had been hidden for their protection. The Regent ruled until it was to be deemed safe for Ambrosius to return as the first born son to be called forth to rule. He would take his destined seat upon the throne as the rightful heir and King.

How'ere, the Regent was caught in a treasonous plot and the Prince was called back a bit before his twenty-first birthday to make his warranted return. He was now come to take part in one of the new high Holy Day gatherings of the Apostolic Church and was to receive his blessing as Prince of All Britain. His coronation would be set later in the year when all was ready, including troops to support the event and nobility from other countries to come as honored guests.

This day of ceremony, how'ere, was at a time when many Lords and Ladies were also to receive blessings from the church leaders at this new holy day called Easter. All would be in attendance to greet the grown Prince. It was a grand occasion, indeed. There, in the vast hall, in the romantic glow of the stained glass flickering with torchlight, Aurelius Ambrosius glanced about and his eyes had met hers. Lady Adhan. She was a beauty. Her eyes sparkled and a warm smile danced shyly upon her lips. A strong feeling of destiny washed quickly over them both. It was one of those fleeting moments of truth. Her blue eyes shone true with heart's desire and his dark eyes smoldered with passion. Over the next few feasting days, through hidden missives *(carried by their devoted yet silent servants),* information of their total willingness to meet and a location had been arranged quickly between them. A tryst was set in motion.

Whilst they had met under the auspices of the au courant Church, they quickly realized that both were quiet followers of the Old Ways in their hearts. If they had to be ecumenical for society's sake, so be it… they would walk the path.

It was when she signed her first missive, "Blessed Be" and he sent a return of the same that they knew there was more to their story. They met one spring day in a pre-arranged meeting, on a bench in a quiet courtyard. They spoke of their conjoined spirituality as Druid clans of old have passed on their wise words to generations hence. It was if they had known each other for lifetimes.

E'en so, they determined they would also continue to worship in their traditional ways as best they could. These were unstable times. Best to be all inclusive and honor what feeds your spirit, and also that what keeps you alive by the fickle laws of men. For Druids believe that "All the Gods are but one God" and that "Spiritual power comes from living in a Sacred manner."

They also both knew that their love would not be an official priority sanctioned as her dowry from her father, a lesser ruler, who did not approve of Ambrosius as her suitor. He did not approve for no one was good enough for her in his eyes. She was a daughter of a King, aye, but without her father's approval, she would not be given permission, nor the dowry to afford him. Whilst she would've been Queen for all of High Britain, politics would arrange alliance with another country for him, and not have him marry merely for love. Marrying for love, it was felt, was a passing fancy and a trend that would not last. Alliance, how'ere, could save a nation.

Being young and confined to the rules of courtly love, they both were restrained by duty and station, yet burned with an inconsolable desire. They both wished their wishes and felt hard pressed to put it into action and soon. Whilst they could've gone the route of courtship and begun the mating dance and made compromises to make it so…this would take a lot of luck, politics, coinage, not to mention approval from so many more than their own hearts. How'ere, their love and lust burned too great to wait patiently for such things. They could not wait. They would not wait. It would take a year's length of dreary proprieties to be approved and granted.

For they knew what the Druid path knows, is that "When all choices are taken away, a perfect path remains." Destiny pushed the cart and lust churned the wheels. The only halting restraints upon this particular cart were the nods to propriety and family duty.

Ambrosius knew of a small secluded cave in the hills, a former solitary Druid's haunt which would surely serve well for a discreet meeting on the eve of upcoming Beltane. If ever there was a ritual that presented itself as a sanctioned time of tryst, this was it! It would be necessary for some quiet love time away from the court and all their damnable prying eyes…and ears.

This May Day's sanctioned opportunity for blanket indiscretion, would prove to be an apt rendezvous indeed. Granted, the whole world went Bedlamite at this time and so, it seemed, could they as well!

The new apostolic priests all turned a blind eye the other way, aye, for on this traditional day of madness and frolic the Old Ways still reigned supreme, and they knew it. At least for now.

One bishop said, "If it keeps the serfs happy and unawares of their financial yoke to the Pope and to his Holy Church, then by all means, do let them forget politics and let them enjoy their rutting frenzy." Another younger cleric looked out the window, sighed and said to himself, "Would that I could run amuck for one day…" He glanced wistfully outside whilst he was bid to close the latticed shutter away from the day's sunlight and nature's beauty.

On this particular evening before May Day, the entire village was abuzz like bees in honey, all in anticipation of the ancient custom. Dry brush faggots and tinder were being stacked and laid in bonfire pits, being hastily made ready for the fire rituals. Starry-eyed virgins, as well as oft-bedded women, donned garlands and made love charms of flowers and special herbs. Many a tuzzy-muzzy bouquet for the evening was made with herbs and flowers sure to persuade the Gods to bring a lover to their bed. It was a time of procreation for all nature. It was tradition that the stag-horned Green Man would rule for one night as the "Lord of the Woods" and the May Queen would meet and romp together in effigy as well as in the likely participants of the land. It was expected that many gentles would revel to all hours of this night and no one would be held accountable for what happened in the woods that night- would stay in the woods- as it were. It was a yearly sanctioned night of madness!

In kitchen cottage lore it is said that Parsley was "to remove bitterness and encourage easy digestion of new emotions." Sage was "for a lover that was healthy, strong and wise." Rosemary was "for love, fidelity and remembrance." And lastly, Thyme was "for the deep healing of any former sadness so as not to ruin nor taint a fresh new love." Some of the garlands contained: Dandelion for happiness and faithfulness, pink Hyacinths for playtime, and Lilies for the irresistibility of a Maiden's charms. Lavender was liberally woven into garments for a most magical and complete enchantment.

The women brushed their hair and entwined flowers midst their lovely braids, and made their amulets. These were heady potions which voiced their wish for their all-consuming need of love be fulfilled. Many a maiden and adventurous maven cooked and wove kitchen spells and made their brews to beguile and lay low virtuous, handsome men! Aye, he who would then succumb to the wiles of lust and *(mayhap)* the bond of matrimony. Women all dreamed of being crowned May Queen!

A favorite recipe to help their chances was handed down from mother to daughter; from aunt to niece was Love Potion Tea. It was best made on a Freya's Day, made still more potent when made and quaffed on a waxing moon. It was believed to make someone fall in love with those who ingested its delicious contents.

LOVE POTION TEA
1 pinch of rosemary
2 teaspoons tea leaves
3 pinches thyme
3 pinches nutmeg
3 fresh mint leaves
6 fresh rose petals
6 lemon leaves
3 cups blessed water
honey

Whilst drinking the tea, the lass would say thusly: *"By the light of this moonlight, I brew this tea to make me Irresistible to the man whom I desire. Goddess of Love, hear my plea, let him desire ME, so mote it be, so mote it be, so mote it be!"*

It was during this time, after meeting and dreaming of handsome Aurelius Ambrosius, that the noble Lady Adhan was no different than any scullery maid. She, too, did envision her own dreams of romance and designed her own magickal brews and garlands! She hid her secret concoctions from all and was set to meet Ambrosius as they had planned.

The young men of the shire *(aye, and, verily, those whose passions needed desperate release)* also prepared for the evening by cutting down greenery to bring the new summer indoors. They would fashion a May Pole for dancing by cutting down a small tree and decorating it with ribbons at the top for the entwining dance in the evening. Being a good dancer and a good singer and possibly getting "accidently" twisted in the ribbons was always a boon to secure a beautiful young bride…or at least a lovely sensual companion for the evening.

As dusk overtook the day, in a grove tangled with grapevines, revelers gathered. The Beltane fires were lit here and there around the country side. Men appeared like the Green Man himself, decorated with leaves and looking as though they had just rolled in a field of ivy. Some of the men sported horns and furs and danced freely, letting go of their work day and turning their thoughts to the winsome sport of wooing maidens. The smell of wood smoke, roasted meat and the sound of singing filled the spring air. Meade flowed freely this moonlit night.

Drummers and singers encircled the growing fires and burly men yelled and jumped the flames. Women floated through the woods in gossamer gowns of thin linen, with flower garlands in their hair. They embodied the ethereal siren beauty of the May Queen herself. They flirted with, and then scampered away from, men and boys, tantalizingly so. This would be the dance of the evening! Flirtation, enchantment and sensuality were the evening's delight! No longer were they the hausfrau, the farmer's daughter; no longer did the men think of themselves as the serf, the beggar nor the rich man. They just WERE. Alive and free! They were as wild and rampant as any other animal in the woods!

Couples would join hand in hand, then run off to rut in the wild wood, to slake their thirst, to throw off bonds of convention. This was the night of Joy and Abandon! It was luxurious, natural and uninhibited savagery. This was the one night when no questions were asked and, thankfully, no promises given. This was a night when those who had yearnings for another, could try out their urges with a feverish passion! This is the night that would result in a new growth for the community with the mid-winter births of many new bairn on Imbolc! A winter's laying in for many mothers was the best time, when all was quiet and the wee bairn could be nursed and kept warm. The earthen cycle was good for winter births as well as summertime frolic, and this was the beginning of the wheel. The cycle was as ancient as the Old Ways themselves and worked with the seasons and the four directions. It was right and good to do so.

The simple jingle of a horse's bridle and low whinny gave away the couple on this evening of Fate. The gibbous moon on Beltane was chosen for their perfect union. A day of beginnings and of sensuality. It would have to be thus, as they had both agreed. Her family would not purchase a Kingly dowry…neither could he, by law, marry beneath him to a lesser-stationed lady. But, aye…where there be a will…there be a way.

Ambrosius met Adhan at the appointed time. He easily dismounted his horse and walked over to her mount. To celebrate this evening's tradition he wore the horns of a goat. She smiled broadly when she saw him, and said, "M'lord o' the Wild Wood, I am blessed and honored by your presence."

He held the reins of her steed and whispered soothing sounds to the horse until it accepted his friendship. He then looked up to her with eyes full of promise, and she carefully slid down into his arms. Her body was warm and her hair and garland had the scent of peonies, lemon balm and sage. Ambrosius pulled Adhan to his heart and enveloped her with his cloak.

"As I am honored by your presence, my Queen, thou art my love, my dearest One," he murmured and nuzzled into her hair and pulled her close. God and Goddess met within their intense gaze of love and lust.

Strong and sincere, he circled his hands around her waist, to her, his body felt delicious and new to her under the bower. She had dressed early this day for travel and had slipped out before dawn's watchful eye beheld the village. This would be a day of no questions for any missing person, but she did not want to answer to any querant that came.

Lady Adhan raised her face up to him and met his warm lips and felt his breath upon her cheek. He smelled of the ride, leather mixed

21

with horse sweat, and freshly scythed sweet grass. His scent was familiar, as though she knew him of old. So new, and yet, a scent of mystery and hunger hung in the air liken unto a deep craving.

Ambrosius was a young man of striking qualities. His visage had been seared into her heart since first she saw him in the Great Hall on that day not so long ago. He was a tall, new man of twenty, dressed in leather jerkin and britches for riding. His dark, curly hair flowed far beyond his collar and his ebony beard was soft and fresh. He was in earnest when he whispered his desire for her, huskily into her ear. Her auburn hair fell around her waist and brushed his fingertips. A need of great longing flowed between them. They did not have much time.

A capable rider, he had arrived a day early having made his itinerary with a clever excuse of a week's retreat and solace with a Holy One to consider his royal future. He had come back into knowledge of his station only recently, having been kept in the dark for safety's sake all the years of his youth. Yet it was seen to, that he and his younger brother, Uther, had been offered all opportunities of learning that they needed to resume their royal stations when'ere fate called the tune.

Knowing full well what now his new life would be like, he was granted leave, one last carefree jaunt, knowing full well the time of year it was. It was made for just such frivolous pursuits, which would be rare in the near future for him, as the crown was surely coming to his placement. The new Prefect had conceded to let him go but only with his agreement to his precise return for the coronation and its important agenda. Ambrosius would need to follow what'ere desire he seemed so secretive about, and sow his wild hair 'ere he took the scepter in hand and crown upon his inexperienced brow. Whether it be wenches or blokes, gambling or drinking, it would be folly not to allow it and keep it pent up in a stallion such as this. His advisors were amused, smiled approvingly so, and let the future King go on his last impetuous quest.

This obscure cave was a boyhood treasure to Ambrosius and always had held good memories of adventure and freedom. This is why he chose it for her now…for *them* now. He was determined to have her as his bride, and he would try to convince her father of it. Dowry be damned, he wanted her… for his own.

He had laid the interior of the cave with victuals, swept it out with cedar branches and started a small fire. The old Druid who lived here long ago made it habitable once upon a time, and the spiritual man had even vented it for a winter hearth. The priest long ago was lain within the stones upon the hill. His well at the entrance remained as a testimony and a nod to Brigid. On this adventure, now, a separate pack horse had accompanied the Prince with a pallet of the best bedding, He had arranged for a fine, soft bed for their secluded courting, and it was meant as their bridal bed.

There was no one there who would disturb them. Lady Adhan's servant had been instructed to pack a hamper of necessities of food, candles and blankets and a note was sent to let her father know that she was "treating a sickness in the hills as part of her Godly work." All had been arranged with care and with detail. Aye, it was Beltane, but best to have an alibi under the circumstances, and an alibi that would match her station. A true Lady couldn't be too careful.

All was in readiness. She had agreed to this union and would give up her precious maidenhead, only if they first be hand-fasted and mated in the Old Ways. It protected her Spirit and was at least something that they could both share in their hearts, forever. They would be wed, if not in legal binding terms of the Church and the Law, they would be One under the Moon and the Stars. He was a King's son yet she could not have him, neither could she deny him. So it was then that they met on this magickal day and soulful hearts took kindred hands by candlelight of the nearly full moon.

The couple lit a candle which had been rubbed with rose oil and they called the Powers of the Four Winds to preside o'er their ceremony of love. They wrapped a ribbon for kindness, devoted love and faithfulness about their hands, all the while they promised these things to each other. An Earthen bond given in love and truth is as sacred as a Heavenly Bond given in any kirk.

All elements Earth, Fire, Water, Wind, and Spirit- were called to witness it. A promise truthfully given is sacred promise bound. The Mother Goddess answered their nuptial kiss with the song of an owl who hooted three times for Power, Wisdom and Great Change. A log tumbled into the fire whilst they enjoyed their first kiss of passion.

Thus began the wedding night and laying in of Lady Adhan to Prince Ambrosius which commenced hastily and without further ado. They only had this one night together, and well, time was a-wasting. Their lovemaking was tender at first, and Ambrosius was gentle with her, taking her maidenhead with kindness and tenderness…and then as she rallied to this new wisdom of carnal delight, their lovemaking turned raucous, energetic and passionate, and the Goddess was indeed pleased! The night was delicious, tantalizing, filled with kisses of honey, and punctuated with a couple's new-found fleshly delight! It was passion of a wild stallion and mare in heat being fulfilled. It was far beyond anything they had ever dreamed. It was surprisingly Soul-deep.

The night did not end until well-nigh onto the lark's song in the morning. Ambrosius promised that after the coronation, he would send for her to start the process, somehow, someway, for their nuptials in the church to read the Banns. They reluctantly pulled themselves from their tangled sheets and their entwined embrace, and made their heart-felt promises to remember that they were once and forever One. This time spent together would stand until the day came when he would take her legally as his Queen for the whole nation to view.

They resignedly and dutifully returned to their stations. He returned to be crowned High King of Britain and she went back to her father's house in Southern Wales. Two separate houses, with two separate destinies. But both with this night's lusty secret kept hidden for'ere in their hearts. A moon afterwards, how'ere, developed a definite change of plan.

Their former secret was to be revealed when Lady Adhan discovered that she was with child. She vowed that she would ne'er go in disgrace to her only true love. She was sure that all at Court would mock her as a harlot and deride him as a rake. She quaked at the fearful (yet ungrounded) thought that e'en he may deny her and force ridicule on her family's house. She could not trust court to raise her beautiful bairn without being knocked about as a bastard to the King. Even though they should've waited and made him a legal son, she could not, in all political sense do it now by coming to the newly crowned High King, with her dignity rent asunder, heart in hand, full swell pregnant with his child, like some common doxy. T'would be a fall from grace that she would NOT bear to either of their houses. Alas, she vowed to her Old Gods to keep her secret and then, for all pretense purposes, she laid herself away from society and court and got herself to a nunnery posthaste.

If she could not be Ambrose's Queen in the Old Ways, she would now need protection of the Church that was growing in power. And she knew in her heart, as her true natural Druid faith said, "The power which can destroy a thing, can also be used to preserve it as well." She hoped this new Jesus would be kind, for he, too, was once a much sought after and hidden bastard child at birth as well. In the deepest part of her pagan self she believed that "All the Gods are but one God...thusly the One God is All the Gods." She knew that God is Love, and those who live in Love, live in God. Aye, she believed that by any name ye shall know the Universe and its secrets. T'was all good in the grand scheme.

So she feigned piety to the Apostolic Church as a virgin novice in order to enter into the nunnery. T'was their rule, not hers, yea, for when in Rome, ye do as the Romans do. Yet months later, the cries of a newborn son, on one cold and early February morn, revealed the veiled knowledge to all who heard it. This private tryst and resulting boy child were known only to a few nuns, a silent Druid and an apostolic Priest who were all told the truth, along with her confession, in order to keep the boy safe and remove him as a target of treasonous assassination. To ensure his safety and that he would have Eternal Life and that the Church could not deny him, according to the new ways, she had him baptized at birth as Merlinus Ambrosius, giving him his father's name. He was born on Candlemas Day. His birth was noted in the book of births kept by the religion of the Christ. The date was February 2nd. For in sooth, the new bairn was a *naturalis.* As such it meant that he was the offspring of a couple who could have married and indeed might possibly do so in the future. This type of birth was treated fairly indulgently, by the Church, for the babe was the product of young love which got carried away. Only a handful of sturdy souls knew of the baptized child's true lineage. They, too, promised to keep Lady Adhan's secret safe for all of their own sakes, until such time as circumstances may change. There were too many inconstant branches, and no one could truly be sure of the vain pride of Uther, Ambrosius's brother. It was he, who may want to have the baby killed, like some grand Herod gesture, so that Uther could ascend more directly. As long as there was no heir to the throne from Ambrosius's line, she felt the baby was safe. Lady Adhan prayed that Uther was kept smug biding his time, unaware of the boy's existence while making his own plans for ascension.

For propriety's sake, Lady Adhan stayed safely away from court life both before and after the birth. She took on the ways of the new Church by beginning her new life as a nun. She had immediately taken a vow of celibacy and sealed her Fate as a novice to serve her new Lord, to preclude her father, King Meurig ap Rhain, making some hasty arranged marriage for her to another to cover her impropriety. Yet she so loved Ambrosius that she could not bear to think of ever being with another. So much in love was she that she vowed her love would stay pure for him always in her heart. Thus she remained constant, pure and true to her vows to the Powers, honoring both Gods and her own vow of faithful love to Ambrosius.

There were worse ways to spend a life if you were a lady of some wealth and standing. She would be cared for, in a goodly apartment, left alone to her own ways, music, art, poetry, and now adding in her church work of healing the sick. She would be a good Christian for her landlord's sake. For her Druid heart, she would be able to work in the gardens, help make the food and wine to keep the Old Ways in this way. She would be safe from suspicion from everyone if she was careful. She was an amazing strategic planner, if not a barren one.

Aye, but deep in her heart of hearts, neither would Lady Adhan have this beauteous child of nature be raised to be a suffering, pious, young priest, devoid of laughter and denying him of his childhood, burying him in guilt and denying him of the pleasures of love and the beauty of this world. Instead, she sent him to her mother's Clan, to be raised in the family of the Druid faith, and he would be taught by Taliesin of Anglesey Isle. This Druid priest had learned at the traditional school for males steeped in the Old Ways of nature. It was the male school companion to the female halls of Avalon. He would be safe there with her family and taught specifically by Taliesin, who would be his able mentor and entrusted by Lady Adhan to be his only guardian. The child would grow to learn all he could and to be a help to all of mankind and the Earth Mother as well. For in the Druid faith, this February 2nd day was also the Sabbat of Imbolc and the Feast of the Goddess Brigid. Lady Adhan would, by the Gods, honor both faiths and try, as most women oft do, to make everyone happy best she could.

For his part, after his coronation King Ambrosius *(whom his new subjects oft referred to as "King Ambrose")* never married another. His heart had been broken when it was announced at court that Lady Adhan had officially converted and had gone into her life as a celibate woman and went into a nunnery. He knew nothing of the impending birth, nor of the recent arrival of his only son. All was kept from him for now, for the bairn's sake. So he too threw himself into the task of his own daily life, which was governance and leadership. His heart stayed true to Lady Adhan and he always remained hopeful that another love would present herself to him as his ultimate bride. Whilst there were ladies who would avail themselves of his personage and his bed, no one ever drew upon his heartstrings nor fulfilled his wish for a mate, as she had.

Lady Adhan's mother lion's protective plan to keep safe her only bairn was complete. He would be raised away from court and away from his noble heritage. This would also keep him away from assassination, away from gluttony and falseness and away from lies and guile. He would also be raised away from rigid society, the Pope's rules, gunnysack clothing, retribution of his Soul, and fear of his impending damnation. Instead she had given him a great gift. He would be raised wholly in nature, as a Shamanic Druid, reveling in the seasons, birdsong, wild grapes, honest intuition and magick, and he would learn to trust and harness his own special Powers. He would be raised to honor many Gods, remaining joyful for the day and reverent of the night. He would keep the Old Ways, honoring the Earth, as Lady Adhan had promised herself, and the Horned God and May Queen Goddess on the night the babe was conceived.

So 'tis true what they said of this baby: he was the son of a King and a nun! He was also a Love Child of the May Queen and The Horned God.

Aye, for what's in a name? He, who in Welsh country parts, would be called "The wild man, Myrrdin Wylit." In Lady Adhan's secret heart, he was her "Blessed Bairn of Beltane" whom she sent away to live safely elsewhere. He was also Prince Merlinus Ambrosius, named after his father, King Aurelius Ambrosius.

But knowing none of this, most of the townsfolk just called the little tyke, Merlin, for short.

I

A Druid's Prayer

Grant, O God thy protection
And in Protection, Strength;
And in Strength, Understanding;
And in Understanding, Knowledge;
And in Knowledge, the Knowledge of Justice:
And in the Knowledge of Justice, the Love of
It;
And in the Love of it, the Love of All
Existences;
And in the Love of All Existences, the Love
of God and All Goodness.

I bolted out of bed and ran to the hills to meet my mentor, Taliesin, who is my teacher in all things. Most days I spend learning Latin and Greek, reading and memorizing the knowledge of our parchments. There is so much to learn. I enjoy mathematics and love to tally sums, and have devoted myself to learning many Bardic pieces and play several instruments (my favorite being the lute), but this day was to be our day of magickal study! And a most fortuitous day it was! This was the day we would spend following the wind!

Taliesin was sitting under a blossoming apple tree when I found him. I said, "Good morrow, learned one!" Just then several petals fell from the tree, as if activated by my voice. He watched the flower blossoms trickle down like snow around him and said, "Aye, good day to thee, young Master Merlin! Howarten this fine Beltane day?" More blossoms fell when he spoke... and stopped when we ceased speaking.

I was amused. "Wondrous!" A few more blossoms fell. Taliesin saw that I had noticed the correlation and he said, "Aye, the tree is impelled by our voices. Once, I sang to a tree during the changing of the colors and for every verse ending, a shower of autumn leaves fell. It was mesmerizing." More white blossoms fell all around us. Taliesin continued, "Another time I did play my harp under a maple tree whilst the wind was dead still, how'ere, a single branch waved and waved whilst I did play...and stopped... when I stopped. The tree seemed to be playing with me!" Another shower of blossoms fell and we waited till all was quiet and still again before he spoke next. "This day, we shall speak of grand things as part of my instruction for thee. I must needs teach you the three goals of the Old Ways that lead to Enlightenment. They are Wisdom, Creativity and Love. Now, Merlin, recite for me the Instructions of Cormac."

I cleared my throat and spoke my newly memorized verses whilst apple blossoms lightly fell around us:

"Be not too wise, be not too foolish,
be not too conceited, be not too diffident,
be not too haughty, be not too humble,
be not too talkative, be not too silent,
be not too harsh, be not too feeble.
For if you be too wise, one will expect too much of you;
If you be too foolish, you will be deceived;
If you be too conceited, you will be thought vexatious;
If you be too humble, you will be without honor;
If you be too talkative, you will not be heeded;
If you be too silent, you will not be regarded;
If you be too harsh, you will be broken;
If you be too feeble, you will be crushed."

Taliesin spoke up, "Well done lad! This day, we shall embrace Creativity, Wisdom and Love, by allowing our day to develop as the Gods see fit. We have no plans. We shall follow the wind! This is a day of Omens and Portent!" He then held out his palm and the tree let down more blossoms than ever and some trickled into his hand. He looked at me, smiled and blew the petal off his hand. It flew up, made a big circle and came to rest upon my shoulder. We both laughed and sat a bit in admiration of this beautiful tree. We placed our hands on its bark and felt the vibrations of the blooming tree. It seemed so alive, so much so it tickled our fingers!

"Plants are simply very slow animals. They do react to us and to the world around us," grinned my teacher. I then closed my eyes and let my body rest against the tree. I could detect feelings like vibrations coursing through the tree. I envisioned sap running up and down and through the tree and how it felt like a pulse to me. It seemed to hum and throb a bit and I "petted" the tree and became friends with it. I then asked it what it would most like to do if it could do anything, and then a thought came to me like a picture what this tree would look like if it had legs like an animal and could move like one. I imagined its roots to be its feet and its branches its hands reaching out to the sun in a joyful stretch. This tree wanted to walk, dance and stretch! So I told the tree that I would walk, dance and stretch for it as well, and I moved all around the tree and spoke to it for quite some time. It seemed to feel joyful for my sharing and it thanked me and I hugged it back.

Taliesin and I sat a bit and then a butterfly flitted in front of me. I could feel faint gusts of wind when it flew past my nose. It tingled with energy. "Let's follow it!" I said, and was on my feet trying to detect its direction. First it touched the lemon balm bush, then flitted to the clover…then it flew up a bit higher and sprinted off towards the hills. This certainly was an adventure, and I was following the sign! I ran after it, and all the while I enjoyed the sunshine, the breeze, the flowers, trying to keep my inspiration in eyesight. When I lost sight of the butterfly, I looked around and realized that I had never before been at this location. I turned round to tell Taliesin, but he had not caught up with me. Or mayhap he was off following another sign from another omen.

At the edge of a drumlin, I climbed the stony hillside and started to make sense of the outcroppings when I realized there was an old path here. It was a path that had been traveled long ago, and there seemed to be a charm or some spell upon the area. I was certain of this for, to me, it looked "wavy" in the light, as if it was too hot when the air came up off the earth in washes of heat. But no, it was not that hot on this May Day as it was newly in the season. There was definitely some effort of a magick spell to keep it hidden. It was easy to interpret this sign.

It was then I was reminded of what my plump nursemaid, Moravik, would always say of my gift of Sight. I would guess correctly the simplest of things, and she would notice. Once when I was very small, she was tucking me in at e'entide, and she said, "Aye, ye have the gift, lovey. Now just be careful who ye tell, and how ye uses it. Always use your powers for Good. Ye dinna want them to think thou hast the evil eye." I always wondered about that. I mean, if I had a "Gift" then how could it be bad? I decided not to think about it and to just enjoy this day of adventure with my teacher. I liked Taliesin. He was a learned taskmaster, aye, but he did, at times come up with fun outings. He was an older man with a long grey beard and a kind face, but he was healthy and strong. I had often wished to think that he was my father, but Moravik would only say that the man who sired me was liken unto no mortal man…and she would tell me no more about him. Neither would she say anything much about my mother, whom I did not know. Moravik would only say, "She was above reproach," what'ere that meant.

I scrambled up some more rocks and heard the trickling of water. It was sounding so clear to me now. I spotted my butterfly leader again and off I went following it! It had a dark body and its wings were roundish and white, other than the brilliant spots of orange on the ends. I knew the long flat green worm it came from. Last fall, I made a point of keeping one and feeding it the Cuckooflower on which it sat. Over a night or two, it transformed into a cocoon, and when it came out it looked exactly like this butterfly. It laid its eggs on the Honesty plant. This much I knew from playing with them and watching them spin their webby home. The cocoon looked like bark on the tree and blended in and became invisible! If you didn't know it was a worm's house, you would've sworn it was part of the tree! This adventurous orange-tipped butterfly came to rest today on a pile of small stones, which was also where the water sound originated. It looked as though the water was flowing from the hill down the side and pooling into this little well of stones. There was my butterfly playmate, sitting so placidly, now drinking deeply from the damp rocks.

I looked around and took in the new sights. Just to the right of the well, there looked to be a vine-covered entrance on the side of the hill. Ooooh! A secret sacred cave, right here in Carmarthen? I had ne'er heard tales of it! There was ne'er even mention of it in the kitchen when the women gossiped about mysterious superstitions while they shucked peas or wound flax on their distaffs.

I gathered up my courage, pushed the ivy away o'er what concealed the entrance, and I entered it. There was something familiar here...I could almost taste it. Then a rush of sound, and then a flood of feelings swelled up inside me and energies seemed to swirl around me. Colors and heat and sparks and voices...and then...nothing.

I woke up with Taliesin talking softly to me. "Merlin, 'tis I. Can ye hear me? Boy, answer me if ye can." I opened my eyes and there he was, with a bit of concern on his face. It was dark here, so he looked around, and found the stub of a candle and lit it. All around there seemed to be the feeling that this old cave was someone's home. There were furnishings of a sort from a long time ago.

"Aye, master, I'm here. What happened? Did I fall?"

Taliesin said, "Well, know ye, I believe ye fell into the mountain of time. Did you feel or see anything afore ye dropped?"

"I remember feeling like I was drowning, and feeling faint, but I was hearing sounds, laughter, crackling fires, a man and woman's voice. They were here. I'm not sure when, but I think it was a long time ago. Where am I? What is this place?"

Taliesin said, "Aye, it was twelve years ago to be exact, to the very day. I had wondered if the Otherworld would let ye find it or not. This is the cave of Fraxinus, a Druid Priest of the area. He died long ago, but afore he passed into the Otherworld he put a spell o'er this place. He believed that it was to be the founding place for a powerful Wizard yet to be forged. It is also the place where you were created, lad. This is where the Gods formed ye. Ye must be the One of whom he prophesied."

I knew that what he said about the Priest and the couple was true because I could feel all that…but I couldn't prove that I was "The One." I didn't have to. My Sight had told me and it all seemed to be "right and true" as he said. I had seen the Beltane evening twelve years ago. No one had been in this sacred spot except them and the Druid Priest. This cave had so much history, and yet it felt so familiar to me. This much was all true.

Taliesin lit a fire in the cave. The fire spit and crackled as he added a log and nudged it with the toe of his boot. He sat back down in the circle of firelight and said, "Most gentles have always thought that you were devil spawn, but verily, I did not believe it no matter what others said, for my heart was clear that you were conceived in love, fashioned in the Old Ways. Magick has always been your path since you were but a gleam in your father's eye. Say what ye will, but I know other things. I too, have Seen it this day…and other days as well." He gazed into the fire, and his words drifted off and he fell silent.

After a bit, Taliesin continued, "Ye have a distinct path to follow, my lad. I shall help thee all I can. Evidently the Gods have seen fit to appoint me to be yer mentor and guardian. I am honored by their faith in me, and I accept this charge as mine own to keep ye on the path. Yer instruction will be different and more intense now in magickal ways. I shall encourage ye to work hard, for I will be teaching ye all that I learned in my time at The Isle of Anglesey. Ye shall have that wisdom as yer own, but ye will now be instructed in the ways of the Craft more than so 'ere before. I foresee that ye shall be a great and powerful man in the future. Ye shall be trained as an Ovate, a Bard and ultimately as a Druid…mayhaps…even an Arch Druid someday. Ye shall be a Gazer of stars, a Listener in the wilderness, a Judge of Kings, and a Healer to All. Ye shall have the Gift of Prophesy and the knowledge of when to use it."

At that moment, we both heard the distinctive call of a nightjar in the darkness.

"Another sign!" I blurted out.

"Aye," noted Taliesin, "A nightjar, that some call a Nighthawk. Did you know that it is a bird that builds no nest? It lays its two eggs on the ground. Not pretentious at all. It has no need to fear, nor need for security, nor for glamour, for it be a fairy bird. Some call it a 'Goatsucker' for its love of milk! It hides its eggs in plain sight. Let us take a page of its wisdom and do liken unto it as well. We shall follow the signs and take its feathery advice, and we too, shall also become invisible. For being 'One with the Wild' and being able to disappear at will shall be thy first lesson in Transfiguration! To be able to hide in life…and nature, has merit. Aye, are ye ready to be as they are?"

I cleared my throat and stood up. "Aye, sir. I am feeling much better now that the visions have stopped. I learn at thy elbow. Teach me what I need to know."

Taliesin firmly said, "Tis well. We shall now advance from the simple education of memorization, recitation and book work that you have been receiving to more advanced "hands on" magick tutoring. The Gods have spoken with this new vision and experience this day. Now, to the matter at hand, which will be to learn the magick of 'Shapeshifting.' The object is to merge with your surroundings, to become one with the Woods and the Wildlings, to be as they are….to be able to run in the dark, no matter what the terrain. This first act of magick is to absorb and *blend*. To disappear, as they do. It

42

may save your life someday." He stood up by the fire and walked outside into the night. Evidently, I had been asleep in my vision for quite some time. Taliesin bade me follow him.

"Look round where'ere you are. We shall start instruction in the ways of animals. For there is much to learn from them. They are not 'dumb animals.' Nay. We can connect with them, and share each other's thoughts, *if* we be careful to listen. Ye can receive their energy, if ye ask them politely for access. Then just try to think their thoughts. Imagine yourself in the colors of the world around you, no matter where'ere ye be. Be like that Nightjar we just heard. Many gentles ne'er see them at all, but only know they are there from their sounds. Try to be one with the bird. Feel its feathers as your own. It has a color liken unto the ground and the leaves around it. Be like they are. For "True Magic is the Art and Science of changing states of mind at will. Action follows thought."

My mentor made a bird call just like the one we heard afore and, suddenly, a Nightjar flew to him out of the darkness and landed on his open, outstretched palm.

"Yes, little one. Thank you for coming. We wish to learn from ye. Will you teach us yer feathery ways?" He whispered to the small bird. It had big, black eyes, whiskers on its beak and it had wee legs! It was the color of dusty, dry leaves. When it opened its wings it looked exactly like a tree's bark.

"Might I also imagine that I have whiskers such as they?" I smirked.

"Hehehe," Taliesin stroked his beard. "Soon, lad, soon ye shall have whiskers soon enough! Dinna rush aging, it shall happen for thee quicker than ye think someday. How'ere, I, myself dinna need to imagine that bristly bit." As he spoke he stroked his beard and smiled at me.

I laughed and closed my eyes, and imagined my eyes to be big as dark saucers, with whiskers on my beak just as a nightjar doth have. My teacher's words came through my mind: "Can you feel it? Do you feel like a bird?"

It was fun starting to imagine it. It seemed like a simple, mischievous game to me. I pretended to have a beak and little, wee legs and dusty wings.

"Tis well! I think I almost see whiskers on your face liken unto our feathered friend!" He pointed at me, and then Taliesin released the fowl to the airy, dark woods.

"Master," I giggled. I flapped my wings. For the next few moments, in my mind's eye, I flew! Then I tried to blend into the surroundings and become invisible. It seemed different than before when I played at it in the woods.

Then he said, "Ye have done well, lad, for I know not where ye be! Come back to yourself, son! Now, we shall try something different. Think not of the Nightjar, but change liken unto a scurrying creature. Crouch like this." He bent down low with his back flat to the earth, knees to his chest, head looking forward, peering ahead. "Although, odd and somewhat awkward until you get used to it, this be the magick way of traveling fast in the night. It is the way that the earthen Fae have long mastered to run in the dark. If you learn to proceed as they do, ye shall have fighting chance to escape danger whilst in the nighttime. It is a way to be unseen and to move swift and silent in the twilight and moon-dark night without falling. If you do happen to stumble, you are already in position to curl up liken unto a pill bug. If ye fall, just tuck yer tail under, roll forward, o'er and then back up onto yer feet and keep moving. Shall ye try it with me? Ye may need to escape in the night sometime..."

It sounded merry, peculiar and a bit dangerous and appealing. He looked so mischievous and so queerly at me, how could I not try to emulate him and the Fairy Fae? I stood up, then bent o'er as he bade me and followed. It was awkward at first, and I did fall a few times, but t'was without having far to fall, and whilst not getting hurt, I realized I was now fearless! We ran through the woods close to the ground, one with the earth, silent as foxes, brave as deer, quick as rabbits, invisible as nightjars and as brave as stoats. Over hill and dale, ravine and knoll, we scurried like enchanted ermines.

I had my first lesson in shape-shifting and a whole new world was now available to me. It only made me more deeply desire to learn how to handle mine own Gifts, to learn the secret ways of Old, and there was so much to learn! I vowed to become adept at it and learn from all the animals in their turn. Taliesin was a firm yet fun, mischievous, talented, creative teacher with a mission, and I his willing student-was aware that I now owned Powers which would in time be honed. We spent many hours learning to "be" other creatures and I reveled in this my new way of seeing life! It became my daily occurrence to "become" some other creature. I got very good at it.

Yet, I had much to learn. I excelled at memorization of the Druidic poems and songs and truisms. It was important to Taliesin for me to develop a good base for my future as a Healer and a Seer.

****

On my sixteenth natal day, Taliesin said that it was time that I had my Spirit Quest.

"The tenets of Druidism require us to know Wisdom, Creativity and Love," he said. "This day, you shall seek them in the form of your own unique path. I have been informed by Spirit that ye shall best find it in the realms of the mind, whilst in the cave of your conception. Ye shall go on yer manhood's Spirit Quest this very day. For it is said, 'If you seek to understand the whole universe, you will understand nothing at all, but seek to understand yourself and you will come to understand the whole universe.'"

We walked up to the cave on this cold February morning. There were tracks here and there in the snow- a wolf's tracks. I pointed them out to Taliesin and looked nervously around. A lone wolf was something to concern you.

"Be ye not afraid, Merlin. Wolf is the Greatest of All Teachers. I see his tracks have early come here to yer parents cave on this morning of the anniversary of your birth. Wolf will be your Guide this day. I have been led to create our traditional Journeying potion for thee. Drink this bit what I have made of Mandrake, Datura and Belladonna. It is an ancient remedy and it will help ye to achieve the Sight ye need to see yer Future. This potion is not meant to be taken lightly, and I have made it with thee in mind, that it be mild but will be intense enough for yer purposes. I will be hither, lad, and I promise that I will not leave ye. I will stay and be thy protector and will help to hasten yer journey with my harp playing. Again, lad, be ye not afraid. Ye have me and your Wolf Spirit Guide this day for your travel companions." Taliesin put his hand on my head and asked a blessing of Protection for me from the Gods. Then he said, "I shall play the harp to show ye the way for thy Journey Quest, for it is said that "All music, or natural melody is but a faint and unbroken echo of the Creative Mind."

I took the cup of remedy that Taliesin had prepared for me, and tasted it. Thankfully, he had placed these heady, stalwart herbs of power into an infusion of Meade. It did not have a bad taste. I drank two good swallows, which was all the cup held, and prayed with each sip that I may find my way safely on this my day of manhood. I sat inside the cave looking out at the winter sky, with my legs drawn up underneath me cross-legged on my cloak. Taliesin wrapped me in another covering, this was of fur, and it was a wolf's pelt.

"A wolf pelt? How did you know we would see tracks this day?"

"I Saw it last week. This pelt was sent to me yesterday by a patron who asked for my help with Divination. I knew it was meant for ye from my vision."

Taliesin started a fire to warm us and then sat down in the corner with his harp. It was quiet and pleasant here in the cave. I felt warm and at peace. Soon, I found myself feeling odd. It seemed as though my eyesight narrowed into two tunnels of light. It was liken unto looking through a hollowed-out tube. At the end of the tube I could see everything so clearly. I could hear soft music and vaguely remembered something about a harp. The music did soothe me, and I relaxed. I forgot all about myself, the cave, Taliesin, my home.

My vision which had previously narrowed was now growing larger and coming closer. No longer was I seeing the opening of the cave, but t'was as if I was hovering off the ground, and I stretched out and felt as if I was flying through the opening of the cave, yet my body seemed not to feel at all. I felt numb to wind, sun, and pain and yet, my eyesight and hearing were magnified. In the distance I saw my Wolf Guide, and it seemed as if he was waiting for me to follow him. When I approached the Wolf, he looked at me and seemed to smile and turned away and started trotting down the path away from the cave, which we quickly left behind.

I trailed after him. I knew that he would show me what I needed to know. I trusted him implicitly. Wolf stopped at the edge of a cliff and sat down. I sat next to him, and he let me touch his soft fur, and that's when Wolf spoke to me. For some reason, it seemed to be all in the keeping of the Journey and was not strange-some that he spoke. His voice was a voice liken unto mine own, and he said to me, "Behold, look to thy future." And he stretched out his paw towards the cliff. I followed where he was pointing and gazed out over the expanse before me.

No longer a cliff edge, we sat at the edge of water, so close that I could touch the ripples it made next to me. There was a fog which covered the view now, but I could not discern anything but the mist.

I said, "I can see naught there afore me."

"Trust your instincts," growled the Wolf. I looked back and relaxed my eyes. I watched the fog for quite a while.

Over time, I became aware of a Hazelnut tree at the edge of the water. It seemed to glow from within somehow. Then I watched the tree let down a branch. One of the branches was liken unto a hand, and it plucked from itself and dropped nine hazelnuts one by one into the water. I distinctly heard each and every "plunk" and watched the ripples fan out in the water as the nuts bobbed to the surface. Then I saw a fish swim up and gobble up each one of the nuts as they fell. I sat in amazement at this and then was astonished to see that the fish swam straight towards me and lingered by the edge of the water. The fish's eyes seemed to be very wise, and they too, now, glowed with the same glow of the tree. I reached out my hand and petted the fish. My finger caught on one of the scales and I started to bleed a bit. Instinctively, I put my hand to my mouth and tried to soothe the pain and stop the blood. It tasted strange. It was like a mixture of flowers, metal and smoke.

Immediately, my mind swirled with thoughts of things wondrous and queer. I saw objects float past my mind: machines, pyramids, what-nots, flying carriages, wars, pestilence, medicine, fear, hope and odd creatures and things not yet manifested.

I then saw human shapes starting to form within the mists. There were Three Kings. There was a family resemblance to all of them, and the first one looked like myself. The monarchs then nodded at me and bowed deeply, then were gone. I rubbed my eyes to see if I could see more. After this there was some movement in the water and there seemed to be something…or someone….rising from the water. Would it be another sea creature? Nay. It was a Woman rising from the depths! She seemed to be floating above the water and the last thing I saw come up from the deep was a sword that she carried in her left hand. She had chestnut colored long hair in one long braid which fell over her right shoulder. She looked at me with a piercing glance of her green eyes… and that intense look of her inner Sight produced a profound, deep longing within me, so much so that I heard myself involuntarily sob out loud. I had not realized until this moment how alone I had felt until I saw her. She called to me with her hand to come and she seemed so like me….yet….seeing her seemed to amplify how completely bereft and lonely I felt inside. While I had caretakers and nursemaids and the odd playmate, I have never felt completely at home with anyone in my life. I beheld the vision of her, and the reality that my heart was cavernously empty suddenly grew in enormity. Yet, somehow, just seeing her seemed to resonate within me that she would be the One to fill my vast desolation with Love. Then she too, vanished in the mist and returned to the water from whence she came.

When I awoke, I was not by the stream any longer but here in my cave. Something was different. I felt stiff and heavier and older than I had ever felt in my life. My hands were wrinkled and gnarled. My hair was white as snow. I seemed to be in the same position of sitting cross-legged looking out of the cave, but there was no open doorway. It must have been sealed with something liken unto glass, for fish seemingly swam in front of what was once the doorway to the cave. I was alone, but no longer lonely. Although, by myself, I knew that I was not alone and that She would be returning for me. We had a Plan for the World and all would happen in good time. I then felt the brush of fur of my Wolf Guide seemingly on my fingertips.

"Eat this," the Wolf said. He had made something for me to sup.

"Salmon?" I asked. "How fortuitous, for I just petted a strange fish."

"Aye. Tis this fish. He is the Salmon of Knowledge. He carries within him Great Wisdom. When you eat this, you too, shall have great knowledge." I ate heartily and more visions came to me of Times Past and Times Yet to Come. After eating, I kept stroking my Wolf friend's fur, feeling emotions of trust and grief and love and lust and then came a feeling of being trapped and then released. I longed for the woman that I had seen in the water and pined for her with a feeling of intense love mingled with grief that I had never felt before. It felt as though my mind had expanded in all directions. I knew things of both the Past and Future now, to my amazement. There were thoughts in my head that I had ne'er e'en imagined afore. So strangesome it was to me, and all the queer inventions, and yet they seemed to be acceptable, as though they had always existed, but I did not know of them. I continued to stroke his fur, even as bit by bit he was fading from me…until he too, was gone.

When I next came to my senses, I could discern the cave once again. I was now lying on my back looking up at the earthen ceiling. My hands held the freshly tanned wolf pelt which I clung to for warmth and security. Taliesin stopped playing the harp when he saw my eyes flutter open.

"Are ye present? Merlin, are ye here?" Taliesin asked me. He helped me to sit up. I felt dizzy. He gave me water. I felt sick in my stomach. I proceeded to vomit several times. "I believe so." I answered. "I feel so queer." I sipped water and steadied myself. "I have much to tell thee."

Taliesin sat and listened while I told him of the Tree and the Fish and the spinning world of new and old things and the Kings and the Lady. He just sat there with a wondrous placid smile on his face.

"My Lad, all will come to fruition," he said. "I have been given the Gift of Interpretation of Dreams and Visions. Ye have been given the Gift o' Wisdom straight from the Gods. Some things must first be believed in order to be seen. The three Kings are in your future. They bowed to Thee because it is said that 'All bow to the King, but the King bows only to his Druid Priest.' These kings are in order: Your father, Aurelius Ambrosius, -your uncle-Uther Pendragon, and your cousin yet to be- Arthur Pendragon."

"My Father? My father is a KING?!"

"Oh aye, lad. Ye have greatness within Ye. Now, what ye must needs do is to meditate thoroughly on this query: 'Do I wish to be King after mine own father?' Is it my path? For if ye will it, it shall come to pass."

My head was reeling. Not only had I just had tremendous visions, but now my heritage had been revealed to me that I came of noble birth! Me! The boy who was said to have come from the Devil himself! Did I want to be King? What, o Gods, have ye done to me? And what is the path for me and the world's greatest and highest good?

Taliesin said one last thing to me as we walked back home to our resting places: "No well-defined boundaries exist between our waking world and the Otherworld; both must be taken seriously. Who is to say wither this world in which we stand is real or wither reality begins when we close our eyes?"

I decided to let this day's revelations sink into my bones and I let them all go into my memories as something to think of another day. My mind was over full now of visions of kings and wars and air carriages and pyramids and machines whirled in my now wide open mind. It made me dizzy and I had to find a way to make sense of all this new information. It was too much for me. I needed a way to cope whilst I managed my feelings. My Druid heritage came to me with comforting words now: "For in dreams the mind beholds its own immensity. What has been seen is seen again, and what has been heard is heard again. What has been felt in different places or faraway regions returns to the mind again and again. Seen and unseen, heard and unheard, felt and not felt, the mind sees all, since the mind IS all."

I knew that men and women had always been kept apart in their learning and teaching on our Druid Path. Yet, I also knew that pagans find and craft their ways through experiences of life and its relationships. Of relationships with a lass, I knew nothing. But now, I felt, somehow, kindred to that lady who had beckoned me in my dream. A deep knowledge welled within me that if we could only meet and join forces the world would be a better place. It was like she knew my Soul, and I knew hers.

I decided, instead, to dream of a reality that I wished for with all my heart. I envisioned that the woman of the water was mine and that I held her in my arms. I quickly fell asleep, safely imagining her stroking my hair, and in my dreams we held each other close.

ne day I asked Taliesin about Wales and where he had been and what he most loved about the land. This was the day that he taught me about the Isle of Anglesey. When he started to speak about it he became wistful. "Anglesey is an Isle which sits up on the northern tip of our beloved Wales. The Druids there live in harmony both in spirit and in trade. I grew up there and learned much from the oral tradition of the Old Ones. How'ere, I desired to catch all this wisdom on parchment. This was something that the Druids had ne'er done before; only passing on from one to another in word and deed. It was frowned upon at first, but when the other Elders saw that so much is forgotten, they allowed me to chronicle it. So I have made this my mission to fashion and keep for knowledge's sake, a record of the Sect. Because of this I was chosen to become a Magickal leader and keeper of the Wisdom. I was relied upon to gather, collect and to record many things. I spent many years fashioning scrolls of knowledge. These are what you have been learning from all this time."

He went on, "The Isle itself is a jeweled lady. She is green and lush and speckled with many standing stones built for community and left to community. Blue water and green surround her liken unto an ever changing flowing gown. Winds constantly speak to her both with gentle whispers and with fierce truths. Sunrises and sunsets are revered high on the mounds within the standing stones, serenaded by the occasional crash of sea waters round the shore. It is a powerful place. Moments of Universal daily splendor are what we expect there. Druids collect their energy from the spiritual transfer of light, wind and water and absorb the Power of the Earth." Taliesin told me all this, verily, t'was as if I were there, with him, the way he spoke about it.

****

One day, word came and he was called to leave Anglesey and to become my personal mentor. He may have left the Isle, but the Isle had not left him. It was within him as a part of his breath and being. He brought with him all his parchments of note and I devoured all he taught me. It was as if I was there, with the other Druids, learning and absorbing. I digested the knowledge like nectar of what'ere he did offer to teach me. Once learned, we quickly moved on to more advanced studies. My teacher was gratified with my aptitude for learning and enhanced his offerings to me. The retention I showed for past lessons was amazing for I could recollect with my mind's eye in perfect detail. My knowledge increased daily. The real talents I developed though were for Divination and for manipulating objects. Tools of my trade were the pendulum, runes, fire gazing, and dowsing rods. I approached all the divining methods with a heart of respect, the concern for others and the resolve to use it for Good. All one need do is to open thyself to the Universe and to ask for an answer and to listen and discern what comes of it. Once an answer is given, the querant, (I have found), does well to thank the Gods that be with him, and to ponder upon the solution. Much good comes of such applications.

****

When I was nearly eighteen, I had completed all my levels, I was taken to Anglesey to be tested by the Elder Druids there. It was an amazing journey and it was as Taliesin had all told me it was. The splendor of the adventure, the scenery and the breathtaking beauty was true. I was introduced to the Druids there, and they tested me on my knowledge of the tenets, the laws and our culture. My memory is not like others for I am able to recollect things perfectly from the first time I heard tell of them. This combined with my aptitude for magick was all extraordinary and the Elders did agree that I was ready to become a Druid Priest. Taliesin told me much later, that the process usually takes many more years than this. There was a ceremony wherein I rose into becoming a Druid priest and I was given my robe. We went back home to Carmarthen and along the way the people would notice our garments and stop to inquire of us and to bade give them advice and help. Immediately after this, the townsfolk would come to me for knowledge, to assist heal them and to predict the future. I did what I could for them all, and word went out into the countryside of a new and grand Seer.

One day, a messenger came to Taliesin and informed him that warlord Vortigern had a problem and had sent for a Seer named "Merlin of Carmarthen" to help with divining an answer. As Druid Wizards we had been summoned for solving his dilemma. We were packing our bags and Taliesin looked at me and said, "This is the Call that you have been preparing yer whole life for, my boy, and its time has come. Thy destiny awaits thee." I, too, could feel the hand of Fate pointing the way.

We set out at first light and made good time. We left with our packs upon our back, walking as the crow flies straight as an arrow. In a fortnight, we had arrived at Vortigern's castle in the western midlands of our beloved Wales. When we arrived at his fortress, we saw it standing there so stalwart and foreboding. The stones were cut with a very dark rock and there were gnarled trees all around the surrounding area. I remarked to Taliesin, "This stand of vegetation seems to be twisted, I hear it crying as if in some great pain." He nodded to me and we knocked at the gate. We were ushered in with great haste. It seems that there was some problem building a new tower, and every time it was built, it would collapse over night. Superstition had halted construction.

Taliesin and I went to the building scene and Taliesin said to me, "'Tis your chance to shine with your exceedingly accurate prophesies. Have a go at it. I will support ye, no matter what the outcome. This is the day ye make your name."

I walked the length of the stone wall and did some calculations. I was then directed by Spirit to consult my runes, pendulum and divining rods. I brought out my pouch of wooden tiles which I had marked with particular symbols.

I asked the Gods to send me a sign, I stated my query matter of factly: "To the Gods, I would ask what be the story of this place? I am listening to hear the tale. Rock and Stone, I wish to hear from thee through my instruments of rune, pendulum and divining rods. Teach me what I need to know, I beg of thee."

I gathered up the runes and threw the divining stones up into the air to bless them and to fall where they may. I did then note whence and wherefore they fell and thusly made marks upon my parchment to scribe the answer. Picking up the stones, I did thank the Gods for their voice and I put the tiles hither in my pouch again to rest for another time.

Next I took out my pendulum satchel and unwrapped the crystal which hung from a chain of silver. Blessing it, and asking the Gods for a sign, I made the same query as stated before with

the runes. Steadying my pendulum silent I said
to the crystal the words: "Show me 'aye.' " The
pendulum started to move slowly in a circular
fashion. It gathered momentum until it was
circling round at a goodly pace. I stopped the
divining oracle from moving, said "I do thank
thee." Then I proceeded with the opposite and
said, "Show me 'nay.' " The pendulum started
moving, but this time it slowly swung back and
forth in a straightsome line. It proceeded thusly
until it too, swung at a goodly pace. I thanked it
for its voice of direction. I then queried the
pendulum certain questions that could be
answered with an aye or a nay. The pendulum
gave the answers, I made my marks upon
parchment to note those answers. I then thanked
the pendulum for its help, rewrapped it and put it
away safely in its satchel.

Next I took out my divining rods and
walked the length of the wall. I queried the
divining rods as I covered ground there.
Deciphering the notes of the answers of all three
oracles, it was quite apparent to me. Here it was.
All three of my divination tools told me much
the same. It was an answer that I was amazed at,
yet, when I consulted with Taliesin, he bade me
inform Vortigern of all the newly gathered
information. I would present it at the upcoming
dinner this e'en. As Druids we live by the
motto: "Respect for the Truth measures the
quality of our very Souls." So Mote it Be.

At the e'en's festivities we sat to the right
of Vortigern's table by the dais in his feasting

hall. The repast was aplenty and many nobles attended the merrymaking. The wine and wassail flowed copiously and the victuals were hearty. We were fed to our fill, and at one point in the evening's festivities, Vortigern called me forth.

"Hail and Well Met, Merlin of Carmarthen! Hail and Well Met, Taliesin, Priest of Anglesey! We bid you welcome! We have heard much good news of thy accurate predictions and of your magick."

We arose and took our places at chairs next to the noble's rostrum. As we sat where directed I said, "We await thy pleasure, sire." Then we gave our respects to the nobleman of the castle and soon they pressed us for the matter at hand.

Vortigern began, "Hast thou found the reason why my wall doth crumble after every day's progress of building? Is it true that we are a-cursed? What sayest thou? Is it true that there be dragons in the foundations? Or are they merely superstitious notions from somnolent peasants?" The gathered guests laughed at his last remark.

I stood up to my full height and raised my arms for effect. I began talking- in a solemn, deep voice- of portentous events to come. "Aye, my Lord Vortigern, thou art cursed, and verily, for there indeed be dragons in thy midst. It seems, my esteemed good sir, that there be two dragons that harry ye there by night, and vex ye there by day. Your wall shall not stand. No matter if you build it daily or weekly or tear it down and build fresh again. Nay, it shall not stand unless ye make peace with these dragons. They wish to feed upon thy fealty and devotion. They wish for nothing less than thy constancy. Unless ye do so, ye must abandon thy cause. Bow to the Powers that Be and give thy allegiance to where it is due, and thou shalt be blessed with prosperity, wealth and grace! Then, and only then, will your walls stand. This is what Spirit has bade command me spake to thee, good sire. I pray that ye accept this enlightenment in the good Spirit that it was given, as honesty forthwith. God save you, Sire."

To say that Vortigern was upset at my words is an understatement. He bellowed, "WHAT dragons? I have seen no dragons! This is only the peasants and their superstitions croaking. This is what becomes of the clicking of their bones and the fall of feathers!" A murmur arose from the gathered assembly as all speculated what Vortigen would do next. He was known to be an impatient and intemperate man.

I cleared my throat and continued to deliver what would surely be the more unpleasant and dangerous news of the e'en. My eyesight dimmed as though I was looking into a pool of black water. My voice took on a spectral quality and an eerie silence and a ponderous mood fell o'er the listeners. I channeled the Spirit of Truth and was led to speak the maxims that had been concealed and not previously been told in the light of day. My voice loomed large and I continued, "Aye. The dragons that vex ye, m'lord, are not beasts of scale, nor fiery talons, nor brimstone, but they be the brothers, Pendragon. King Aurelius Ambrosius and his brother, Uther. Both are sons of Constantine, whom ye have murdered in days of yore, and the rightful rulers of this land! They are the ones responsible for the curse that be upon your lands and ...your wall...and your life. If you would only submit to King Ambrosius as your liege, and make peace with him and his brother Uther; your foundation will be strengthened and peace will surely reign once again in your land. The Gods have spoken! What you do with this news is of your own accord and upon thy conscience. We be merely the messengers as thou hast requested this prophecy by your own hand. I faithfully submit this verity to you and apply that you take it in the manner it was given, as a gift of the Sight called forth by thine own request. We, as Druids, are bound by our vows to answer the call of all who need our gifts. We do thank you for this, your benevolence and hospitality this day. We ask only to have your favor of safe passage whilst we journey homeward to Carmarthen. Blessed Be to thee and all present hither." And I sat down and tarried for what would befall us.

The hall erupted into a multitude of conversations and Vortigern glared whilst he met his head together with his advisors. Taliesin and I abided whilst the drama ensued. After what seemed longsome time, Lord Vortigern spoke: "Merlin and Taliesin, we thank thee for thy pains

in coming. We wish to have this curse lifted and
we desire to show you our good faith and hopes
for a truce with the Pendragons. I know not how
they have cursed me, but indeed, you spake the
truth that they vex me and harry me day and
night. They killed some of my men in the woods
and what with all the highwaymen; my people
are not safe. I would offer a boon feast for those
Lords and Dukes who follow the Pendragons
and who would greet them and hammer out an
accord with them for all of our sakes. Wouldst
thou help with the reconciliation betwixt us? I
shall meet with Pendragon's heads of state here
at my estate and will start the alliance meetings
now. Ye shall go to the King as my ambassador
and tell him of my plans. God save you."

All the while that Vortigern spoke, it was
as if I saw an image of a snake with a tongue that
flicked, as he formed his words. I did not know
why the vision appeared, nor from whence it
came, but I said nothing. I would spake later to
Taliesin in our quarters. Surely, the primary
desire was that Vortigern would avoid risking
the wrath of a sorcerer. Instead I answered him
with "I would be honored, Sire." and sat back
down in my place. Taliesin and I would be
emissaries to ensure the process. We had been
called immediately and undeniably into the fray
of war.

When we were both back in our rooms,
we discussed the evening's events and shared
our stock of intuitive feelings and visions. We
did not trust Vortigern, and our spirits were

adept at discerning trickery. We slept fitfully that e'en, and our dreams did not bode well as they were filled with bad omens.

The next morn, we saddled up our mounts and were surprised to find that we were now to be accompanied by a troop of Vortigern's guards to "be sure we found our way to King Ambrosius with the news of the upcoming olive branch." In sooth, Taliesin and I were now prisoners instead of "honored emissaries." Something was definitely afoot, and we both put up our energy shield of magick by envisioning ourselves wearing cloaks of white light. We knew we were safer with our active defense mechanisms in place. All would be well.

****

As we rode along, with guards surrounding us on all sides, Taliesin and I could detect a pricklesome energy emmanating from the guards. We were reading their auras and detecting their malevolent energies. We knew then that they were not our benevolent "protectors." They had been ordered to take us away and put an end to our inclinations of planting seeds to join with Ambrosius by killing us along the way. Nay, Vortigern would not entertain sech thoughts of alliance. We did not tip our hat to them, and instead my friend and I nodded to each other knowingly and conversed by speaking telepathically. There is great power in silence. We could both feel the hostility growing toward the men who "guarded us." We intuited from the guards unguarded thoughts were that we were not being transported to "keep us safe from highwaymen," but rather, as "objects to dispose of." We also were attuned to the fact that the nobility that currently favored the Pendragon royal line, those wealthy men who were being invited to a "feast" were also not safe. Nay, many would die. Taliesin saw it in his dream last night. If these guards only knew that I was King Ambrosius's son, surely, I would not draw breath for long, nor my wizard friend either.

Taliesin and I vowed to do what we could to escape from our sentinels as soon as feasible and to thwart their plans for our demise. "*To know, to dare, to keep silent.*" This was our Druid motto for this journey. We also took great comfort in "*To know thine enemy is to defeat thine enemy.*" We decided to speak as little as possible and to simply listen as much as we could. We decided that a spell of Protection for our sakes would be in order as well as a spell of a Thought Changing.

We waited until that evening and when we were about to bed down, without speaking, but with our minds as one, we cast a circle. We stood with our backs to each other. Raising our wands towards the moonlight and scribing it in the air around us, we inwardly prayed this thought:

"Hail fair moon
With Thee commune
Ruler of the night
Guard us on this flight.
To not befall,
Nor deadly pall
Surround he and me
With safety be
By dragons light
Give us your might
Surround us hither
And safely thither
So mote it be!
So mote it be!"

Taliesin and I both also did magickally plant a thought in the collective minds of the soldiers to ransom us instead of disposing of us as Vortigern had ordered.

"Create in these men
A wish not to slay
but to defend
By the Powers of Good
Do as ye should
May the mind be swayed
Whilst our hearts obeyed
To do no harm
With this spell and charm."

The guards knew we were Sorcerers and were alarmed at first, but whence they did not see anything come of our posturing, our silence was taken as petulant defiance. They scoffed at the antics and chalked up our actions to being sheep-herded along to King Ambrose's castle instead of traveling at our own leisure. As the journey continued, and when our spirits showed that we were carefree and unaffected by them, yet still not talking, it unnerved them yet again. Nevertheless, we listened intently and ate quietly and did not speak to them nor to each other. So complete was our reticence that they soon forgot that we could even speak and treated us as if we were deaf mutes. The guards started to feel less angry and started talking freely amongst themselves. They boasted loudly on the ride, made plans whilst making camp, plotted in their sleep, contrived when they availed themselves of nature's call, it mattered not. We learned much from their discourse and smiled to ourselves. Over the next week of travel with our steeds and their soldier riders, we did not die nor were we murdered. Nay, rather we had started to look like abundant riches to the soldiers. They cooked up a new plan over the spit one night as the fire crackled and illuminated their conniving eyes.

Throughout, Taliesin and I simply remained quiet and calm and let their own greed motivate their agenda. Our spell of Thought Changing had surely taken effect. For now, whence listening to the men, we now heard an entirely different plan than what Vortigern had envisioned. Indeed, we were to be made a fatal spectacle before King Ambrosius and all his men. The soldiers were to make a dramatic demonstration if the King failed to ransom us for the set price. The "set price" for our freedom was a walk away reprieve from altercations for the kidnappers, and a handsome chest of gold to share. How'ere, that which they each vowed outwardly to split afterward was only in word alone. All the while, their inner thoughts betrayed them. For we heard clearly their innermost contemplations and of how each man plotted against the other, in their hearts and vowed superiority over each other. For each one of the rapacious sentries proved to have grasping thoughts of each owning ALL the coinage by any means. They would've sold their own mother afore all was said and done. And what would become of us, their hostages? Well, our lives as living breathing grateful Mages, would be subservient to King Ambrosius, whether we liked it or nay. It sounded plausible to the guards who thought their plan was fail safe. To justify going against their sworn Lord Vortigern, they even reasoned that this new improved plan would even work into his plan. For whilst Vortigern had offered a conciliatory dinner feast to all the supportive nobility of the Pendragons, the guards knew verily that he planned to kill each and every one of the guests and blame King Ambrosius to start the upheaval he'd been desiring. King Ambrosius would be kept busy with this distraction whilst Vortigern slayed all the King's nobility even as they spake. Vortigern wanted the crown, and he would have it. The guards had heard him say so. They were only helping him to do so. So the new and improved plan of ransom worked nicely into the guards' deliberations as well, for it was now a well-known part of warfare these days. For a knight, nobility or special personage was indeed worth a King's ransom if captured but worth nothing if he were to be killed. Without a banner of heraldry declaring our personage, we would need to have a dramatic event to gain the attention of King Ambrosius. The sentinels set about devising one.

Over roasted coneys the guards devoured the rabbits whilst they hatched the idea that would do the trick. A peasant messenger would be "persuaded" (by knife point) to run the errand and inform the King and company that Great Mages had arrived and would be "sacrificed" in full view of the castle. This, of course, would only serve as a diversion whilst two soldiers would hasten in another route and pinch what they could and double their take and meet them in the woods hence. Even on the outside chance that the King would not pay the ransom, at least the guards would get something for their pains and desertion.

It was interesting indeed to observe the degradation of a kernel of an idea bloom into total rogue machinations. We had wanted to avoid our imminent deaths, and so it seemed we would. It seemed like a plausible plan, and the soldiers had been working out the details for hours. It could work. Aye, to remain quiet, to plant a seed of an idea and let them cook the monster into a whole spider web of creation was a thing of beauty.

Per contra, we had already "seen" that we would be saved. It was a collective thought in the minds of locals; t'was HIGHLY risky to roast mages -what with curses likely to fly whilst in the roasting flames. The possibility that a Magician could invoke the wrath of the Christian's devil upon them was, indeed, terrifying to them. Little did these unenlightened simpletons know that Druids don't believe in the devil. Nay, our Horned God is a benevolent being. So we did not distress much over it but decided to do what we could to enjoy our ride through this area.

Once the soldiers had their new and improved plan (*which would also make them rich*) the adventure took on a whole different feeling. The guards relaxed and behaved much more like jovial friends as they imagined and planned how to spend their upcoming riches. It would be the first of my many journeys throughout Wales and Britannia. I confess that I enjoyed traveling very much. My love for horses and being one with the trees and air, what'ere the weather was, certainly was a boon to me no matter the circumstances. In the evening where'ere we stopped each night I would take the time to observe the flora and fauna and make notes about our travels in my parchments. One of the soldiers once asked to see what I was writing, but when I showed him, he couldn't read the notations that I had been jotting down, so it was illegible to him. Other than commenting on the renderings of birds, snakes and crawling creatures that I had been drawing, he dismissed the whole thing. I found the experience fascinating and informative!

Taliesin spent his nights seeking omens and jotting down the stars in his parchments. He was a Bard and so, while not being able to speak upon this journey, he turned inward and wrote poetry. He was a great Bard and constantly serenaded the sweetness of life. This venture along these roads untraveled was done in silence for us both. It was likely a challenge for one who loved to sing, and yet there was a beauty in the silence. It made us both turn inward, and we bloomed in spite of the quiet, or mayhaps, because of it. Yet it was our silence that kept the guards spellbound and on their mission. We dared not speak, we dared not disrupt the illusion.

Taliesin and I were in the realm of the Gods daily for we were in Nature. We spoke to the trees with our internal voices, and we sang with the birds in spirit. Taliesin and I both gathered herbs when'ere they availed themselves to us. We already had amassed bunches of agrimony (a beautiful yellow flower which stops bleeding of all sorts and helps relieve pain) along with couch grass for potions (which dissolves stones in the bladder and opens obstructions in the liver and gall) and medicinal wood betony (a nerve tonic and grand for the aged and their digestion) along the way. We were especially ecstatic when we stumbled upon a patch of vervain, which is sacred to Druids, and we felt blessed and on the right path now because of the appearance of it on this strange journey! Every time we stopped to rest, drink or to privy, we found some new wondrous flower or herb for our healing arts. By day, we amused ourselves by taking turns silently cloud busting as our horses plodded along. But in sooth, we also constantly prayed to the Gods for our safe passage and arrival back home. The omens we received along the way (in bird sightings and in natural elements of wood, tree and animal signs) gave us less and less to fear the farther afield we traveled.

Taliesin and I reveled in the time spent and enjoyed the journey which made our journey seem short-some. To us it may indeed be somewhat of a sojourn into the realm of the Gods, to witness creation and observe unfamiliar oddities and territory. This is in direct contrast to the tramping itinerary the soldiers experienced and who grumbled along the way making their campaign ever long-some in time and deliberations. It was a lesson in relativity, indeed.

Finally, when the soldiers spotted King Ambrosius' castle, we were told to dismount and were immediately tied to trees within sight of the fortress. Branches and firewood were placed at our feet. We assumed they meant to burn us in front of the castle if the ransom did not come through in a timely fashion. Vortigern's soldiers were not so much his true defenders, but merely mercenaries, bought and paid for. Obviously, they had not been paid enough in their minds for a job like this, and now they felt that their fortune was within their grasp. A likely messenger was found in the form of a peasant bringing back his sheep from the pasture and he was threatened within a blade's promise and cut enough to make it seem a likely oath to come. The sheepherder then ran posthaste to the gate to deliver the demands for our ransom, whilst his sheep wandered on this new grass. Two other guards slipped out round the opposite direction and desired a way in to the castle to pilfer what they could. We all then tarried amongst the flock now scattering aimlessly about, to wait upon the King whilst he received the news of the fiery display of roasted Druids to come. An hour passed and then another. The sounds of the bleating of sheep, the feeling of the bonds that cut off our circulation, the smell of the lavender patch that our funeral pikes had been set up on, the beauty of the castle from the distance, the activity of the soldiers playing dice whilst waiting, the thought of being roasted to death...all made for a most twisted pastoral scene. If not for my belief in our powers of spellbinding, and if I were a different man, I might have felt fear at this moment. How'ere, it was all quite amusing in its absurdity to me.

Suddenly the drawbridge opened and a flying column of the King's troops swarmed the rogue soldiers holding us, and there was a sudden melee. Many of Vortigern's men were dead and the rest mounted up and fled. The two that left previous as thieves did not stand a chance and were easily detained and caught at the gate. They had alerted the squad and handily disclosed where their brothers in arms were hiding. The moles turned coat in an instant and pledged allegiance to the King.

The King's guards watched and let some of the rogue sentinels escape. "That'll be just enough tale to give Vortigern something to cry about," said one of the King's guards. The rest of them scoffed and shouted at the retreating guards, while others cut Taliesin and me free from our bonds. We were promptly escorted to the castle.

The castle of the King of All Britain was, indeed, impressive. The walls were cut from Kentish rag-stone and each stone was expertly honed to a millimeter of precision. One could not even put a hair between the stones, so finely set were they! The streets we passed through were clean and the mortared walls were high, nigh unto five stories tall! As our horses followed where our new King's guards led us, I looked up and all around straining to see all that I could behold. I had ne'er seen such opulence! There were banners and crests blazoning upon the fortress walls, there were armored guards holding presence at particular doorways and carts full of produce and livestock aplenty. It seemed as though everyone we met, whether a horseman, scullery maid, lady in waiting or valet, were dressed exceedingly well for their station. The castle residents were excited to receive news from outlanders, and we were hustled into chambers of our own. Inside there were all kinds of pewter plates and gold and silver decorations. Tapestries lined the stone walls and embroidered fabrics lined all the tables and shelves. Up flights of stairs and down several hallways we wound around until we came to our quarters.

The houseman who led us to our lodgings opened the door for us. Inside were two beds laid with goose-down pillows, and fine sheets with silk duvets. There was a chamber pot within reach under each bed. The room had been swept clean and flowers bloomed in a vase next to the wash bowl.

"There will be servants in to help thee prepare for audience with the King. Baths are being drawn for thee, even as we speak." The well-dressed servant sniffed the air and squinted his eyes at us. "Aye, dinna spare the castile soap suds, have at it liberally." Taliesin smirked and wrinkled his nose at me and I at him. We blamed the horses. So we were given linens and towels and went to the baths.

In a large room filled with what looked to be a pond, there were others bathing in the warm water. It was a nicety from the Roman conquer that still remained here in Wales. It was all the rage, evidently. We quickly stripped off and relished the clean water, the smell of the soap and lingered in the decadent water whilst a servant or two helped to wash our beards and hair. We were then asked to step lightly and changed into our new formal robes that were laid out for us upon our return from the baths. The garments were grand, embroidered with suns and moons. My robe was blue linen, covered in symbols of nature and Taliesin's robe was an earthy brown linen covered with images of herbs. They were handsomely rendered and felt fine to us. We had much for which to be thankful.

We returned to our room from the luxurious baths and found a servant had left some victuals for us. There was pitcher of brown ale, two mugs, and some herb goat cheese and fresh bread on a trencher. We ate and drank the ale which was dark and bitter and cut the dust of the journey very well. The goat cheese was quite hearty and we did appreciate the food. Evidently, the King looked forward to hearing our tale of Vortigern and wanted to sate us and revive us a bit 'ere we did meet to sup with him this e'en.

After we ate, we both laid on our plush beds and napped until we were called to attend the festivities in the e'en. While it was strange being in this new affluent environment and knowing full well that I was soon to meet the man who sired me, I felt strangely calm. Liken unto knowing my destiny was upon me and all was in perfect order. I was reminded by a Druid saying that I had memorized: "Only when your mind is tranquil, at peace with your destiny, will an answer come."

All my life I had wondered about my father, and who was my mother? Ever since my Spirit Quest, I have known of who he was, but not from meeting him nor of knowing him as a person. I still knew not a whit of my mother.

I had given all my yearnings to the Gods and trusted my safety to them. I sent a prayer of Gratefulness to the Gods for this, my dream of meeting the man who sired me, would finally come to fruition. I also must've been exhausted because I fell immediately asleep after our long ride and ordeal.

In the 'tween hours afore night, a rapping came at the door. Taliesin was already up and had lit a candle. He opened the latch and a footman greeted us with "Good Sirs and most noble Mages, the honor of your presence is requested by King Aurelius Ambrosius. Prithee, I bid thee hasten to come presently."

I quickly straightened my robes, fluffed out my dark beard, and followed the footman and Taliesin to the banquet hall. I could smell the victuals before we arrived and the grumbling in my belly was liken unto a starved beast. It now reminded me that it had been a long time since we had a repast of this magnitude!

We were seated at one of the tables and took our seats upon the benches. We would be announced and introduced to His Majesty after all of our appetites had been sated. This was a goodly idea, as most gentles are more kind after they have been fed and it would bode well to meet the King in a contented state.

The long tables were laden with a sumptuous array of victuals, the likes of which I had ne'er seen in my time in the hills of Carmarthen. Aye, I had been treated well by my teachers and guardians, but this was something grand indeed!

Course after course came out from the kitchens upon trenchers and platters and bowls. A stew of hare, and marinated and salted stag. There were chickens stuffed with eggs inside! There were loins of veal, and all were in the first course! Taliesin and I ate vegetables and fruits and berries afore this, with fresh breads and grains along with some ales and wines. We did not want to insult our benefactor, how'ere, so we availed ourselves of all that was offered to us. It was always good to savor what the Gods had delivered as bounty onto our plates, and this was definitely the most sumptuous feast I had 'ere supped!

The second course dishes were more intricate, and there were dishes with sauces and creams, sugar plums and pomegranate seeds. There were meat pies containing venison, capons, chickens, pigeons and rabbit. There was a stuffing made with meat, eggs, saffron and cloves. I had ne'er had some of these flavors afore, so I often inquired of the steward. I did not want to appear daft, but indeed, this was a world of opulence that I had ne'er encountered and I wanted to remember and to learn as much of it as I could.

The next few courses were also heavy on the flesh of animals. There was a sturgeon cooked in parsley and vinegar and covered with powdered ginger, cheeses a-plenty and plums stewed in rosewater! There were bog beans, calabashes, squashes, peppers, cucumbers, shallots, leeks, lettuces and tomatoes with vinegar. For fruits there were bowls heaped with apples and plums, pears and elderberries, rhubarb sauce, quinces, grapes and finally sweet strawberries in a white cream. The last course contained a variety of port wine to wash down some preserves and pastries.

To say that my growling belly was silent t'would be a lie. It was now so full that it made gurgling sounds and I knew it would be time to expel some of the vapors soon that were building within me. Of course, belching and wind was to be expected, and Taliesin and I heard much from our surrounding compatriots at dinner! Evidently the custom here upon the expelling of some gaseous air was followed with someone shouting "Leave nothing for the devil!" Taliesin and I were very much amused by all the fanfare that the vapors heralded. We supposed it was a compliment to the cook. We vowed to pace ourselves if we were 'ere to dine so lavishly again with nobility! My mentor and I smirked and noted that we may indeed waddle like ducks out of the hall or mayhaps need a cart if we dared rise to go to the privy. Thankfully, we found our way there and back afore we were called to come and stand before the King.

I had not been able to see the monarch from where we had been seated in the hall which was filled with revelers. Up until now, I had been content in my life with my Druid teachers and studies and learning all about Mother Nature and the Gods and Goddesses and how best to please them.

E'en though I had long wondered about my father when I was a child, it was no longer a pressing matter to me. I was now a man, full-grown, with a man's muscles, desires and beard. My hair was long because I had ne'er deigned to cut it. I no longer needed to feel like an orphaned child, for I was complete in myself and in the Gods' ways for me. The magick that I had been learning was enough for me. Still, I oft wondered how my father, this King of my Spirit Quest, would look and behave.

We had been seated off to the side, and he had not seen us, at least not up close yet. I have no doubt that he had many detailed accounts about who we were, and Taliesin was renowned as a Seer from Anglesey. I was just starting to have tales told about me, how'ere, and it seems that my story had preceded me from our encounter with Vortigern, and my expertise with magick had grown greatly since I divined at Vortigern's wall. Mayhaps it was the guards who had rescued us were amazed that we were delivered as living beings and not brought in as corpses. For Vortigern's fame lie in his malice. Many in the land felt that Vortigern's style of warmongering and predictable terrorizing had not been inflicted upon us for some unseen magick, which we may have *devised*. They would be right about that. Our shields of protection, silence and inner talk had cast an armor of defense and glamour around us that Vortigern's sentinels failed to penetrate.

After a grandiose calling to order, the hall fell silent and the crowd finally assembled. Honors were given to His Majesty for the sumptuous feast and relative safety of the land. Next came the inevitable presentation of certain nobility, their wives, their accompanying progeny, all for to greet His Majesty for reasons of political or social alliance. Lastly the herald read aloud the news of the land. We waited patiently through all the expected flattery and posturing of the noblemen and all their deeds until we heard the Herald call out:

"Grand Mage Taliesin of Anglesey and Mage Merlin of Carmarthen come forward and present Thyselves!"

We both rose and proceeded to walk down the side of the banquet hall to the front of the dais where the King sat with his ambassadors and barons. A hush had fallen o'er the crowd. It was always curious to me to be greeted thusly; for whilst some gentles did not believe in magick, nor in the Old Ways, they certainly did not want to offend -nor cause any insult- to a possible sorcerer who may then be convinced that the clod might make a better newt than a man. No sense in tempting Fate, as it were, and so the crowd gave us leeway and a broad path opened up for us to process to greet the most noble Lord of the land.

Taliesin and I both bowed to His Majesty, but when my eyes met King Aurelius Ambrosius, a wave of recognition came o'er his face and mine. It were as if I was looking at mine own self 20 years advanced in age. I was stunned. My visage seemed to affect the King as well, and I could detect his urgency to speak to us in private. Taliesin looked at me and I at him, and we knew that the King had many questions and not only concerning Vortigern.

Abruptly King Ambrosius broke protocol, and His Grace said, "Good subjects, I have much to discuss with these learned sages of a disturbance in my lands. I shall withdraw to my chambers to discuss strategy with these enlightened ones. I bid you a pleasant e'en. I take your leave and ask that you continue on hither and enjoy the e'en in my absence." He then leaned towards his own valet and said quietly, "Bring the magicians to my chamber and make certain we shall not be disturbed."

When the King rose, all the of the subjects rose as one in accord. "God Save the King!" they all cried as one.

Taliesin and I were directed to follow hastily after the King, and we were ushered along as His Majesty kept a good pace. Down corridors and through halls we trailed along behind him and his servants. We finally arrived at a massive door at the King's quarters. Two sentries stood watch there. They saluted their leader and parted the way by moving aside their double-bladed axes.

     The door was shut behind us, and the King sat down in his private chamber and motioned us to do the same. When we were settled, he looked me in the eyes and said, "Esteemed Mages, I welcome you here, and we have much to discuss on how you can be of service to me and I to you and am very much interested in what news you carry about Vortigern and his plans. How'ere, I must ask you something removed from these subjects first. Merlin, when I saw your visage in the hall, a wondrous feeling of astonishment came o'er me, and I was compelled to speak to you in private. You are the image of myself when I was young and also of someone I loved; a woman by the name of Lady Adhan. If I were to dally in the realm of conjecture, I would say that we are of the same kith and kin. It is because your visage is liken unto mine own, and that your eyes be liken unto that of my Beloved of long ago, I cannot look past it. A curiosity is befuddling me as to how can this be. She, who is a nun devoted and secluded in the Church and you who are a Druid Priest, surely you must know the answer. Tell me, prithee, from whence your lineage comes!"

     The King had dropped his guard and played his innermost thoughts to us, strangers unto him. I admired his courage and candor. In sooth, it was disarming to see someone who is feared yet also revered, being reduced to being seen as just a man, his heart rent open to view and who hoped, beyond reason that his loved one was nearby.

I began, "Your Majesty, I do not have a 'lineage' as you say. I was sent as a boy to learn of the ancient religion at the feet of this, my master, Taliesin of Anglesey. Whilst he may have the information that you seek, I know not, for he has ne'er shared it with me, but has let me evolve and grow under the Gods' care, without influence of my missing parents. He kept my instruction strictly to the laws of the Old Ways. In sooth, this is the way of who I am. How'ere, in the realms of the ether and mysteries, I give you what else I know of. Upon a Spirit Quest on my sixteenth birthday, I did venture into realms of the unknown, in which, I did learn of three Kings who are my Destiny. The Spirit Quest told me your name, your brother Uther's name and your future nephew's name. From this, I do believe I am from the seed of your direct line. I pray you, hear me as I tell the tale of what I believe was my conception." I proceeded to describe to him what I thought were the details of one Beltane night eighteen years ago. The description of the cave, the man (of whom I was his exact younger replica) and a woman, and their tale of a hand-fasting all were recanted in full detail as if I had just experienced it for the first time.

The King sat in amazement whilst the story of his bedding Lady Adhan commenced. When I ended my story, he looked at me and spake: "'Tis the truth, by the Gods, I swear it. It is as you say, e'en down to the last word. By Zeus, thou art my son!" Aurelius held out his hand and grasped mine and pulled me into his bosom and the love that flowed betwixt us was real and powerful. When finally we drew apart, my father and I were One. Like a gift of the Gods, we absorbed it like nectar. There were grateful tears in both our eyes.

King Ambrosius went on: "Where is Lady Adhan now? I had heard rumor of her joining a nunnery and whilst I sent many messengers to try to reach her for many years, I have had no response from her. She must've counterfeited her love for me. For low these many years, I thought she was constant, but alas, I have no word to prove it." Aurelius looked away and stared at the tapestries in his room.

Taliesin spoke next. "Your Highness, verily, Lady Adhan loved you…too much so to risk shame upon your houses. She wanted her child to be raised away from the treacheries and politics of court and away from the Church so that Merlin may become the great Druid that she foresaw. This day has come. Lady Adhan put herself away in the keeping of the Gods and had the boy raised, low these many years, by me. She was generous to me and her family, and we kept Merlin well fed and clothed. She knew he was a Seer, even as she looked into his eyes at birth. She kept him safe and was always faithful to you by joining the Church as a celibate woman. Alas, though, my liege, I have bad news for thee and also for thee, my friend, Merlin. Lady Adhan passed into the Otherworld several years ago yet she is with you both now. This I know. For I believed that she has arranged by spirit this very meeting for you both to carry on, together, now that his teaching and growth into a man is complete."

While I never knew my mother, I felt her loss at this moment, but it was nothing as compared to the loss that Aurelius felt. He sat for several long moments, and we three prayed for her to find release and happiness in the Otherworld. We took up our goblets and toasted to her beauty, her care and concern, her Love for us. Then Aurelius toasted to his new-found son, which made us now a family reunited.

We spoke of many things late into the night. He wanted to know of my life growing up, my wishes and hopes and he told me his. There was more wine, and the servant brought us bread and cheese whilst the candles waxed long. Taliesin and I counseled the King about Vortigern and his duplicity and treachery and of his plans to thwart King Ambrosius at every turn.

It was a strange feeling that I had, sitting now in my father's rooms as a counselor to a King with my friend and guardian and mentor, Taliesin. It was the most like home in my heart I had e'er experienced. I was now, Merlinus Ambrosius, as my mother had always wished. And somehow, somewhere I felt that she did smile and was content in this knowledge of our unity. My life would be very different from here forward.

Afore we retired for the night, King Ambrosius said, "Merlin, I want to name you heir to my throne. I want you to consider that you could be King after me. Verily, I know that this is much to consider, and I shall give you time to adjust. We have much to discuss and to make up for time lost. On the morrow, I shall announce to the world that you are mine own son. I should like to start the process of including you in my heritage, in sooth."

I begged him prithee tarry with the announcement until after I did beseech the Gods and pray upon all this new information. I needed to consult with my oracles and my friend, Taliesin, before I could go forward. Aurelius did oblige, he understood that it was a new world for both of us.

Afore the night was out, Taliesin did officially complete and transfer his sworn guardianship vow to me o'er to Aurelius as my rightful father when he told the King this:

"M'lord, many years I have been a faithful servant to the last wishes of Lady Adhan. I have protected Merlin as my student and my ward. Indeed, I have taught him all that I know and he has risen to the challenge and hast become a Druid Priest in his own might and authority. I wish to transfer my Guardianship over to you as his father, now that he is a grown man, he needs not my protection any longer. My Liege, I shalt always be thy faithful servant, and

Merlin shalt always be a boon companion and friend to me. My title changes not my heart. May the Pendragon line live long and may the Gods guide you both…All ways and in all things."

Ambrosius accepted Taliesin's wish and my mentor was now freed from his vow to Lady Adhan. He had certainly done his duty.

Taliesin then asked of the King, "Your Grace, may I be permitted to travel back to my home in Anglesey? Now that my duty is accomplished, there is no need for me to remain hither nor at Carmarthen."

Aurelius thanked Taliesin with great affection, "Aye, and for your good service, I shall gift thee with treasure for your pains. Ye may stay hither as long as ye like, and when it is time for your journey, there shalt be packed for thee a train of goods as my thanks for my son and all that he has learned from thee. Also I shall provide soldiers for your safe passage back to Anglesey. Ye shall not be harmed."

Then Taliesin told me what I was saddened most to hear, "Merlin, 'tis well that ye are hither. It is your place, and no longer mine, for I shall be leaving on the morrow. Ye will now be with your own father, he who is your true family. 'T'is time to bond with him and for me to now to take my leave of thee. I must needs make my goodly path and go mine own way, and for you to take your path separate from me."

I spoke to my mentor, "Taliesin, I had often fancied that it was you who was my father, and indeed, you have been in so many ways for low these many years. I do thank you for all that you have done for me, shown me, taught me, and made me think for myself and to trust the Gods for the rest. May your path be easy and may you find joy."

Taliesin retired to his chamber for the night which gave Aurelius and me some privacy. I felt a pang of sadness when this wondrous man left the room. Aye, though I did stay a bit longer, and I too, did swear my love and fealty to King Aurelius Ambrosius, my father, the King.

Yea, it had been a most magickal and fateful day. Verily, for though I did gain a kingly father this day, a family line, a history and a name of fame to add to mine own, I also did lose a part of me, my mentor, my daily life with Taliesin, and tragically, the ability to ever know my mother.

I parted ways with my father this night and went back to my chamber to think about all that had transpired. When I entered our lodgings and I got into my bed, the sound of Taliesin's snoring across the room was truly bittersweet music to mine ears.

93

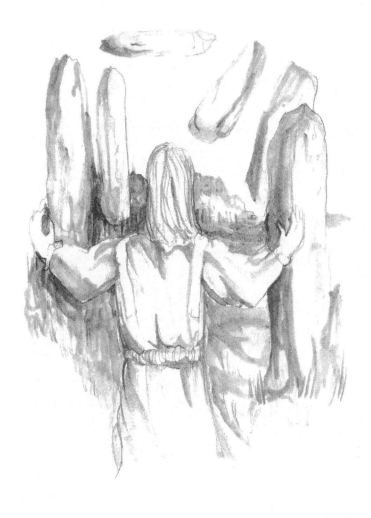

efore Taliesin left, he gifted to me one grand and priceless treasure. It was the incredible and rare Knowledge of Atlantis. He bade me take a "Vow of Silence to all but One who was Worthy." This I vouched willingly so. Then Taliesin taught a final lesson and I participated with my gifts as well and taught him too. We were to Dream Quest as one great adventure together. We found a safe and secluded place in the forest and laid down on our backs and gazed up at the trees. Slowly, and deliberately we relaxed into a meditative state, and then we did go into a trance, there in the woods. It seemed that our Spirits left our bodies and we became as small as dust.

We joined our collective consciousness and stayed together and darkness shrouded us as we moved in the sky, the great unknown called to us and we traveled past the stars. Our detached Spirits started to become aware of a beam of light in the distance. We followed that light that called to us and we saw the first of many levels of existence. This first level was filled with horrific shapes and shades, it was the makings of night terrors. We traveled past these ghastly shapes and went to the next level. Here there were deformed human beings with oddly sized body parts. We quickly left that level and went on to the third level, where hooded, grey shrouded entities came closer and closer to us. These were the Guardians of the Akashic records. This was more of a space in another dimension and not so much as a time period. We passed these entities with respect and the next beings we saw were lighter and brighter and less ominous. The light then traveled upwards and we floated up and followed it where it led us thither.

We then entered a world which was quite pleasant. There were trees and homes and yet there was no movement, no signs of life in this plane, only the shapes and colors and images of what we knew of from our own existence. At first all was quiet, yet the more we looked about we could detect some sound. We wouldn't call it music so much as harmonious sounds. We found it to be quite soothing. There was sound getting louder in one direction and so we made our way following those notes and resonances. We arrived at what we knew was a Hall of Records. I don't know why we knew it was called that, how'ere, we just knew it somehow. There were no floors, walls nor roof. Yet it as called a Hall. There in this hall was an ancient one. He handed us a book that said the word, 'Atlantis' on it.

This ancient one said, "Here is the wisdom firsthand which is now legend. Learn from it and grow in your work."

We opened it together. It was a most amazing story. Taliesin read out loud:

"It was beneficent time. BEings accepted prodigious feats as their birthright. Energies now unknown to man were common place and man and woman lived in harmony as One and with the world. All humanity was in kinship with the earth. There was an understanding that man would live in accord with the Earth and all her creatures. Man Beings lived their lives by the stars and in empathy with nature. All was well and as it should be. Yet there came a time of some discontent. Some BEings were not satisfied and wanted more that what was known to them. Some humans started to learn the art of treachery and of violence in order to garner Power over others. The Earth rebelled and Legend tells of the time when Atlantis then fell into the sea. Most of those discontented ones were drown and were no more. Many remaining Atlanteans swam to shore at Anglesey and made their life there. The new residents made it a land of knowledge, power and altruism. Down through the ages, enlightenment was transferred of the many fantastical Atlantean contraptions and amazing devices. The ability to understand contrivances to move heavy objects with the slightest touch of hand was available to the entire population. This is where the Druids of Anglesey and the Mavens of Avalon first acquired proficiency in magick."

Taliesin and I knew in our hearts that this was the Truth Incarnate. He continued reading from the book…

"When the Druids and Mavens decided to forever split their teachings up as single-gender scholarship, something sublime was lost and the Atlantean Way of Life was for'ere absorbed back into myth and legend. It is not as it was. It is not as it should be. The two need to be joined in Spirit and become harmonious again or all will be lost. Human BEings need to learn how to love and trust again or mankind will continue to repeat this pattern over and over until all is lost."

Taliesin closed the book and we handed it back to the Ancient One that kept the records. We traveled back the way we came and safely found our sleeping bodies on the ground in the forest, lying peacefully entranced. We entered them as ourselves, only now we were much more than we were before.

Taliesin and I spoke for many hours about this Dream Quest. We had both learned the ways of Atlantis and we vowed to be faithful to keep the philosophy and consciousness, safe until we found another whom would also promise its safety.

It was with this journey quest that I became Arch Druid of Albion and keeper of the Sacred Knowledge. Taliesin would make it known throughout Anglesey that I had arisen to this level. I would take my place with prestige and honor.

Soon I would say farewell to my teacher, my friend, my kindred brother, Taliesin and I vowed to remain in contact by every means and by Spirit and Omens always. We both had a mission and a destiny to fulfill and would know it when its time was near.

****

My life took on new meaning and a different direction when my dear friend and teacher left for Anglesey. Per contra, life was indeed opulent at court and a far cry from Carmarthen and my beloved Druid cave. I found myself constantly surrounded by those who would woo me, beg of my talents, seek my advice, and otherwise try to gain the King's favors through me.

I convinced my father to keep me close to him, but not yet to announce to court that I was his son and Prince of the Realm. I wanted to be a man of mine own bearing and talents and not only "the King's Son." I wanted to be a Priest and Wizard in my own right. I had my own name, and it was a hard-earned moniker. All one had to do, how'ere, was to look upon us both sitting side by side to see the resemblance. They could all see for certain that I was the King's own flesh and blood. But no matter, Aurelius made me his Chief Counselor and provided to me in all ways, and I did want for nothing. I became his staunch advisor in matters of court, to strategy of his lands, to dream interpreter. I was by his side whether I was his Prince or his Seer or his kin. It was all the same to me. I was his son, and we both reveled in the knowledge.

But the winds of change blew swiftly. Word arrived that Lord Vortigern had proven his mettle by serving the feast he said he would. He had arranged a gathering for many of the chieftains that showed loyalty to the King and invited them to a treaty feast between Saxons and Britains. It was delivered on counterfeit means, how'ere, and whilst enjoying their grand dinner, Vortigern had designed to have the Saxons slay them whilst they supped. Assassins rose up next to the chieftains, pulling out concealed long swords and slaying the unarmed nobles e'en as they arrived on peaceful terms. There was much blood and death delivered as a message to King Aurelius Ambrosius. This massacre was for'ere to be named *"The Night of the Long Knives."*

War ensued with the Saxons, and Vortigern was to blame for the latest flare-up. The land turned fierce, and battle-ready men rallied to the King's side. It was to evermore rid Britain of the oppressor, Vortigern and his villainous followers; he who would slay unarmed men who came to make a peace treaty. King Ambrosius and Uther and all their men then marched on Vortigern's lands. All had pledged to remain camped there until the walls were breached and his holdings were laid to waste, and his castle was besieged and burned. For a month, the fortress held until finally the tower was decimated and crumbled. The Pendragons had indeed clawed and tore at the very fabric of Vortigern until he and all of his family were put to death for their treachery. Peace finally came hard-won to Ambrosius's lands, the Saxons appeased, for now, and the usurper, Vortigern, was no longer a point of contention. Now there was reason to celebrate, and yet also to mourn the fallen. King Ambrosius desired to build a monument to honor the dead of the Night of the Long Knives. It was to be a reminder to all warmongers that peace would be celebrated and valued.

The King cast about for ideas and came up with one to inspire awe: "In keeping with the beliefs of your mother and me, and our holding fast, come what may to the Old Ways, I believe that there should be a stone circle erected. It will be a massive monument, built of Britain stone and raised on Salisbury Plain for all to see, for'ere, for posterity's sake."

Yea, though verily, which stones? I then dreamt about building a circle from stones gathered at Marlborough Downs and also blue stones from the Preseli Mountains. It was to be called *"The Giant's Dance."* I awoke and knew what was required of me to make it so.

I met with the King and told the idea to my father, Aurelius, who supported me. He said he would send me along with his brother, Uther, and his troops and all myriad of implements and ships to retrieve those stones. I told him that I did not need sech things and that all I needed would be a horse and a ship and a travelling companion. I knew that as a Seer, I would not travel well o'er the water. (It be a notorious fact that anyone with the Sight cannot pass o'er deep water without discomfiture). All the King did was laugh and send me on my journey with more man power and weaponry and conveyance than necessary. It was an expense that he did not need to spend. I implored them how'ere, he and Uther would not believe me when I stated my truths, so we started our journey to fetch the crags for the monument to be placed upon Salisbury Plain.

We arrived at each of the locations in the fall, much later than expected, for what with hauling men and gear, it took far longer than I had originally anticipated. We easily discerned which stones would be the ones to transport as they had been carved long ago and remained for this purpose, awaiting us as their litter to carry them to their niche of power.

Uther made a big show of commanding his troops to rope and tie and try to lift the stones. Try as he may, try as they may, no number of men, no team of horses could budge the gigantic stones. I merely watched as they availed themselves of all their strength and burned their passions without much ado.

Finally, Uther came to me, red-faced with anger and distress, and said, "Aye, these stones shall stand here till the world ends! They will not be moved! We will return to Ambrosius and tell him that you have failed!"

"M'Lord Uther, some things must first be believed to be seen." I walked o'er to the stones in front of the assembly and raised my arms and addressed them, "Dear Ancient Wise Ones of Sarcens and Blue, I do honor your strength, your wisdom and your resolve. I would ask you, prithee, to release and remove thy selves from this place, and to come and settle down in your exalted and rightful place of honor." The men all scoffed and laughed to hear me talk aloud to the old hewn rock.

Yea, though, verily I heard the stones tone a reply in their deep voice of gravel and granite, "Merlin of Carmarthen, we are ready and have been biding our time for your arrival. We lift only for Thee." It was a clear a voice as any, but the scoffing men heard it not.

I then thanked the Spirits of Granite and pulled from my satchel an instrument that I had fashioned, by Atlantean means of olde, which had been shown to me previously in my dream vision with Taliesin. I invoked and engaged its Powers. The stones easily lifted themselves of their own accord and hovered off the ground by several yards.

Soldiers and workmen fell upon the ground and beat their chests and prayed to their God to save them from such awesome Powers; these that I commanded. In sooth, it was an ancient means of propulsion and of leverage, but they could not, and would not, accept such a tremendous yet simple idea now in these Dark Ages of Man. These disbelievers were surely coming around to the ways of my magick and Power and would for'ere tell tales of this feat.

I proceeded to climb upon my horse and propelled the stones to follow me. Slack-jawed with disbelieving eyes, Uther, his men and all the craftsmen trailed along behind me and the moving giant quarry. We loaded ourselves onto the ship, and the stones glided along behind us above the water. Men would not leave the railing of the ship but instead remained to stare and cross themselves to counter the evil eye, and otherwise found themselves lost in amazement of the floating stones the entire voyage.

We landed again and travelled to Salisbury Plain. Whilst the stones would serve the purpose that Ambrosius wished, I had also planned to arrange the stones mathematically in sech a manner that in the future they would also serve other purposes. I had been calculating the stars and the dragon lines and worked with my instruments to bring this idea to fruition. The Giant's Dance would now serve as a calendar for calculating the stars to mark the Solstices and would be a meeting place for the future gatherings of Druids to come. A great awakening would come from communing with these stones. I had seen the future and knew that these massive hewn rocks would inspire disbelief, wonder, amazement and conjecture. It mattered not. All that mattered was that I would please my father by fulfilling his wishes, and by doing so, I would have set up a monument to Druidism for time eternal.

There was one more critical reason for my arrangement. I dowsed with a blessed willow branch, the fourteen major dragon lines to be absolute where they intersected. This took quite some time, but I had men available to help me mark the locations precisely, so it was completely accurate to the world map (which I foresaw would come in time). At the center of these lines is where the boulders would be placed to create a vortex of energy that would also become a place of vibrational healing. People would come to this stone circle and stand within it and ask for healing of the stones; they would thusly be healed. The energy that would be swirling 'round them would be palpable and cause direct alignment of their own energy centers.

The stones spoke of all this and their pleasure to me, and I thanked them for their help in this matter and vowed to set them down in a circular pattern. When the exact places were marked, I made a bit of a ritual, setting each stone and talked to each rock while I maneuvered the boulders into their new home. As I had listened to the stones murmur the entire journey, I also knew of and followed their yearning to place certain stones upon the top of other particular stones in their wish to stay connected as pairs or trios. Aye, there were relationships betwixt certain rocks! Most men dinna believe that rocks have spirits and feelings, but it is certain that they do and a part of Druid beliefs. I was true to the stones' urges, and they in turn promised to stand- no matter the climate- for eons to come.

When all was done, the circle was complete, something very magickal occurred. Just as the crags had whispered to me, the force and activity of their vibrations started a vortex of energy swirling into a geo-spacial spiral. I could feel the surge and throb of the stones' resonance emanating from the boulders. This circle would flow along on these dragon lines to bond them with other cultures 'round the world, sech as the Great Pyramids and the Nazca Lines, e'en as close as the Marden Henge in Wiltshire. They were now all placed in line together following the dragon lines.

A great vision came to me. The Giant's Dance was now in Salisbury Plain for the world for all eternity. Druids would now have another place to join, and this place would connect them and their pulse with the other monuments of the world, following the dragon lines from antiquity. I envisioned the future and was pleased. There was great delight to me in the fact that people in ages to come, would watch the sunrises on Summer Solstice and the sunsets of the Winter Solstices hither. I knew that if these Seekers would only think on what is here, they would find much more wisdom in this wondrous Earth. When all was settled and finished, I concluded my ritual and knew that the Gods and Goddesses were pleased indeed.

Uther and his men, how'ere, were terrified beyond reason and vowed to keep me at arm's length.

When we returned, King Ambrosius was well pleased and there was a ceremony to dedicate the The Giant's Dance as a permanent marker to his fame as a remembrance for those who were slain on the Night of the Long Knives. Aurelius, being a sympathizer to the Old Ways, invited Druids from o'er the land to welcome them to commune there. A great and wondrous ritual was to happen on the e'en of the Winter Solstice. Bonfires and torches were lighted and as the sun set, their blazes radiated and shined off the stones to mark the night! The Apostolic Church was not happy with the new monument, but they fussed not. Their priests and bishops were busy with the start of building their own stone monuments which they called cathedrals. To each his own. It is all well and good. Druids welcome all faiths as long as they are kind and love the Earth enough to take care of her.

****

O'er the next several years, I lived and learned in my father's counsel and he in mine. We tried to make up for lost years and ate most of our meals together and spent our free hours talking. We also looked very similar. He and I both had long, dark hair and beards (although his was now speckled with grey). Buxom lasses did occasionally fill his bed, and there were many offers from them to fill mine as well, but I was disinclined to slake my thirst. E'en though I was a full-blooded, able male, and I had my own urges for female company, I resisted one buxom lass in particular. She seemed to remind me of someone, I know not who, for I knew no lass before that looked like her. The lass was sweet and fun and had long golden hair. A bit of a ready smile and blue eyes. What I liked most about her, aside from her comeliness, was that she was a great listener to whate'ere I spoke about. Once as we were walking in the gardens after dinner one night, she pulled me aside and kissed me full on the lips. It was certainly a surprise to me, and I admit, I did enjoy it. The stirrings in my loins told me of it without a doubt. How'ere, I did not want to leak my Spiritual Power out her or to any other. Access to me meant access to my Power; that would only confuse those who could not deal with what that entanglement would mean in their life. Linking physically with me would entwine our spirits. I did not want to get diluted by a young lass and her lusty cravings, nor did I want to become enslaved by mine own delight with her and forget my work. Conjointly, I resisted her temptation for I knew she was not the One who was foretold for me. Alas, though she had not made herself known to me…yet. So whilst my handsome father did cool his desires occasionally with a bed-warming maiden, I did no such thing and endeavored to contain my Power.

$$* * * * * * * * * * * * * * * * * * * *$$

Aurelius took me on grand hunts. I was a good rider and archer and had learned to hunt to feed myself, if need be, back when I was a boy in Carmarthen. How'ere, I usually ate only eggs and fish and not much meat, (only when my blood called for enhancing). I personally did not agree with hunting for sport and for the thrill of the kill. It was not the Druid way. I saw that vast amounts of damage were done to the forest and to the numbers of creatures. But I did appease my father and go, as it was time I could spend with him. We played chess and dice far into the night whilst we spoke of many things. I told him as much as I was able about the mysteries of life and did help him in his administrative duties and in counseling his subjects. Every blue moon, we would go into the woods in the glow of the stars.

Once in a pleasant happenstance, we came upon a faery ring. Gazing at the natural circle of mushrooms growing in a largesome ring, and conversing with my father, I did tell him that these rings are sometimes called Sorcerer's Rings. Most of the peasantry avoid such places due to their level of danger associated with the trickery of the fae. I did see, that it was a good time to call upon the fae, how'ere, this time, I felt safe enough with this place and knowing a bit about the signs and the proper behavior when dealing with faeries, we stayed *outside* the circle this particular full moon night and instead of barging in where angels fear to tread, we walked round the ring nine times in a deosil direction. If we had walked round it the opposite way, and done it widdershins, then we would've been under the fae's beck and call. This would be most unfortunate, and any unsuspecting fool to blunder through a faery ring on a full moon, mayhaps would be forced to dance and dance till eternity ends! How'ere, 'tis best to err on the cautionary side whence dealing with the sidhe. Whence we had gone round nine times, but never ten, we called to the King instead. I did introduce him to King Auberon. King of the Fae met King Ambrosius, and as both were monarchs, they were equally honored. It was only right and good to do so. Both Kings of the Land were respectful and did honor each other in their own unique way. It truly was a magickal e'en and one I will ne'er forget. This realm of the 'Good Neighbors' was magnificent and we were careful to only stay a moment, for a moment therein can be like no earthly time and we were lucky to step in and out so fairly. It was a magickal moment that we did share and spoke often of, yea, though, verily only in the King's private chambers.

****

Over the next year, I enjoyed my time and learned my way around court and its inhabitants. The King helped me to learn the ways of courtiers and how to be a perfect stranger whence visiting others in their castles and how best not to offend. I learned much from my father. I was counseled about who was and who was not to be trusted in his eyes, (how'ere, I could see into a heart and knew the secret thoughts therein, but he wished to show me his leanings and they were very correct using his intuition). My father was a fair man, per contra, he had to dole out harsh justice occasionally. I went on progress with him during several summers whilst the King visited his subjects in the country. I enjoyed the lands that he ruled. I would meet Druid Priests in each place, and we would gather and share information and encourage one another and learn and share our talents and gifts. It was a wondrous time of adventure, honesty, love, friendships and family, and I relished it.

The King's library was my favorite place to be other than in mine own dwelling. I was given large chambers, and in them I had set up a workshop to dry herbs, make poultices, study, and do my spell casting. I was left to my own devices, and I enjoyed the life and absorbed as much as I could whilst here. I spoke to several alchemists of the realm and we enjoyed many philosophic discussions together over wine and stirred the pot of transmutation with each other.

****

I was curious as e'er! Life was indeed fascinating and proceeding exceedingly well. Almost *too* well, evidently, for circumstance, much liken unto the wheel, did turn round once again and bring with it new complications.

The King was taken to his bed with a wasting illness. Whilst he tried to rally, and whilst his doctor and I did all we could in our realm of healing to comfort and soothe him, it seems that m'lord would not have long to live. I was summoned to his bedside one e'en along with Uther and some of the King's Counsel. He was attempting once more to sway me to becoming Prince of the Realm, then High King, and to make the decree 'ere Aurelius passed into the Otherworld.

I knelt on the side of his bed and looked into my father's eyes. He was a virile, handsome man of forty-four. This sickness was thought to be liken unto a poison and he was fading fast. Surely, there was treachery afoot.

Aurelius held my hand e'en as he was slipping away and asked me yet again to let him crown me King in his stead. He had no heir other than myself, this I knew, and yet I also knew that the crown was not meant for me. It was for Uther, and his son after him. This had all been made apparent in my Spirit Quest when I was just sixteen.

"My Lord, my dearest father, here in front of your Counsel and your brother Uther, I contend that I cannot assume this role. I have seen visions and this is not my path, although it is an honor to be asked, and I understand that, as your only child, it is your wish for me to take the scepter. Verily, I have seen my future, and the

Gifts that I have been given are for other events that will carry on for future generations. It 'tis my duty to continue on my own path. I do respect and love you greatly, and wish not to vex thee, but nay, m'lord, I shall not take the crown. I plead for your mercy and understanding in my decision. How'ere, I will vouchsafe to carry on as I have as your Mage, and instead, be Counselor and Mage to Uther as well, should he need me."

My father's weak smile faded at my words, but still he held tight to my hand and squeezed it with what remaining strength he could muster and he said, "As you wish. Alas, ye shall not be King. Blast, son, but you have the Will of your Mother! Yet I always loved and respected her for it. Ye shall be provided for, as my son, though, e'en if thou dost protest."

A scribe and parchment were brought forth by the King's command to capture what he said next.

"Counsel, be it known that this is my son, Merlinus Ambrosius Pendragon, known as Merlin. He passes the birthright of his name onto his uncle, Lord Uther Pendragon, who shall reign as High King of Britain. I grant that Merlinus Ambrosius Pendragon own the land of his birth, and that he have the rights and riches as my son, for'ere. Be it known, also, that Uther Pendragon shall take my crown, and barring no heir apparent from my brother, Merlinus Ambrosius Pendragon shall reign to further our

Pendragon line. So it is written, so it shall be done."

Uther came forward and spent some time with his brother, and there was a closing of their lives together and their brotherly love shone through. Uther was extremely relieved to hear that I was not taking authority o'er him, but was instead pledging my allegiance to him as his Seer. I would do what I could to ensure that the events of my vision of the Spirit Quest fell as they were foretold to me.

I would not leave my father's bed and endured to be his Guide and Priest all the long night and remained by his side. There was a sickness within Aurelius that was rampant and his fevered brow showed no cooling. His doctor, manservant and I were the few who stayed with him throughout that fateful night.

I prayed with him for a peaceful passing over to the Otherworld. I performed the Druid *Prayer for the Dying* and anointed him with pure water and burned sage and myrrh and prayed thusly:

Time has passed,
the Wheel has turned,
Tis time to move on.
Thou shall walk hand in hand
with the Ancient Ones.
Thou shalt be with your loved ones
who went before ye.
Great Father Sun and Great Mother Earth,
welcome your servant,
Aurelius Ambrosius Pendragon, home.

I continued to pray and clear his energy until the morning light when he took his last breaths. His last words were "Now I shall be with my beloved, Adhan."

The manservant closed the drapes against the sunshine, blew out the candles and wept. Bells tolled forty-four times to ring out the years of the King's life, and the sound carried for miles. With each strike of the bell, a knife pierced my heart.

So ended the book of life in this world of King Aurelius Ambrosius Pendragon, my father and friend. So it was that I had built the tombstone monument for mine own father. So opened another new book and life to him in the world beyond. Blessed be. It was decreed that King Ambrosius was to be buried within the circle of the Giant's Dance. Indeed, the last time I had been thither in the Giant's Dance I was so elated and proud to offer it to my Lord the King. How'ere, now as we formally ensconced him there for all eternity, my heart was heavy. I had not Seen at that time that it would also be my father's resting place.

After the month long grieving process for the King throughout the kingdom and then the subsequent festive crowing of the new King, Uther Pendragon, my life changed once again.

****

I resumed my studies in the library and spells and alchemy in the workshop; I spent little time at court anymore. Whilst Uther made a fine leader, he was a bit too rash and loud for my sensitivities, and very much I missed the relationship that I had made with Aurelius. Forasmuch as I loved my conversations with my father, I disliked my dealings with Uther. He was a proud man and ever after he was suspicious of me after the moving of the Giant's Dance. Henceforth, he dealt with me as rarely as possible.

How'ere, one day he came to me with a vexing problem. He was smitten with Ygraine, the Duke of Cornwall's wife, whom he had met at court during the funeral events. There was no calming him. He had seen her and he had desired her with his whole being and craved no one else. He felt that she would be the perfect Queen (aye, if it were not for the pesky fact that she was already a happily married woman with children of her own).

One day shortly after this, Uther came to me and said, "Merlin, I canna eat, I canna sleep. My duties as leader are suffering for the love of Ygraine. I MUST have her. There be nothing more to do for it, but command ye to help me. I am in agony. Ye have Powers, do ye not? Make it so."

I knew this was a pivotal moment for the fate of the Pendragon line, and for my crucial involvement with the King. This was what my link to him would be, for'ere. Whilst I always seek to be for the petitioner's Greatest and Highest Good with my magick, I ne'er try to interfere with fate, I knew that there was a son and future king to come of this union, and I must, somehow, arrange for this bonding.

"Aye M'lord Uther, I have Seen it and so, indeed, it shall be. I do wish that ye shall wait for time and for Fate to contrive her marriage to thee. I do not wish to deceive anyone for the fulfilling of lust."

"Merlin, do what you have to in order to please me and make this deception so. I *must* have her."

"Verily, well, Sire, by your command, I shall work a powerful spell of alchemy on thee. Ye shall be made to resemble Gorlois, the Duke of York, himself, and ye shall bed his wife in his image. This way, the Lady shall be true in her heart to her husband, for she is a faithful and kind, and loyal noble Lady. I happen to know that Gorlois is now off fighting against the Saxons in the hills. If ye permit me to transform thee into his very likeness, ye may have her this night. The spell shall last only until the morning light, then ye shall return to thine own self. So, needs be, ye must be gone before the sunrise."

King Uther readily agreed. With my art and with alchemy, I was able to cast a Transmogrification spell upon Uther, and he became the physical embodiment of the Duke of York. We hastened a quick journey to Tintagel Castle, and I accompanied the King to aid with the illusion.

When we arrived, the gates were opened easily to us by the Duke's guards who saw their Master riding in. "Gorlois" dismounted quickly and was ushered in by his servants bustling about to bring him in to meet with his Lady Ygraine. When he saw her, he kissed her hard and with a ferocity that surprised her. He barely hugged the daughters, Morgause and Morgan Le Fay.

I watched all this, as I was there under pretense to "officially" encourage Ygraine to permit the damsels to be educated upon the Isle of Avalon. Verily, the girls had the Sight, and in sooth, they knew it was not their own father as they could easily see through the counterfeit visage. Morgause and Morgan were wide-eyed with amazement kindled with fear at the stranger taking liberties with their mother. The girls tried to warn their mother that it was not father with them, but she did not heed them, but only bowed to her Lord. Ygraine was a trusting soul and did not have the Sight. She could not see the Truth as the wee perceptive lasses could. It was her saving grace.

And so it was that Uther deliberately and hastily took Ygraine to the Duke's own bed and enjoyed the Duke's marital pleasure; even as Gorlois was that very moment currently fighting on a battlefield and in the thick of defending his lands. All this occurred even whilst the King was cuckolding the Duke's wife.

Ygraine felt that her husband acted very differently, more virile and more amorous, and did not know why he was home instead of being out in the war camp as he said he would be, but it mattered not. She loved her husband and was subservient to him and his needs. She was otherwise convinced it was the Duke himself.

The girls, how'ere, remained alarmed and watched the story unfold for themselves. When "Gorlois" and I left in the wee hours of the morning, we did so under the guise of being called back out to melee. When word came later that following day, that *(the real)* Gorlois had been killed in the fighting, he was brought home the next night by his men. The soldiers carried the slain Duke with them and the sad tale of his strength and valor and death the night before.

"Surely, you mean another night? For verily, m'lord was with me just this last night in our own bed."

"Nay, m'lady, he was killed at the hour o' ten bells last e'en."

Ygraine was morose and confused and went to her bed to mourn, thinking all the while that her husband's spirit must have come to make love to her one last time afore he traveled to the Otherworld.

After the funeral, and o'er the next two months following, King Uther hastened to come to the grieving Ygraine. Gifts and gowns and presents for the Lady and the girls and all manner of delicacies were sent from Uther to her. He started sending her love notes and then, a proposition of marriage to save her from widowhood.

She could not refuse the King, as she had her daughters to provide for and to raise. There was also a new development, which was not yet apparent but soon would be. Ygraine was now with child. Aye, for in her mind, so it would seem, she was pregnant with the child of Gorlois's ghost. She told Uther the news of her predicament and the King promised to raise the baby as his very own. With those promises, Ygraine consented to marry Uther and the sooner the better, under the circumstances.

After a ceremonious funeral was held for Gorlois, and a formal (but short) grieving period was accomplished, a hasty wedding ensued. Uther had his Queen. How'ere, the stink of deception and the betrayal to the Duke of Cornwall would remain as a shadow o'er the marriage, and the baby for'ere. This I had seen. Even so, Uther loved Ygraine and she in turn, did learn to love him well and truly cared for him. They were rarely apart and when they were, they pined for each other greatly.

Per contra, after the wedding of Uther to Ygraine, when she and the children were now ensconced in the High King's castle, the birth of the new bairn came to the newly wedded couple as a mixed blessing. The parents loved him without end, but the sisters Morgause and Morgan le Fay felt they had been usurped and displaced in the Queen's eyes. The girls' previously loving hearts turned to stone at the funeral of their father. The lasses feigned to love the new Prince but in sooth, they did not. To the sisters, he was Uther's child, in looks and by spirit, and that they were nothing more than bastard baggage to the King.

When I saw the lasses at the time of the birth, I knew their thoughts and what they felt in their hearts. They would always blame me for the deception and death of their own father. In their eyes, I was cruel and false, how'ere, I had to do what I did. It was not of mine own choosing, but the path that Fate had decreed for me. Arthur had to be born to rule Britain. This I knew, whilst the lasses did not.

The new boy Prince was to be named "Arthur" by the King's decree… and slanderous other names by the older sisters who desired to destroy him. After the bairn was weaned, Uther forcibly removed the babe from Ygraine's safe arms and handed him to me. I was to take him away, keep him safe from harm and ensure the boy was raised elsewhere. I would conceal him by magick until the time came for him to take the crown.

I arranged to have Arthur raised with nobility, away from court, at Sir Ector's fortress to keep him protected. Sir Ector was a good man and promised to raise Arthur as his own and to turn him back o'er to the King when he was called to do so. I promised that I would, from time to time, go there to teach the child and to keep the King informed of his progress. A spell of invisibility surrounded the child.

The King would not allow the budding, talented young Mavens, Morgause and Morgan le Fay, to attend Avalon, but instead they were to be married off posthaste in an attempt at alliance. This would also handily free Ygraine from motherhood to be Uther's full-time attending and loyal bride. This decision further enraged Morgause and Morgan who were denied their goodly mother and sent far away from her. The young ladies conspired to learn dark magick in order to avenge their father, the Duke of Cornwall.

In time, the young lasses grew in talent, wisdom and cunning. I would find out first hand, later on, that their combined dark powers of magick would prove to be formidable, e'en to me, the Arch Druid Priest of Albion.

IV

gave much thought to the placement of the boy prince, and arranged to have Arthur raised with nobility and graces, away from court, at Sir Ector's fortress. The Lord would keep the boy protected and also exposed to new ideas. I had written to Sir Ector, and a furtive communiqué was sent to him. I would work an enchantment of invisibility around the babe and surround the child with magickal protection.

When I saw the lasses, Morgause and Morgan le Fay at the time of the boy's birth, I knew their thoughts and also how they felt in their hearts towards me. And yet, it was in the fates for me to fight them in the end. How'ere, this was not that day. This day, the girls cried and clung to their mother, even as they were given the news that they were now to grow up much faster than they all thought.

No matter how I tried to reason with Uther, the King would not allow the budding, talented young Mavens, Morgause and Morgan to attend Avalon to receive goodly training for their gifts. Instead they were to be married off posthaste to the brothers, King Lot and King Urien, respectively, in an attempt at alliance. The girls would be well provided for and would be Queens in their own right.

As Uther forced Ygraine's daughters from her, he also unwittingly set up their forever cold hearts. For the girls only truly desired to remain with their mother, their home, and now that she was Queen, the girls fancied themselves daughters to King Uther. Even if they were not of his own seed, they felt it was their due because of the beguilement of their mother. The lasses felt that Uther *owed* them that much. King Uther, how'ere, thought nothing of the kind. He wanted to rule his kingdom as he ruled his house, and that was with complete obedience, regardless of his own actions.

The King told the court and all gathered that he was disappointed to see me go, leaving him as an advisor; how'ere, I did feel with my intuition, that with my absence he would also feel relieved a bit as well. His only son, the Prince, would now be safe and I, his nephew, would not be hovering as another rightful heir. Even though I had signed off my claims to Ambrosius's throne, Uther would for'ere be suspicious of me and my magick.

Before I departed, Uther walked me to his stables and gave me a wondrous gift. It was the offer of two fine horses to hasten our departure. One filly he picked for me was a Welsh Cob who was pitch black save for a ghostly white face. "She's always reminded me of your powerful magick. Her face is haunting with that pale visage," said the King. This mare had a long black mane and two white boots on her front legs. "Such spunk and fortitude I have ne'er seen possessed by an equine. She is truly a King's horse. I have named her 'Bowrider,' she is swift and surefooted. She shall keep you safe."

As I greeted the mare and petted her, I felt instinctively that we were a match as grand new friends. Then Uther gave me the pick of his stable for another horse to carry the boy and what'ere I would need along to Sir Ector.

Spirit called me to marvel at a sand-colored palomino mare with a long pale mane. She was curious and seemed to take to me forthwith. "Now that one is a funny one. She can muster a way out of damn near any fence or gate. She is quick-witted and inspects everything," Uther said.

I looked her over and said," I should like to call her 'Nosy' because she wants to learn everything!" He laughed and said, "I give them both to you, for your usage. Godspeed." He also granted me the tack, reins and what would be needed to keep them. I thanked him and yet returned all but the most simple of tack and accoutrements. "I cry yer mercy, Your Majesty, how'ere, I shall be traveling lightly and incognito and need not the ornamentation which would note me as royalty whilst journeying." The King nodded in agreement. I knew the King also wanted me to hie away from him and his crown, these were but parting gifts and I took them willingly so.

Ygraine made sure her stewards packed for me some grains, dried meats and fruits, wrapped cheeses, several loaves of dark bread and a pipe of wine to start my journey with her son. With my horse saddled and the other packed with supplies, I mounted early one summer morning with Arthur nestled in front of me, and I bolstered him in my arms. The child would grow up in a saddle. He would be a good rider. It was slow going as we four (the horses, toddler and I) all had to learn to get along together. At one point I devised a bit of holder for the bairn on the back of Nosy, and linked her to walk alongside Bowrider. I needed to have a respite from holding the child and could more easily control the reins. I did not like his occasional crying, so I was constantly finding ways of amusing him, comforting him or helping him to sleep. I admit, I loved his laughter. The animals and I got along and learned about each other quickly. They seemed to be very intelligent and soon I heard their thoughts, which were mostly about clover patches and wondering when we could get a drink. Sometimes the horses would send thoughts to each other about the path, some hornets up ahead or that they felt they needed to be scratched. I did what I could but wanted to make good time. I would have interesting conversations with both the horses and with the babe as we walked or trotted along. This was an adventure for them as well as for the infant and I, but soon we all felt the camaraderie of being a team on a grand adventure!

It was at this point in the journey, with the earth in full bloom, with the birds singing, the sound of my horse's footsteps on the dirt and cracking twigs with every step, that I began to bond with this new little man. It was a journey of freedom for both of us. I was finally free from court myself and felt like I had been given the keys to a new life that was now mine own choosing! No longer was I indebted to anyone. No master, no father, no King. I was mine own master. I was mine own father. I was mine own King. And this wee babe would be liken unto mine own son. I could raise him as I saw fit. He would be King one day, and I would have influence o'er what kind of a man he would grow up to be. This was an opportunity of grand proportion, and I thanked the Gods for the chance to do so.

And this new boy Prince. What of him? He had just lost the only parents that he knew and would, no doubt, always wish for their love someway in his life. I prayed that he would not let his need for affection stand in the way of decisions when he would reign o'er the entire Empire.

I now understood the great responsibility that Taliesin must've felt in raising me. He was a good and kind teacher, and so I would try to emulate him. Once I had found my father, I knew that he was a strong and powerful man, and so I knew that I would be as well. I thought of Uther and how he made decisions that were uncomfortable for others in order to make his life and country the way he thought it should be. I suppose that he was only doing what was best in his mind for his path as well. This too, I would have to do. The hard and uncomfortable choice was sometimes for the Greatest and Highest Good. I promised the Gods that I would be true to mine own self and to act in ways that would make the world a better place. From here on out my thoughts, words, deeds would be to benefit humanity, sometimes even if it was not to mine own benefit. But surely, I would need to care for myself the utmost in order to care for this child.

I also reveled in caring for my horses, Bowrider and Nosy, as well. They were a pleasure to brush down in the evening. We enjoyed each other immensely! I only hobbled them lightly in the evenings and they stayed contentedly nigh and safe by me. I would listen to their soft whinnies and murmurings and could tell when they were bothered by something or someone. I learned to listen for their communications with each other and with me.

****

Arthur was a toddling child of three when we arrived at Sir Ector's castle. It was a rainy, dreary day when the drawbridge was opened to us. My horses were glad for the dismounting and the hay that was surely to be delivered to them for a job well done. It had been a long trip, with days of unending riding and nights under the stars by firelight. I managed the entire journey alone with the bairn with little event, for I did have magick by my side. I put a dome of protective energy around us as I slept or left the child to forage for firewood and food. The horses too, seem to look after him when my back was turned and would whinny when they thought he was in danger. We ate well on what the forest and fields provided. We did not want. I had brought some supplies with me, as a gift of the King and Queen for the journey. We also carried some treasure for Ector in payment in kind for his fostering of Arthur. Ector would be recompensed for his duty, no doubt, now and in the future in the King's graces.

Sir Ector was also known throughout Wales as Cynyr Ceinfarfog, Lord of Caer Goch. His name meant "the Fair Bearded." He was a Lord in Dyfed, and one of my mother's countrymen. I could trust him. He was a wealthy man and had several fortified estates including Castell-Coch. This was where Arthur would be raised in anonymity and assurance.

On the morning we arrived, just as we were coming up over the burn, Sir Ector's Castell-Coch loomed large. I carefully dismounted and asked for admittance. It was indeed, a formidable fortress, but modest in comparison to the High King's castle. There were several towers and baileys and a large keep. Arrow loops positioned into the masonry surveyed and protected every angle of approach. There was a small, sturdy main gate which was accessed only by a single lane bridge. It was simple and unadorned on the outside, save for Sir Ector's coat of arms declaring his ownership of it and the surrounding land. Inside, though was an entirely different story.

For his castle building, Sir Ector had hired all sorts of craftsmen from his own locality to benefit from doing the iron work, the paintings and the art. Passing travelers with skills were courted and fed whilst they installed intricate scrollwork and stood on scaffoldings at the rafters. It was done with a free heart and a full belly, so those talented wayward travelers would decide to stay on here at Castell-Coch for extended periods of time whilst they enjoyed creating. They would be warm, dry, safe and fed whilst applying their craft and talent for posterity's sake. What could be better? Hundreds of painted panels adorned the rooms with fairies, cherubs, ivies and playful imps. Thousands of gold-painted fleur-de-lis made an interesting border from room to room. It was obvious that the artists felt at home hither and the artwork made the onlooker feel joyful when they viewed it. Indeed, Sir Ector and Lady Anna were joyful people and it was evident that their servants worked with willing hearts for them. It was a goodly arrangement for all.

The kitchen was simple, and yet, set up well and able to cook and feed many in its arrangement of pantries, cheese cupboards, wine racks, and wooden counters buffed o'er the ages of many a trencher and platter. Mice were kept to a minimum by the house cats which were allowed in the kitchen. The dogs were allocated a more respectable position, which was anywhere Sir Ector was. He loved his hunting dogs and treated them like family. They were underfoot but well-behaved hounds for the most part. Sir Ector was wise, for the outside of his fortress showed great strength and a Spartan adornment. Once inside the gate, how'ere, the furnishings, paintings and decorations showed a Lord and Lady who enjoyed the finer things in life. There was an opulent room made for matters of justice and for entertainment. The walls were painted intricately and there was much lattice work. Several balconies were on the open-air floor above for viewing from different angles. There were benches for the community to wait their turn with Sir Ector during times of judicatory duties. Ector was a fair Lord, but taxes did have to be paid, and he did try to keep peace in the land and his peasantry safe. It was *Noblesse Oblige*; the responsibility of the wealthy to act with generosity to those in lesser standings and he took that responsibility seriously.

Sir Ector and his wife, the Lady Anna, came out on one of the baileys to welcome me. As soon as she saw the boy, Lady Anna scooped him up and ushered him inside undoubtedly for a bath and some food taken from her own hand. She would definitely be a good mother to him, and I smiled when I saw the joy in her face as she cooed and snuggled him under her wing. He would be well.

Whilst Lady Anna was off spoiling her new toddler, Sir Ector and I talked of many things into the night: King Ambrosius's death, the new King Uther, and mostly of the boy and of his upbringing. I agreed that the ruse should be complete, and to let the boy assume that Ector was indeed, his own father. This was to be his lineage, at least for now. I told Sir Ector that the time would come and be apparent that the boy's fate had arrived. The opportunity would present itself without a doubt and then his nobility and heritage would be acknowledged. This was a promise of the King -and I then produced documentation of proof with the King's own seal in wax. Uther had thought of almost everything, and Ector seemed content in this knowledge.

After the long discussion in the knight's private rooms, I did also present the King's gifts and the child's gold for his keeping. I knew that there would be more coming sporadically from Uther, to keep Ector happy, most especially at holidays and the observance of the day of his birth. When I saw the boy being loved by Anna and her servants, and playing with the Lord's dogs and cats, I knew that he would be raised well here, and safer than at home and much more the better than to be around his sisters, who could not be trusted around him.

I knew that Arthur would grow up in the perfect setting. There would be food, structure, lessons with a teacher, lots of animals and local children for him to grow up and play with. I wanted to provide a chance for Arthur to be gregarious rather than growing up to be the hermit like myself. I had grown up accustomed to being alone or with only a few people around. This place would be different than my childhood for the boy, and yet also suit the King's plans whilst also giving the lad a safe and pleasant environment.

But just to be assured of his safety the morning that I was to depart Ector's lands and leave Arthur in his capable care, I wove a complicated spell of protection. It focused on the young master, Sir Ector and his family and o'er the entire estate of Castell-Coch. The spell also contained a mirror component to it. Anyone who tried to harm the boy or anyone included in the protective spell would have their perniciousness reflected back upon their own self and sting for it.

I hugged the child and gave Sir Ector and Lady Anna my promise of intermittent visits until Arthur was called back to the King's castle home. And at the times of my future sojourns hither, I would be available to do some out-of-the-ordinary studies with him, liken unto the lessons I learned with Taliesin.

I then set off for points unbeknownst to me, for once to abandon responsibility, at least for awhile. It was a novel sensation and quite peculiar for me to feel so untethered. I remembered my Druid lessons and reveled in this old adage: "You fail only because you limit your thinking, because you assume your own rule-restrictions. You must learn to make up your own rules in life, for when you accept a limitation, it becomes yours."

Leaving at dusk, I took my horse and pack horse and set out. Looking up, I reveled in the full Buck moon. I left my old self behind. I had no rule for my new person, only in that I would do always what was in my Greatest and Highest Good and that for others as well. As I gazed and analyzed the night sky, something became very apparent to me. There was a new conjunction in the evening heavens. It was Venus and Jupiter only a small width apart. I knew about this occurrence from wisdom gained from my knowledge of Atlantis transfer. It was no coincidence in my opinion that I saw it now. It was a Sign of a new leader! This starry harbinger in the sky was to me, an interesting omen reoccurrence and a timely one, seeing as how I had just hidden a young Prince from harm. I smiled to myself, and it cheered me no end in its symbolism! I believed that this child, Arthur, would bring a great period of Enlightenment and cultural edification for all of High Britain in time hence when he would rule as King. With the conjunction of Venus, the symbol of Love, and Jupiter, symbolic of Law and Social Order, it seemed to me that Arthur was ushering in a whole new kind of justice system. It was one that the world needed, what with clans fighting clans and our island being invaded every so often by neighboring warring nations. People feared one another, and in their process of killing each other and drawing their boundary lines, the earth, our Great Goddess of all, was being harmed. It was time for some Enlightenment in my opinion. How'ere, I had also looked far beyond Arthur's time to eons ahead, and it seems that man is a daft animal indeed. Humans will need continual offerings of Enlightenment until we finally all evolve in the Golden Age to come.

So because of the noteworthy sign of Venus and Jupiter bringing love, law and social order into alignment, I did what I always wanted to do. I meditated and then turned my horses' heads straight towards Avalon. I had wanted to meet the Lady of the Lake at last. I had dreamed of her for years. It was time for this too.

Wonderful does not describe the level of spirit that I was feeling inside. There was no deadline. There was no one to check in with. There was no King's schedule, no permissions needed, no task master's assignments to produce. I was able to let my mind wander, to meander to my own inner drumming. I stopped when I wanted to, I lingered as long as I felt was prudent, from hours to days to weeks, my time was mine own. I daydreamed and worked out spells and alchemical reactions in my head as my horses trotted along leafy paths, they seemed to know the way that I needed to go, without my direction.

I would sometimes ride far into the night gazing at the stars and watch the Universe unfold before my eyes. I would sometimes rise before dawn to hear the first bird and watch sunrises and pray and meditate in the morning revelry. I bathed in crystal-clear water. I would lie naked in the ferns, gazing up at the clouds and sunshine and basking in the air and the precious day. My beard and hair had become very long and was sometimes matted with twigs and leaves from lying in the bracken. My chest hair was thick and my limbs were strong and my eyes were keen. Sometimes I bathed and soaked in the water. Sometimes I did not and took dust baths instead like a dog in summer heat. I watched a snail for several hours make his way and leave his slime trail and watched its head and horns and was amazed by it. I did many amazing things. I did nothing. It mattered not. I cared not. Once I met a farmer on the road in the Caledonian Forest. I was naked and appreciating nature on a most beauteous day. I had felt the urge to make up a song and so, I was sitting playing my harp, singing a song to the trees when a farmer came walking by. The man asked me what be my name and I told him, "I am the wild man, Myrrdin Wylit." He looked at me, sitting there cross-legged in the woods, without a stitch on, playing music for no one, shook his practical herdsman's head and said, "Aye, that'd be aboot right," and he just continued walking. I simply smiled and kept singing to the trees.

Divine timing and guidance showed me my new path. I was now twenty and eight years old, with no master save mine own self. My studies of nature, science, art, literature and mathematics consumed most of my waking thoughts. I gathered herbs for medicines and hung them to dry off the saddle of my pack horse. My horses kept me wondrous company and we grew in love for one another, and I learned all about their personalities, and they learned my ways as well.

Occasionally, I would think of the woman of my dreams but not for long. I tried to put her out of my thoughts until the day that I would meet her in the flesh. Some women that I had met had told me that I was very handsome indeed. I did not think on it much, but now, as I was riding by myself for long periods every day, I did think back on some of my memories. There were, for instance, several comely women at court who had tried to pursue me and persuade me to come to their beds. They wanted me for their very own. The lovely ladies said it was not only for my wisdom, but for my stately visage as well. I had grown tall and strong and my hair was very long, as was my beard now. I did not want to be bothered with cutting it as some men did. I believed in cleanliness above all things, even if it was not a priority for some of the courtiers who believed that bathing would cause their death. Thusly, I may have been attracting women by being sweet smelling for I lacked the odiferous scent that obviously surrounded many of my peers. My dark eyes looked through and past most people and saw things that they could not even dream of. In sooth, I believe it was my inexperience and quiet nature that called to these women to chase me the way they did. Whilst I contented myself with charts and graphs and drawing likenesses of flowers and herbs to study, all they could see was a reticent virgin who needed deflowering. I would have none of it, although, when I felt lonely, or when I saw signs in nature of procreation, such as happening upon deer in full rut, I often wondered what bedding a woman would feel like. This was a natural way of being with the female of the species, a natural thing and blessing of the Gods, and yet, I knew it not.

Along the way I stopped at a stream to water my horses. There in the middle of the running stream, just south of a small waterfall, was a young girl. But she was no ordinary lass. She was doing something I had ne'er seen before. She was stacking and balancing rocks, one on top of another, next to each other, building an archway of small stones whilst the water flowed through and around her. The precariously balanced rocks formed an inconceivable, improbable balance, and yet the whole arrangement of the stacked stones looked beautiful and artful. There was harmony and symmetry amidst counterbalance and tension. Some rocks were on end, or balanced on one side, with two or more stones looking as if they were holding up the whole weight of the composition. It was truly a feat of both artistry and absurdity in the same moment.

How this young woman-child accomplished sech a feat was mesmerizing to watch. I dismounted my horse as quietly as I could so as not to disturb her trance. The mares drank deeply from the flowing stream whilst I stood contentedly and observed her movements.

She was young, and looked to be a waif about thirteen years old, yet she was focused like a sage and seemed to be glowing with her own personal energy. Her skirts were tied up around her legs and she stood in the water up to her knees, oblivious to my being there. She was so caught up with her meditative stone building that she was in a reverie the likes of which I had ne'er seen in someone so young…except perhaps mine own self in earlier years.

While she was in her spell of achieving stasis, I noted everything about her. She was calm, indeed, and healthy, with a manner of a young Maven. Good lord. Green eyes. She had green eyes. And…Gods save me…a long braid of chestnut hair fell o'er her shoulder. Was it possible? Was THIS my lady of the lake that I envisioned so long ago? Mayhaps it was. For I was only sixteen then and this lass looked to be only a few years younger than myself then. I wondered…did I foresee her as she is now…from a young man's heart then? For on this day, I must be fifteen years her senior. But there was something about her…her spirit called to me.

When she saw me, she was at first startled and looked around quickly to see if she should need to plan a hasty exit. I spoke to her in my most soothing voice, "Good day, my dear, be ye not afraid, I will not harm thee. This is indeed a most amazing feat that you are creating!" She did relax at the sound of my tone and the friendly greeting.

"Good day to thee, sire. It is my way to give back to the forest and to the world. I like to let the rocks have fun. They speak to me." She stood up and spoke in my direction and I replied. "This I do understand, for I too, have heard their voices and have had my ways with them, but this…this be a unique gift! What be your name, child, and how came you hither? What be thy family's name? From whence have you come?" I inquired.

She started wading to the shore, leaving the stone archway there, like the entrance to some magickal realm. She answered my queries in a voice so honest it made my heart hurt to hear her speak.

"I have had other names, by those who have tried to raise me. I have answered to Niniane, Viviane, Nimue…but each time, I would see dreams and foresee the future would go awry in those whose care I was in, those who had given me those names. So I abandoned them all and have put them behind me. I belong to no family. I'm afraid I have no last name to give thee. I stay here mostly since then, on mine own. I have taken a name for myself, and you may call me Nivienne. And I know who you are. You are Merlin, son of King Ambrose. I was told of your coming, but you surprised me on your arrival time. I imagined I would see you later on in my life…when I was older."

So. It was she! Yet she was but a child. Albeit a wise sage of a child. I watched my horses drink their fill whilst I took a moment to ponder what I would say next as she looked me over. She did not seem afraid, nor displeased in my countenance.

I bowed to her and said, "I am pleased to meet thee, Nivienne. Aye, Merlinus Pendragon, son of King Aurelius Ambrosius Pendragon, just as you have said, at your service. I, too, have seen thee in visions, alas, I did not know that ye would be only a burgeoning Seer nor did I foresee your age as being so young. But no matter. It has been foretold to both of us by the fates that we are to be acquaintances. It is Fate that has brought us both to this day. You do have the Sight, this I do know by the light of your Spirit."

I could see her aura, the spiritual energy rings round a human being, much like the inside rings of a tree whence it is cut down. The aural rings round a living soul are liken to such layers, how'ere, only on the outside of a body. Many a Seer may detect such things if they train their eyes. Her aura was shining and dancing around her in hues of purples, a most wondrous luminous violet and *gold*. Indigo was the color that I had seen before, it was the hue which surrounded Taliesin when I thought back. But the gold color, I had ne'er seen before but only heard tell from my master. By these colors, I could perceive that she was a Seeker, a visionary of the future, who could see into other worlds and dimensions. The gold aural ring told me that she was protected by Divine entities…Angels, if you will. The fact that she already knew who I was, was more than encouraging. This was a fortuitous meeting indeed! The age difference was daunting but not unheard of, aye, the Fates must've enjoyed the humor and possibilities in this pairing.

I continued, "I, too, have magickal powers. I shall teach ye many things, if ye are willing to learn. She nodded her head, but she looked a bit worried. "Nay, lass, be ye not afraid. I am a gentleman, and you are my charge. Thou shalt be safe with me and I promise to protect thee."

"Merlin" she said, "May I inquire of thee something that burns in my mind? I have oft dreamed of a place where I am to take refuge. I have been given the gift of seeing strange things, and some powers I canna control. I believe I am being called to a sanctuary, yet I know it not. It is there where I am to be instructed and I shall learn to wield my talents with skill. This shelter, I am convinced is called "The Isle of Apples," know ye of this haven?"

"Aye. The Isle of Apples is also called Avalon. It is a magickal place, and one whereto I was proceeding on my way to as well. Would you care to join me, m'lady?"

"Merlin, I would be ever so grateful and follow you where'ere you lead. I do long for safety and conversation. In sooth, I know this horse for I have had a dream of this very same lovely mare. She is beautiful." Nivienne stroked Nosy's muzzle, and the filly nuzzled her right back.

"Her name is 'Nosy' and aptly named, she is, indeed. Very well, then lass, you may have her. She is now your very own steed. I give her to ye."

I helped Nivienne up onto the horse once she stopped hugging and cooing to the marvelous mare, and got her settled and mindful for the trip ahead. "It is a long way yet, but we can take our time. I would like to learn who you are, and I will teach ye what I know, if ye are willing, and we can learn new things on our mutual path. Let us find our magickal destiny together."

"Sir, I have been on mine own for so long. There be nary a soul who has ever understood me nor could they comprehend what magick I can do. Yet, I believe that you are someone who will be very important to me. How'ere I have had so many dreams about you and so many thoughts about other wondrous things that I scarcely know how to decipher them all. All I know is that we were meant to meet, and by the Gods, we are now hither together! I also know that I am here to be a help to thee, as well."

And with that, we clicked our tongues and our steeds set off in the direction of the Isle of Apples. To Avalon.

V

The shadows of late afternoon dappled the forest floor and made for a pleasantly cool and shadowy ride through the forest. Nivienne and I had wondrous conversations and the heat of the day sweltered not under the trees. Often we entertained ourselves by storytelling. It was a game that started one day as our horses ambled along. I cleared my throat and started telling a story as if I knew it, how'ere it was a tale not yet constructed. After a few moments of interesting action or conundrum, I would just stop talking and look at Nivienne with a wink. She picked up that it was an amusement for us to pass the time. She took up the ends of the story that had been started and would weave a tale, and then for no reason or rhyme, she too, would leave off talking and give me a sly smile. So it went back and forth, our tales growing in magnitude, depth and detail that our time passed us as if but a moment. It was a most pleasant frolic of innocent merrymaking that we both reveled in the joy of it.

Bowrider and Nosey picked their sure way through the woods while Nivienne told me stories of what she had learned thus far. She was a buoyant young lady with fortitude of spirit. For the first ten years, her life had been tumultuous. She was an orphan who had, thankfully, lived to see her adolescence. She had survived, how'ere, she was not unscathed. Verily, she not only had survived but she had thrived, and mayhaps because of agony, she was even more open. Nivienne knew that closing up her spirit would be the result if she didn't remain purposely clear.

She had been kept tied by the foot and attached to the scullery as a kitchen whelp when she was only 5. It was harsh, and cruel what beatings she had to endure. When she escaped from her last situation, at age 10, it was to save her life. That last family who had taken her in made her weak, and her spirit was made to feel worthless. When she got her chance to run, she did. She ran far and she ran long. Living among the animals and woods, using her intuition and gifts, she learned to live from day to day. One morning, the rocks and stones called to her, how'ere, she didn't realize t'was the rocks calling her.

She distinctly heard voices crying out to her. The voices sounded like gravel, dusty like dirt. They were low tones, and sort of rumble-talked to her, once she could drop her hearing into their levels enough to discern their speech. The vibrations and low tones and long deliberate sounds gave her comfort, for they did not speak in vain. The voices she heard seemed hard and cold, as was she, yet they were once made of molten lava. Her heart was likewise warm within but had become cold with distrust.

Yet the voices grew louder as she walked and seemed to emanate from a pile of stones. At first she thought that there was someone, or some*thing* buried beneath the rock pile. Tentatively at first, then bravely moreso, one by one she removed rock by stone until reaching to the bottom of the pile. There was nothing there, yet the voices still did ring in her head. Finally she asked out loud, "Who goes there? Friend or Foe?"

What followed sounded like a low hearty laugh, and the voices said, "We be thy friends as ye are our friend. Ye are a jewel in the rough, as are we. Ye are a Crystal Woman and only sech can hear us. Ye will be able to hear others like us, as well. We lie here at your feet."

Pebbles, minerals, ore and boulders conversed with her from then on. She learned the secrets of the forest from these earthy beings who watched everything at all times and at all seasons. The stones were her best teachers. They had given her strength and wisdom beyond her years, for they were from times long past and had knowledge of eternity within them. With each rock that she found and heard its story, she learned more and more. They told her where to find food, shelter, and clothing. They spoke of the Universe, its workings and its magick as they understood it. The rubble told her stories of Gods and Goddesses, cultures long lost and times forgotten, for *the stones had seen and remembered it all.*

The more she stayed listening to the rocks, the more she enjoyed her own self and the Earth Mother from whence they came. Nivienne memorized their wisdom with her wonderfully quick, child's brain, she asked the stones how she could repay them. They wanted to be useful, and they wanted to be beautiful. The stones said, "No one looks to us as a thing of beauty. Only as a weight to be angrily removed about in fields. We wish to give others wisdom with our strength and shapeliness. We wish to make humans look upon us and thusly, themselves, differently." The stones promised to comply with balancing at her hand. She worked with them in her creation and her essence had become unblocked with these spiritual gifts. By lifting the rocks, she became stronger than her ordeals and wounds. She proved she was neither weak nor worthless, but tenacious and hardy.

Listening to the rocks and following their wisdom, she proved she was able to see beyond the ordinary. With each stone she touched, she drew its strength into her being, her legs and arms and her spirit. This is how she had become such a magickal person.

As we rode along Nivienne cleared her throat and asked me bluntly, "Merlin, who were you as a child? What was your life like? I wish to know you and to see you at the age that I am now."

The sun was high in the sky whence I started telling her of my childhood, Taliesin, my life long quest for knowledge, the fruitful sessions that I had adventuring in the woods on mine own and with my mentor. In sooth, by the time I had arrived to tell her about the day that I met her at the water's edge, the sun was setting and we were finding a place for the e'en and were giving our horses a rest. E'en then, I continued on filling her in on my hopes, dreams and desires, and also my Quest for mine own path.

Through my tales of youth, we saw that our childhood years, though divergent from each other, yet we still had similar elements within. Verily, my life had not been as harsh as hers. Yet we shared the same feelings of displacement and abandonment. The more we conversed, the more kindred we felt. We stopped and made our night in the wood, gathered twigs and a bit of brush for a fire, and slept close to each other. She liked staying close by me, especially at night. Safety, I assumed, was her reasoning, although it was wondrous to have her in such proximity. Nivienne doted on the horses, and, I admit, she fussed over me as well. She made sure I ate and would find herbs and gift me with them. For merriment, she showered me with flowers.

She wove a garland of daisies and dandelions one day and wore it in her hair, and I swore to myself that I had ne'er seen anyone so lovely and pure. Not even in court could there have 'ere been a more comely maiden. She was a delight in conversation. Her magick was different from mine, and yet it was powerful too, even in its infancy. I knew that she was just a blossoming child, but I could clearly see the day when she would be woman enough for me. She, too, was growing quite attached to me as well, much like an older brother or father figure, I assumed, until she spoke quietly and surely to me in words I thought I'd never hear from a female.

"Merlin, when I am older, old enough to be a wife, would you join with me in love and promise?"

Whilst I was astonished at her candor, I looked into her eyes and saw devotion there like I had ne'er seen pointed in my direction. I think heat flushed up into my face and a burning feeling made me swallow hard and I said, "My dear, 'tis customary for the man to ask the maiden sech things should there be sech affection."

"And do ye have sech feelings for me then? Do ye have sech affection as this would require?"

Her look of pure pleading nearly crushed my heart with her sincerity. "Aye, lass. But ye be just a child yet. I am many years older than ye. Fifteen to be precise. Ye have much to learn in Avalon. We are almost there, and then I shall have to leave ye there. But I do promise that I shall return for thee at the perfect time. Then we shall be together. There is no one I would rather call mine own than thee. But first, ye must grow from sweet child prodigy to beautiful lady Enchantress. When ye have done so, call out to me and I will come to thee."

This made her smile to herself and it was enough. I thanked the Gods that our union was so serendipitous, and so easy. I admit, that I am not adept at these sorts of things, but my visions of her, and her person were so easily compatible, and the future seemed brighter just thinking of her in it, that I too, was swayed by the notion. At least, so far so good. How'ere, there was one major hurdle yet. We would have to part, in order to be together in the future. This would prove to challenge us both, for we had become quite smitten with each other, and I concede that I would indeed miss her company. This fact amazed me, I, who had always enjoyed being on mine own and preferred solitary days instead of company. Here I saw myself from a bird's eye view and realized that I was alone and would, mayhaps, be stung with loneliness in the very near future. Me. Merlin, the wild man of the woods--with a WIFE? The idea amused me and I pondered it with great relish and got lost in silly young boy thoughts.

This is when I realized that Bowrider and Nosy had come to a halt. We stood on the bank and looked out over the water. There was a mist, and yet we could see the Isle of Avalon in the distance. The tide was low, and being so, our steeds were able to walk across to the tidal island of apples.

Nivienne's emotions clashed like dark clouds in a blue sky. She was at once overjoyed to be here with her education about to begin, and at the same time devastated that our time together was about end. Her visage spoke volumes as tears coursed down her cheeks, framing her soulful smile.

As we traveled o'er to the island, I told her of the legend of Avalon, here on Ictis Island and that it was one of the Gateways to the Land of the Dead to the Otherworld, as well as the best learning place for maidens with budding magickal gifts. When we silently stepped foot on the isle, the mist gave way to a bright and splendid day and standing there were novitiates awaiting us. A line of young women dressed in white robes and green cloaks, tilted back their foreheads to better display a blue half-moon tattoo, the Mark of the Goddess. The women had been waiting for us and were here now for our silent arrival to take us to their Mistress of the Isle.

We dismounted, and the women motioned to us, without speaking, that our steeds were to be bathed, fed, brushed and pampered. We thanked the horses for their efforts on the ride and bade them go with these kind keepers. Bowrider and Nosey had worked diligently to get us here and deserved to be treated well. I knew they would enjoy benevolent care here and rightly so.

We followed the Mavens from the shore up the bank and to the temple. It was of simple architectural design, Greek in structure, liken unto how I had envisioned Hera's temple. There at the altar of the moon stood their leader. She was stately as a Queen and carried herself thusly.

She stepped forward upon our entrance and descended the steps to greet us.

This beautiful woman, dressed also in glowing white, with long, lustrous dark hair and wide eyes, firm brow also marked with a blue half-moon emblazoned for'ere on her forehead, bowed low to us in respect and stated:

"We welcome you here, Merlinus Ambrosius Pendragon, Arch Druid of Albion and son of King Aurelius Ambrosius Pendragon. We are humbled by your Presence. We also welcome and honor your new apprentice, Nivienne, and bid her our esteem and acceptance hither. I am Freya, Maven Protectress of the Isle of Avalon and present day Lady of the Lake. Goddess Bless thee." She folded her hands into the shape of prayer and then opened her arms wide to share the blessing with all.

I realized that she had Seen our coming, and I also realized that this Lady of the Lake was not the one of whom I had dreamed of on my Spirit Quest. Nivienne was Lady of the Lake in my Spirit Quest dream. Would she be Lady of the Lake someday? Hastily filing away those thoughts for ponderance, I returned the welcome salutation and bowed to her in return and said: "We accept your gracious hospitality, Lady Freya of the Lake, Maven of the Isle. And to all your respected Mavens gathered, I bring salutations from King Uther. I also bring greetings from Taliesin and the Druids of Anglesey. I would ask to deliberate with thee on matters of importance and to seek thy counsel.

May the Gods and Goddesses bless all gathered hither and may blessings and prosperity be upon the Lands of thy keeping."

With this, Freya clapped her hands, and many of the attendants dispersed, while others bade us sit, and they brought us fruits and cheeses and a decanter of wine and goblets. "You must be weary from the road. Prithee, eat, rest, and sleep. Then we shall talk of great and powerful things."

Nivienne and I were indeed famished and worn. The victuals did indeed appeal to us, and we sat in comfort and looked out on the water as we drank and soaked in the island view. Birds of all kinds roamed the temple, and we did amuse ourselves with feeding them the fruit, directly from our hands. I watched Nivienne absorb every detail of what would be her new home. I pondered that this island was a goodly place of love, and she would be safe here.

After we ate, we stretched out in our chairs there in the temple in the shade of the sun, and it was not long before we succumbed to sleep. A summer nap in the heat of the day does wonders for healing the soul. We awoke to the sound of a gong and the light had changed from afternoon to a cooler eventide. Evidently, we had been more in need of rest than we had known.

Freya was with us now, seated to my left and Nivienne on my right. I discussed with Freya that I, as Arch Druid, wished to link the knowledge of Anglesey with Avalon and that I had been pondering how to do it. I envisioned a world in the future that would be complete again and that I would, with Freya's cooperation, and the guidance of the Universe, be willing to guide the world with Druid and Maven at the helm. For I had Seen the future as it stood progressing now, without my intervention, it would proceed without Love and Wisdom and the disregard of our Earth Mother Goddess. The world would otherwise be ruled by soul sucking cold machinations. Evil and harm would reign over creation without the beauty of the Goddess.

The Maven Protectress did also confide that she too, had seen such visions that foretold of my coming to her and had seen Nivienne as the link between us. Freya offered to educate Nivienne as a Maven Novitiate and to train her as Lady of the Lake to follow Freya, in time.

Nivienne was wide-eyed in wonder at all of this and yet comforted in the knowledge that all that she had been feeling was also the truth. In her heart and soul she knew it was her destiny.

All three of us chatted for quite some time about the state of the world now, its darkness, and that if left unchanged, would spiral human kind into a vortex of apathy, greed and cruelty. The earth itself needed protection from man and all that would come. It needed kind hearts leading the way. We all three went down to the lake and standing in the water, we joined our hands together in a circle and vowed our faithfulness to the Earth, the Water, and to Fire, Wind and Spirit. In this way, we made a magick spell to join us together and only after we had all made our sacred promises to the Earth and each other to be Caretakers together, did we unclasp our hands. The water would remember our vow, and each and every time we were around water we too, would each remember our own promise and the oath we gave to each other to be for the World's Greatest and Highest Good.

****

Freya did explain to Nivienne all of what would be expected of her during her time of education hither. Utter and complete compliance was to be given as her due to the Lady of the Lake. Nivienne would be given duties as Novitiate and also a job of service to the Isle. Nivienne promised to be faithful and true and accepted the mark of the Goddess and as an Earth Sister to the Moon.

I stayed for several days, learning of the ways of Avalon, and also did help to officiate at the Novitiate ceremony for Nivienne. I spoke with Freya on matters of the world and Spirit. We were guided to put a spell of protection and invisibility over Avalon for all eternity, so as to make a safe haven for those learning how to counteract the ways of the world. We agreed there would be a day when Avalon would be targeted to be destroyed by those wishing to disrespect its wisdom. Womankind, herself, would also be targeted and not respected by the world at large. It would be a shameful time to come when women would be destroyed for trying to bind the world together in love. We were of the same mind and it was good to be with another caring and extraordinary being who could sense the future as well as the path we should take in part.

****

I left Avalon the next morning after promising Nivienne that I would return when she was sixteen at which time we would bond as mates and Spirit Guides together in Love and Wisdom and with Avalon's blessing…that is, if Nivienne was still of that same mind.

As a betrothal promise and token of my admiration for her, I gave Nivienne a dragon brooch for her cloak. She in turn, gave me a crystal stone with which we would communicate whilst apart. I held her in my arms for a long time, our spirits did entwine, and we said a good bye without tears but with great hope for ourselves and the future and what it held for us both as individuals and as a couple to help the Gods.

Before I departed, Freya took me aside and said to me this: "Merlin, I have consulted with my cards and with my Spirit Guides. I am to inform you, that you are to claim all of Wales and Britain as a magickal realm. You need to do this for the posterity for all magickal beings now and to come. You must participate in your own Wild Hunt ere ye return to Avalon."

"Aye," I said. "I have been being prompted in dreams by the Fates on this as well. It is now time for me to do that which I have both longed for…and also dreaded. It is time for me to stake my claim on this land and elements itself, which I promise to defend. I am off to challenge not only myself but Nature and her Power, and I will attempt, Gods help me, to succeed in claiming all of Britain by surviving the ordeal."

Freya said, "On this quest, ye shall be accosted by a most Powerful Being: a dragon by the name of 'Bazzalth, Protector of the Sky.' Gift him with this: it is a looking glass of gold. It is a treasure, fashioned by the Sidhe, the immortal race of winged blue creatures that live and protect Avalon. He will tell you what you need to know. He shall have words for thee of importance and will help you on your journey. Know ye, he will try to kill you, how'ere, be stalwart and true. Man should ne'er show a false face to a dragon. It increases their odds of wrath for they can read the hearts of men. This reflector is a major tool to survive him, along with your wit and magick. Shield thyself. Ye shall overcome."

I took the looking glass from Freya, and stowed it carefully within my pack. Before I tucked it away completely, I did glance at mine own reflection. It was odd to see who I was…and had become. I was a full-grown man now, with black beard and long dark hair. The swain looking back at me had smoldering brown eyes with long lashes. He had the straight and regal nose of his father, and yet, honestly, to me, I thought he also had the look of a mad man. I must be mad to begin this next quest. It was not a balanced act of a sane person. It was a wonder that Nivienne was attracted to me at all, I thought. The gaze in the imager was stern and yet, far off and away, the visage of a man who knew much and also of one who still had much to learn. This journey would surely test me to my limits.

I vowed to the reflection, that I would keep me, the man in the mirror, safe, above all. I would care for mine own self, so that I could care for this world. I packed the imager away and mounted my steed and left Avalon without looking back. I knew I must go forward now for three years and I let Nivienne do the same.

****

I rode Bowrider into the Cambrian Mountains. It is a beautiful yet harsh place and would be the setting for my Wild Hunt. I had a vision of the particular mountain top to which I was to proceed to, its name is Pen Pumlumon Fawr. When I arrived at this mountain in Snowdonia, a poem from the future rang through my mind:

"From high Plynlimmon's shaggy side
Three streams in three directions glide;
To thousands at their mouths who tarry
Honey, gold and mead they carry.
Flow also from Plynlimmon high
Three streams of generosity;
The first, a noble stream indeed,
Like rills of Mona runs with mead;
The second bears from vineyards thick
Wine to the feeble and the sick;
The third, till time shall be no more,
Mingled with gold shall silver pour."

No wonder a dragon protected the land. It was rife with water, treasure, riddle and reality.

I unsaddled and unbridled Bowrider, let her loose and instead made a satchel for mine own self. I would climb the mountain and face the Dragon on mine own terms with mine own magick and wits. This horse that Uther had given me had become my dearest friend. Bowrider was now, truly, my kin. I spoke with her in my mind and let her know that I would meet up with her on the other side of the five mountains after the Wild Hunt was finished. That was, if I succeeded in my quest. I asked her to tarry for a few days and to find her way to that place and to await me. If I did not meet my trusted friend there before the next full moon, then she would be free from this bond with me and could go back to a wild being. I put a spell of protection on her and let go with my love and my dearest thanks. In three nights t'would be the New Moon, a very dark and appropriate time for the start of the Wild Hunt.

****

The Wild Hunt is a Druid's personal journey, a soulful quest that has physical repercussions. It is a time when a Druid goes up against the earth and all her elements in a contest of wills, wit and strength. It is not for the squeamish. Many are they who have not triumphed, but have been bested by wind, earth, fire, water and spirit. I would pit myself against the Elements asking to win the right for magick o'er the land. The stakes were high for me, as it was either for me to win and rule as Enchanter, or I would die trying.

I began my climb from the south side, the only real path up to the top. It is a barren place with sparse vegetation, many rocks, sprinkled with a few cairns built by those burying their dead or those who have also quested hither. These rock piles mark important locations for posterity's sake. There was also a stunning view of all of Britain and Wales. While I picked and chose my foot-and hand-holds carefully, I felt the sun warm my face and the wind whip my hair and I felt truly alive and ready to face this journey. Here is where I would call forth the dragon, Bazzalth.

I had never dealt with a dragon before, but knew of their existence and their power and their trickery and cunning. Dragons are well

165

known for their savage beauty and strength as well as for their vanity. That is why the Lady of the Lake had given me that seeing glass. It would be nigh unto irresistible for the dragon and its love of self, provided, of course, I could avoid it frying me first with its flaming breath. Freya had, indeed, been kind to me with this protection of a perfect gift of passage. I would not let her down.

On the first night I would commence by leaving gifts of wine and bread for the Elements and offerings to the Mountain and subsequently, on each night hence until the New Moon. On the night my quest would begin, I knew I would be opening myself up to almost anything. Carefully, I climbed to the peak, stacked scavenged wood and set the area for the event. I explored the surroundings fully, and found passages during the day (possible escape routes) for I would have to find the paths in the dark. On the third night, I would light the fire and pledge myself to the hunt. When the moment was right, I would throw into the flames the most important ingredient, Mandragora root. The mandrake, in this instance, would become the Spirit of the Chase, and when thrown into the fire, it would release the elements and cause them to rise and give chase after me, seeking to deter me from finishing the quest. If I finished sparring with all the Elements and was yet living, I would have succeeded! How'ere, if one of the Elements bested me, then I would exist no longer.

My best defense against calling out and sparring with the Elements would be to call them and then to put distance behind me and wait to see come what may. I would cover ground as quickly as possible and hide, shield, and push back when the time came as needed. The Elements would be represented in the spirit of the Mandrake, and once called forth, each Element in turn would approach me as the embodiment of the element itself in some way. We would seek to outwit each other and to win our own prize. It was a dangerous game, but one in which I *must* win.

But e'en more so, the prize I did seek was to survive the journey and to absorb the wisdom it would teach me. That, and also to secure all of Britain, Wales, Dyved, and Snowdonia as magickal ground for all eternity and for my title of Enchanter. If I did not succeed, I would lose my rights as Enchanter, as well as my life, for the land and elements would claim ME. The stakes were indeed high. For the next three nights, I prepared myself, ate as much as I could find, and tried to store and feasibly carry as much on my person, yet whilst still remaining light on my feet. I slept when'ere and where'ere as much as I could. Not knowing whence I might be safe enough or be able to sleep enough o'er the trials to come, I tried to rest as much as possible to safeguard mine own health in lieu of the upcoming battle with the elements.

Finally the third night came, and the night was dark, indeed, as black as pitch. I dressed all in the darkest of colors, so as to blend into the night for mine own protection and invisibility.

In the middle of the night, when it was darkest, I built my fire and called the Four Winds to witness my ceremony, whereupon I stated my intentions out loud for the elements and the Gods to hear:

"Salutations to the Four Directions, Powers of the East, South, West and North! Hail to thee also, the Powerful Elements of Earth, Air, Fire, Water and Spirit! I honor you as my strong opponents and I promise to honor you always, now and forever after! I would challenge thee to a Wild Hunt and to play with me in your strength, and I will play with thee in this game of Life! I would have for my Magickal Realm, this Land of Wales and all of Britain, and to make it a lasting magickal place for all of the eons to come! If I win, I shall promise to keep the Earth and this Land safe from the Chaos of Corruption and to hold Peace in the realm and to teach others the Druid Way. If I do not succeed, ye may have me as thy dinner, to grind my bones and to spit me out or to treat me in ways that are just to thee! I commit myself to this journey to know thee and to survive thy onslaughts! So Mote It Be!"

At the last possible moment, when my declaration was complete, I felt calm when the night was darkest and the fire burning brightly, I threw the Mandragora into the flames, then I turned and fled into the darkness before me.

What happened next surprised me, which was that nothing happened. The fire crackled on and there was no reaction in the world around me. Regardless of this quiet anomaly, or because of it, I realized that I had made a good decision.

If I had only turned around whilst running, I would have seen a sight that few lived to see. For there, in the dark night above the sputtering burning flames, rose an immense Spirit, unseen by most; and few mortals had e'er lived to tell its tales.

The Spirit of Fire blazed and rose behind me as I ran into the black of night.

My first opponent had arrived, Bazzalth, Protector of the Sky.

VI

It is said that "the four enemies of a man of knowledge are as follows: Fear, clarity, power, and old age." I vowed that my journey lay within this statement.

Fear. I knew that I must overcome any dread or horror that doth lie within me. I would seek it out and confront it. Being fearless in the face of terror is what is called for if one is to survive calamity. If one would lead humanity, as I was drawn to do as my purpose in life, then one must be lionhearted and stalwart in the face of any misfortune or revulsion.

Clarity can be elusive. It is a gift to be able to perceive within the heart of any situation what is fact and what is false. For in sooth, both are sometimes the mirror image of each other. Accurate certainty is clouded many times by mystery, spell and deception. Thusly, the truth oftimes eludes those who require it most. Good decisions require clarity in the face of uncertainty.

Power is the one enemy that counterfeits as your friend, lures you with words of your own strength and ego, but in the end, may become one's undoing. I have seen Power destroy so many in their quest of acquiring it. I determined that I would not be one to succumb to its siren call.

Old age is the destroyer of health and stamina; it wears away what was once a mountain and transforms it to a molehill. In order for me to continue leading mankind, this one fact of life was one that I must face and conquer. I must strive to remain young at heart no matter what may come. Immortality may be unattainable but I would strive to find a way so that I could continue to guide mankind to a nurturing existence. This is my ultimate quest, to be a force for good for all.

In my heart of hearts I knew that I was powerful. I also knew from visions that I would live to be an old man. Clarity was something that I would *try* to decipher in all things as I grew in wisdom. Yet fear was another matter yet to be wholly mastered, and this I found to be true especially so when a dragon was hunting you.

And so I put my head down and ran head-long into the darkest of nights, heart pounding in my throat, feet finding their way, running into the night remembering the night that Taliesin and I ran as ermines. His words still rang in my mind, "Someday this could save your life."

I then remembered his lesson of the Night Jar, invisibility and shape-shifting. Quickly thinking, I changed into the form of an owl, and my silent feathers lifted me into the night. I could see so much more detail in the dark as I rose up into the sky. Circling around in

the air, and looking back at the scene of my
dedication to the Wild Hunt, I saw what looked
to be a dragon rising from the embers of the fire.
It was magnificent! Aye, but terrifyingly
magnificent! Surely, the dragon would be
looking for a man, at least at first, which would
give me enough time to fly up into the air where
he would not think to look for me. I prayed that
this modification of guise would bid me enough
time to find a suitable hiding place.

The dragon roared up out of the fire
which had grown into a raging blaze. Bazzalth
shone a keen eye all around and then clawed and
pawed his way around the fire, easily picking up
my scent. Walking away from the fire in the
same direction that I took, the dragon narrowed
his cold, golden eyes and saw my footsteps stop
in the dirt. The remaining footsteps on the
ground, the addition of wing prints in the dirt
there, led the old wyrm to the last spot where I
had been a man. It must've been the imprint of
my wings on the ground showed the last possible
place afore I lifted off of terra firma. The dragon
roared and looked up into the sky, only moments
after I had landed and settled into a large
outcropping of boulders.

I transformed from an owl back into
myself again and wedged my body into a crevice
and waited for the dragon. From my pouch I
withdrew the crystal that Nivienne had given me.
I spoke to it and said, "Dear Rocks from whence
this gemstone came through the Crystal Woman,
I need you now. Be with me. Hold these rocks

and stones steady about me and fashion thyselves into a wall of protection to keep my life safe." The crystal glowed red and I knew that I had been heard. The rocks around me seemed to crack and shift and form a tighter acquaintance. Whilst the dragon honed in on me (the intruder), I reached into the pack on my back, and drew out the looking glass from Freya. I held it in my hands, looked at the imager and said "This gift is for Bazzalth, may he be pleased with it" then I lingered and expected the onslaught to come. I was not disappointed.

Bazzalth flew down to the rocks where I had stowed myself and the dragon spoke. He said in his deep and scaly voice, "Merlin, I have found thee! Prepare to die. You have not only challenged me, Bazzalth, Protector of the Sky but you have summoned the other elements to come and hunt thee, and they *shall.* I have power o'er air AND fire. Feel my wrath and be afraid."

The dragon first started flapping his wings, and hurricane gale-force winds shook the mountain. Boulders fell all around me, but I hung on and drew mine own powers around me-- and blended with the rocks there to keep me safe. When this assailment did not prove effective, Bazzalth inhaled and breathed a fury of flame and roasted the rocks all around me. Indeed, they did glow red as well…but I had already caused them to recognize the heat and the rocks only felt warm to me. There was the light of day nearly exuding from the dragon, and all was lit up around it as it spoke.

When Bazzalth's onrush of power had not terminated my life as he had hoped, he said, "Dost thou live? Be thou afraid of me, now?"

I spake at this point to the most fearsome creature I had 'ere seen as I looked out between the crevices that held my safety.

"O Great and Powerful Bazzalth, Protector of the Sky! Indeed, I do live. But I am not afraid, for I am enraptured with the sight of Thee. I have heard tales of the beauty of dragons and their fearsome power, how'ere, I have no words to express my gratefulness in seeing a creature sech as Thee. If only ye could see thine own self, ye too, would be enraptured and know that ye are a gift of the Gods to the world."

The dragon then let out a sound what sounded like a rumbling purr. I continued, "Indeed, Freya, Lady of the Lake, has bade me give ye a gift, insomuch as ye might see the Power of thine own self, in return for my safety on this Wild Hunt. May I present ye with a greatsome gift, the likes o' which ye may have ne'er seen?"

The dragon was curious as are most creatures in this world. He said, "I shall spare thee if what ye say is the Truth."

I maneuvered the imager out of the shelter of the rock and turned it towards the being and it glowed when it made contact with the reflection of the dragon.

Bazzalth was enticed by the shape therein and drew closer and closer in order to see more of itself. I could feel my skin nearly burn with the heat of its breath so close to the looking glass I held in my hand.

"I bid thee, take this gift. It is for Thee." I thrust my hand holding the reflective glass outward even closer to the fearsome creature. I felt scaly talons grip the object and take it from me, ever so delicately. Then there was silence for a few longsome moments. In sooth, the dragon had no words for what it saw therein. It was truly mesmerized. As the creature gazed at its own image for the first time in its long life, a feeling welled up within the being and tears boiled to the surface of the golden eyes and splashed hot water next to my feet.

I spake again, "Indeed thou art a most beauteous and magickal being! Did I not tell thee the Truth? Dinna cry. Thou art an amazing creation of the Gods and never has there been a more magnificent reflection!" I said this in a clear voice to the dragon, oh so close to me. "I spake honestly and sincerely, "I have ne'er seen anyone as wondrous and terribly beautiful as Thee."

My words rang true, for indeed he was all that and more! I could barely breathe for the sight of him.

There was a long silence as the dragon examined every inch of its scaly body. Then slowly, coming back to reality, it went on, "Aye. Ye have done well. You have given me a grand gift and ye know not of the immensity of it. This is the treasure from which ye shall inherit your life from me. *If* ye do finish this quest, I shall gift thee the knowledge of the Thirteen Treasures of Britain, in exchange for giving me this, for I do not wish it to fall into anyone else's hand but mine own. I am certain that the Lady of the Lake did not tell thee, how'ere, about the power and greatness of this imager. It is said that the one who doth possess this looking glass doth also possess the command of ME, for good or ill. The Sidth fashioned it and gave it to the Lady of the Lake for safe keeping. She alone was trusted to keep it safe- if it was not mine own possession. Ye have done a goodly thing to turn it o'er to me, and now that it is finally in my possession, I am truly a free creature. I have been freed from this spell. I am grateful and will keep my promise *if* ye shall survive Earth, Water and Spirits' challenges as well. Come out from thy hiding place, and be ye not afraid. You are a most powerful being in my world now, and I shall ne'er harm thee. I accept and honor thee, Merlinus Ambrosius, son of Pendragon. My shape shall always be thy totem in keeping with the honor of the Pendragon name. Know ye that doubt can kill. Step out and into your Power."

I came out and stood before this resplendent body. It thrilled me to be so close and vulnerable and yet so safe in the dragon's presence. I did honor him and verily, I did keep this image and the dragon's tears ever in my mind. I did ask if it would be acceptable if I were to bottle up some of the tears that were puddled all around my feet. Bazzalth obliged me and I was sure that there would be a time where sech a magickal elixir would be of service. I thanked the dragon and left the imager with the creature contentedly gazing at the wonderment within.

As I walked away from this marvel, darkness again descended. In sooth, I had been so enraptured and intensely occupied for the time I was with Bazzalth that I had forgotten that it was night. And so it was still, and the further I got from the glow of the dragon, the darker it became. It was the new moon, the darkest night of the month. Carefully I chose my steps. To be injured was surely a losing posture so I continued on my Wild Hunt and soon after I found myself facing a dense peat bogge. It was all around me. There was no going back. Retracing my steps would surely signal my surrender to the elements, and I was so close now to succeeding what with the elements of Air and Fire behind me, I dared not make sech a directional change. I pushed on.

As a Druid, I knew much about the Goddess Mother Earth and also knew that bogges could be dangerous if traversed with haste. A quicksand of death and the travail therein had swallowed many a horse and rider and wild beast. Nay, this was a time for utilizing patience.

I saluted the Earth next with an olden rhyme to bless my quest in conquering this next element:

"What is hard and yet is soft?
Tread this patch with care to stay aloft
An earthy path may be your earthy grave
Step lightly and your life you may save."

Before I entered the bogge, I found a stout shillelagh to help me guide my every step along this path. Then I removed my boots and decided that I would walk barefoot and have true contact with the earth and listen to its words through each footfall. "Gods and Goddesses help me," I said and started my bogge walk of sliding my foot out ahead and not giving weight on it until I was certain that the surface was firm. With my walking stick and my slow gliding pace in the dark, I had to remind myself to breathe. I found I was holding my breath and if I continued doing so, the result would be exhaustion. I managed this slow pace for quite some time and rested for a moment.

Before I restarted my journey through the bog I miscalculated and fell into the muck. I was deep in the quicksand. Surely the earth wanted to claim me, and I knew if I struggled that I would become a casualty and one of the bogge's permanent residents.

"Relax…breathe…relax…breathe…relax," I told myself. I decided to turn onto my back instead of trying to swim face first. Slowly I managed to float on my back and then to free my legs. This took a great deal of effort, and I was tiring. But minutes seemed long, and finally I triumphantly unfettered my legs from the muck.

I then managed to urge my body to bond with the sedge grass and soon I was wholly out of the quicksand. I had escaped the Earth's challenge!

I had mastered the worst of the bogge and now I had succeeded in besting the Earth element. I thanked the Earth, e'en as I tried to wipe myself free of the dirt. I found a new problem. Bog leeches. Aye, they were a gift of the earth and I had at least 20 of them gifting my legs and feet with their presence. I did not have any wine nor whiskey to heal myself should I wish to encourage their removal with a bath of the intoxicating beverage. Thusly, I made the decision to let them be. I walked on and allowed them to feed and drink their fill and fall off when they were finally satiated. It would be my gift back to the bogge to let them feast on me, as my gift back to the earth. It was the least I could do to repay the earth for my freedom and my life. It was not long when, one by one, the leeches became full of my essence and dropped off without much ado. And in this manner, they left my body without regurgitating any of their contamination back into me. I had escaped an earthen grave and thusly still managed to feed the worms. It was only fair to give back a kindness. As I shook the dirt from my feet when I left the bogge, I said "Thank You" to the Earth as I gratefully left the area.

I sat for a few moments as I tried to get my bearings. When I heard water running I knew my next challenge. When it was dark, crossing a river would be especially daunting. In thinking

on it next, how'ere, I realized t'would be a
pleasure to cleanse myself of the peat and to
scrub where the leeches came off, as I felt itchy
as I remembered them. I prayed that the Gods
would continue their guidance and protection
o'er me as I finished scrubbing myself and
entered the water with this blessing:

"Water swift and water wide
Moonwash dark with rising tide
Grant me this moonless ride
And in thy bosom safe abide."

My intention was to cross the river, but
the water's intention was to sweep me with the
undertow. Thankfully I remembered my lessons
with Taliesin and shape shifted immediately into
a fish. I became a pike and smiled with my
toothy grin and enjoyed the water and breathed
in through my gills. My eyes adjusted, and soon
I swam with the tide. Other fish saw me and
stayed far away from me and my menacing
smile. Suddenly I instinctively realized that the
current was running ever more swiftly and the
river was about to break over the breach of a
quickly approaching waterfall!

Just afore the current o'er took me to
sweep me with the rushing water, I put all my
muscles into the task of swimming upstream as
fast and furiously as possible! Once safely
enough back upstream, I found a low-lying
strand. I jumped as high as I could out of the
water and hurled my fish body out of the drink

and up onto a bank. There I lay panting and gasping for water, feeling as though I would die, but then remembered that I was a man and not a fish. I thusly became myself once more and breathed deeply of the air. I was most glad of it and blessed the gift of breathing and the air to fulfill my need. Thusly, the Wind Element was honored with my every breath.

I walked a bit farther, the dawning light beginning to grow. The sun would soon rise, and I still stood and had persevered thus far. I then came upon what some would say was an Ally. It is an organic being that is found within a plant of rare and strong medicinal value. I knew when I saw it that I was to confront it as my last test. I sat down by the plant and got myself into a comfortable position. Taking some of the leaves in my hand, I held them up to the sky and said:

"Not taken lightly,
Nor ingested in vain,
Destiny guide me,
Manifest and maintain."

I ate liberally of the plant, which on another day would be a toxic dose to others. But I ate until I felt myself say 'enough.' I focused on the growing light of the sky, and the orange of the sunrise spread across the horizon. Soon, I heard a thumping, coming closer, closer. Was it my heart beating? Nay. I remained calm. In fact, I found that I could not move a single limb, nor finger, nor I e'en blink. I had become paralyzed in effect, and the Ally was approaching. It came within view of me. It was a large squarish shape, dark in matter and walked by swinging corner to corner. If I had been able to move, I would've run, terrified into the night. How'ere, I could not run but was forced to sit and experience this frightening form. The Ally within the plant had seized my limbs and muscles so that I would experience this frightful entity. Looking at it was liken unto a long, dark night filled with nightmarish visions, and its square shape was otherworldly. I could feel only fear when I tried to comprehend its meaning. The more I looked at it and tried to understand it, the more it unsettled me further, even more than that dragon or anything in the world thus far had 'ere affected me. This monstrous shape clung close to me. The longer it stayed, the more I got used to seeing it. After awhile, I started understanding this shape monster. It occurred to me that mayhaps it was my own fear, and I was gazing into the bane of my existence. Was I looking at mine own self and a terror of mine own making? My apprehension started to subside the more I became familiar with it. At one point it swiveled on itself without a sound and started swinging its self, edge to edge, pivoting itself in some sort of strange transport as it continued to motivate, becoming smaller and smaller on the horizon.

Sunrise then came over the hill, and I found that I was alone once again. The dark Ally was gone, and I could start moving my fingers, toes and arms and legs. I had survived my ordeal! And not only that, but I had met mine own terror where I sat, and now I knew that I had nothing to fear. This had been a great gift. I felt that I could connect with this Power at anytime when I needed it and felt that I could learn to summon it at will. I was ever so grateful, and in turn for living, surviving and thriving, I lay prostrate down on the earth and thanked the Gods, Sun, Moon and Earth, Wind, Fire, Water and Spirit for all that they had taught me.

After leaving gifts to the Elements as thanks, I descended the mountain and found Bowrider waiting for me. I was never so happy to see my friend since the day I was given her. Strangely enough, attached to my horse's neck, was a scroll. Within the scroll was a list of the Thirteen Treasures of Britain! Along with clues and markings on a map. "This will be a Wedding Quest for me and my Lady Nivienne," I told myself. I mounted and set off on my own exploration of my magickal realm, which I had now won from the elements! I wished to discover as much as I could of this new domain of mine so recently won and acquired.

****

For the next three years I lived and roamed and soaked in the lessons and the ways of these lands. I felt that life took on an ethereal quality as did my personage for I actually seemed to have spooked some of the locals who saw me as if I were an apparition! They were not used to someone living here in this desert of

Wales and scraping a living from the barren land. I roamed throughout Wales and Britain. I sometimes went to Sir Ector's and counseled Arthur in the ways of shape-shifting as Taliesin had taught me. Intermittently, I would come and go from Castle Coch, and check in on the child who was now almost 6. I deservedly earned the peasants' name for me, "The wild man, Myrrdin Wylit." I would not disappoint them. I decided that I would be liken unto a lone bear, kind, yet fierce if attacked. All was well.

Unkempt and solitary, I became the hermit I was, and yet I would often send messages through to Nivienne through the ways of the crystal she had given me. She was doing well and growing in leaps and bounds. She too, was learning much and growing as an Enchantress, much as I had grown as an Enchanter.

****

One day the crystal Nivienne gifted me several years earlier started to glow with a bright golden light. I knew it was time for me to find my way back to Avalon. She was ready to see me. …and I, was more than ready to know her. I had learned and waited and grown. I was now ready to take a wife.

When I arrived again at Avalon, I must've been a sight. My hair had now grown halfway down my back, I was muscular from living in the wild and climbing into trees for fruit and safety from wild animals. My arrival had been foretold, as before, and all was in order. Freya greeted me graciously and spoke to me privately of all that Nivienne had learned and her proficiency in the ways of magick and of Avalon's secrets. Freya told me that she would allow Nivienne to go with me to be my Mate as long as Nivienne wished the same, and that should the time come for Nivienne to fill Freya's place as Lady of the Lake that there would be no opposition to it from me.

I spoke of my wish to change the thoughts of mankind for the better, and for Nivienne and me to shape man's desires in the future. Freya said that all was prepared for our nuptials, and I was able to prepare myself with new robes and a bath of herbs, and some of the Avalon residents took great care with my beard and hair to prepare me to see my dear one. I knew Nivienne must've grown into a beautiful maiden by now, neither did Freya nor I want to shock my darling betrothed with my appearance, such as I was now. I'm sure we had both changed in the three years that we'd been apart.

The way had been paved with flowers from the Maven's baskets before me as I walked into the woods and under a bower of blossoms I met my beloved. She was even more beautiful than I had remembered, and she beamed when she saw me. I felt a vortex of energy swirl around me and for a moment I felt dizzy, but the feeling passed when she took my hand and I nestled my head into the folds of her chestnut hair. We held each other as if we had been drowning and now had found our life line to the shore. When we had recovered our senses, we stood ready and faced the Lady of the Lake in our determination to be wed.

Freya did handfast us under the eye of the Gods and Goddesses, all of the Elements and Powers of Nature. I was the luckiest man on earth. Nivienne swore that she was the most blessed of all women. There was feast afterward and we were given a separate dwelling place in the faery woods to consummate our union.

The first night was tentative, sweet, demure and shy on both our parts. Neither of us knew a thing about what we were to do, but we soon learned the ways of love. We then spent the good part of the month practicing what we had learned. I had never felt such a depth of feelings for a person in all my life. It was truly a blessed union. Freya had given us a cask of meade, as is tradition, for our "honey"moon, to enjoy this stage of our wedding and to lose our reservations. For the first time in my life, I allowed myself to drink freely and to imbibe in libations, to speak deep thoughts to my new bride, to explore her and to listen intently as to what she also had to say whilst she was in her cups as well. Aye, we were drunk on meade, drunk on love, drunk on lust and drunk on the joy of being in love so completely.

I may have been new to the ways of loving-making, but we both adapted quickly and very much enjoyed each other in connubial bliss. Her scent thrilled me. I adored every inch of her, and she felt the same of me. We simply could not get enough of each other. When we connected physically our spirits as well as our bodies reached out and entwined in each other. It was as if we were ribbons of ethereal beauty twisted together in a beautiful, complicated energy pattern. When we were deeply enraptured in the posture of love, strange and beauteous visions would fill our minds, hearts and souls. An outpouring of our energy, being blessed in the faery woods, flowers sprang up where'ere we went that month!

What the Gods have joined together no one may pull asunder. And so it was with Nivienne and myself. We hoped ne'er to be separated for any length of time in our lives.

After a honeymoon of bliss and the wonderment of learning of each other's bodies, minds and souls, our pillow talk eventually turned to daytime scope of conversations diverse. Our hopes and dreams became each other's pursuits. We walked sincerely through the realms of base physical passion and pleasure through to the sphere of plans for the Universe and our part in it.

When our secluded month of marriage hideaway drew to a close, Nivienne looked at me lovingly and said, "We must go. Let us thank Freya and Avalon for their grand hospitality."

This was when we called all of Avalon together, and blessed each one of them with our sincere gratitude. Our horses were called for and as we mounted them, we bid a reluctant farewell to our friends and the time we had there.

Heading out into the sunrise I said, "Nivienne, our life together is now entwined. Let us make our way in the highlands and lowlands of all of Britain and Wales and explore this green isle! 'T'is wondrous indeed to be riding together again!"

She kicked up her heels and clicked her tongue to her steed Nosey, and said, "Aye! We are a grand team! E'en though thou art an old man on a slow horse!" They sped off ahead of me, and I could hear Nivienne's delighted laughter, even as I heard mine own as I made Bowrider catch up to her in a gallop. The horses also seemed happy to be together once more and on the move. While I certainly enjoyed our honeymoon lounging and taking our rest of sleep and lovemaking, my joy was just being with her, no matter where we wound up. How'ere, we did have an actual plan. Our current quest was to follow Bazzalth's design and so Nivienne and I were bound to find each and every one of the Thirteen Treasures of Britain. This adventure would take us through the entire land, but we would learn much of each other's magick along the way as well as knowing our blessed Britain and tales of many other dimensions. In the end, it took us o'er the next twelve years to complete, but we found all of them. Some were hidden in plain sight, whilst others were hidden by enchantment to protect them.

Hither is the listing of the Thirteen Treasures of Britain, the Powers that be theirs, and from whence they came and thusly found:

Dyrnwyn, the sword of Roderick the Generous. We found this magickal sword hiding in a merchant's wares for sale as an ordinary weapon. How'ere, I knew that this powerful sword would burst into flames from hilt to tip whilst in the hands of a true nobleman. It was hiding in plain sight in peasantry and needed to be found and kept safe. I made sure that I did not touch the sword with my bare hand, but kept my hands wrapped in many cloths while touching it. It would not be seemly to have it burst into fire whilst paying for it with simple coinage.

The Hamper of Plenty. This magickal basket would magnify food, for if victuals for one man could be put into it, food for a hundred would be found when next opened! This basket and ***The Horn of Bran the Blessed*** was a magickal vessel dispensed what'ere drink one desired. It had a mysterious past and spiritual gift which we became immediately aware of. We would keep it safe until the time was right to release it. We found both of these at a location we felt led to and find it encased under stones. Nivienne easily located them by listening to the rocks tell us where to look thither.

The Chariot of Morgan the Wealthy. This carriage quickly transported its owner where'ere he wished to go. This wondrous chariot was hidden by the Fae. Bazaalth had told us how and whence to find it. It was hidden with a spell of Enchantment and to anyone else it looked like a falling down hovel of a stone hut. How'ere, we easily discerned it from the directions on the scroll and the symbols emblazoned upon it.

The Halter of Clyno Edden. This magickal bit o' tack was given to us along the way by a beggar. He did not know what he had, but traded it for some victuals. If it is hung on the owner's footboard by a staple at night, what'ere horse one wished for would be found in the halter. I ne'er used this for myself nor Nivienne, as we already had our dream horses. How'ere, we have used it to serve others and help the deserving find the horses they so desperately needed.

The Knife of Lawfrond the Horseman.
This blade would carve for twenty-four men at a meal. A magickal athame.

The Cauldron of Diwrnach the Giant.
This magkical kettle only boils a brave man's food, and ne'er for a coward's. Interesting for those without discernment to be able to watch and see who is who by asking them to mind the kettle.

The Whetstone of Tudwal.
When used to sharpen a brave man's sword, it would slay any man it wounded. If a brave arm makes a short sword long, then this whetstone, would finish the job.

Padarn's Red-Coat.
This doublet would fit only a nobleman, ne'er a bumpkin. How'ere, once a peasant with great heart did fit it, and it did his heart good, and also mine to see him wear it as he had a noble soul.

The Crock of Rhygend.
This enchanted bowl along with the next dish were both found

washed ashore from a shipwreck. They magickally produced what'ere food one best liked. We found this to be true whence we found them and as we were famished, this crock lived up to its reputation with a grand feast of the sea that we did not have to catch.

The Dish of Rhygend. Another magickally cooking trencher much the same as the crock of Rhygenydd. This one produced wondrous delights of taste.

The Board of Gwenddolau. This delightful chessboard had pieces made of silver, a board of gold and on which they played by themselves. We were led to find this gameboard under a floorboard in an Inn. Someone had carefully hid it, but then was found dead in the morning. We did not fear to stay in the room, as other had, for they afeared his wasting illness. We feared it not, for we did understand the deceased symptoms as a heart attack. It was not catchy, how'ere, we did delight in this treasure for many years to come and it showed us many moves that were clever indeed.

Caswallawn's Mantle. Whoso'ere wore this magkical cloak, would vanish from sight! When I held this cloak for the first time in my hands, I knew would save my life one day. I did not know the whys nor the wherefores, how'ere, I just knew this to be the Truth.

These amazing treasures were found one by one, although the crock and the dish were found together and they all shared the sameness of heralding the worthiness of the one using them. For an unworthy person would not be able to access their powers.

It was an inexplicable journey of great magnitude to be on this quest, to find these treasures of Britain, and bliss to finally be together. It was also our quest to find our own home. Not my parents' cave, nor the land of my father, nor the Isle of Anglesey, nor the Isle of Apples which is Avalon. Nay, Nivienne and I wished to find a place of our own.

One night as we sat by a crackling fire, on a perfect summer evening, we decided to try blend our wishes together and dream of where we needed to settle. We both did dream dreams that night. We walked together hand in hand in our dreams to the edge of Wales. There we came to the bank of the sea, and across the waves we saw it. An Isle of our own. In the morning, we spoke about our matching dreams and felt that this was the place we needed to find. We felt compelled to ride our horses north to the sea. And we did so. There we found the very same markers in our dreams, there we saw the very same hillsides, shores and the view of the land of our dreams! We paid a ferryman to take us and our steeds o'er the water. It was Ynys Enlli, which we decided to call- "Bardsey Isle." Nivienne said, "'T'is a place for bards and magick. It will be a home for us and space for us to be together and to minister to others in peace."

I agreed, "Aye, to live on an island of our own and to finally, finally feel at home with another kindred heart and safe away from the tumult of courts and war."

Nivienne knew my heart, and I knew hers. We quickly found a cave there, and as my father before me, we made it into our own love nest. It was easily hidden, and yet, we did not turn away those who wished healing or guidance. Nivienne and I wanted to learn everything there was to know about each other, and yet, e'en more! We were compelled to learn about how we could help the world with these treasures that we found and the magick that we had in our joint reservoirs. We took the treasures of Britain, and we hid them there, with us, under spells of protection and built for ourselves an abode in the cave on the hill there.

The first thing we did was to plant an apple tree from seeds from Avalon and to dedicate it to the Isle of Apples and to Anglesey Isle. We were the island in between. We were the link to grand knowledge and we would be the keepers of it for'ere. We occasionally would visit Arthur at Sir Ector's and continue his regal education and keep him in the ways of the Druid path as well as to keep him in a mind fair to Avalon's ways as well.

****

Soon, how'ere, trouble did burst our bubble of happiness. News came to us that King Uther had taken ill and lingered on his deathbed. It had been now 16 years since I had been at court, and I was immediately summoned, as next of kin, to come to him. Nivienne and I departed in great haste. We used the Chariot of Morgan and were there posthaste.

Uther was glad to see me as he weakly took my hand, held me in his eyesight, and bade me find his son, Arthur. I was to bring him back safely so that he may take his place upon the throne. He was to protect Britain from the wolves which would come.

A confused Arthur was sent for from Sir Ector's to come directly to the King. The young man was told of his heritage and his lineage and his home. We needed to connect Uther and Arthur to each other and to the kingdom and we did hasten quickly back to the castle. The King knew that many contenders would come to try to step in line for his crown, not knowing that he had an heir, who had been kept hidden away safely for all these years. A mob would not trust an unknown bastard who came forward at the last moment. Uther had spent his last hours bonding with his son, and teaching him what he would need to know, do, and how to behave. Even on his death bed, Uther was still plotting and planning the best for his kingdom.

Verily, though, Uther's breath came to him ever more labored. Ygraine, Arthur, Nivienne and I sat with him throughout a long night and early one dawn, as the sun peeked over the mountains and shown through the tapestries, Uther did breathe his last. His hands were held in love by Ygraine on his left and Arthur on his right. Tears flowed freely from them both- from Ygraine for a husband who was on death's bed- and from Arthur for a father who was longed for, only just realized, and now soon to be taken from him. Nivienne and I comforted them both. We made the announcement that day and the bells did toll for Uther. His reign had ended, yet there was no official heir to take his place, that was all that the peasantry and gentry knew. Many had heard of a child born to Ygraine so many years before, but when no child manifested, many assumed that the child had not lived through the birthing.

Consultations, posturing and solutions were offered up, to no avail. How'ere, there was a way through the chaos that remained for a leaderless nation, and I was set to launch it.

Before Uther's death, we all had planned together a ruse for the Kingdom to rally as one and to become unified once more. It would be in the spirit of competition! This would give the populace something grand to think of, to plan for, and to spend their energy upon whilst waiting for Arthur's appropriate moment to come forward as the leader he was.

Nivienne spoke to her stones and had a large granite boulder hold a sword within the rock, and the boulder vowed only to release the sword to Uthur's true successor, Arthur. A proclamation went out:

"Whosever can release this sword from this stone, shall be the leader of all of Britain." And it was signed by Uther, before his death.

Men from all o'er Britain came to try their hand at pullng the sword from the rock all to no avail. Nivienne had enchanted the sword to remain for'ere ensconced until Arthur's touch released it. For one and only one would succeed Uther as King.

After many men in the kingdom had spent their energy and strength trying to free the sword to no avail, then a stranger, a young man stepped up to the task. There were shouts of encouragement and of derision, but when all was quiet, this brave young man wrapped his right hand around the hilt and covered it over with his left hand and pulled. The sword easily slipped from the rock like pulling a knife from the butter dish.

A hush came o'er the crowd gathered and then cheers of wonderment! The young man smiled from ear to ear and brandished the sword on high! He waved it around and the crowd loved seeing a peasant succeed!

The gathered assembly murmured: "Blimey! He's done it! The wee lad has done it!!" "Nay! He isn't a nobleman!" "Aye, it could've been any one of us!" "T' think of it! Tis wondrous indeed!"

The young man was promptly hoisted onto the shoulders of cheering men and taken to the castle doors.

His name was Arthur Pendragon, it was he who pulled the sword from the stone, and now all of Britain stood behind him and saluted him at once as the future King!

Arthur decided to name this sword, Excalibur and he claimed it for his own. At his coronation, he held the sword on high, in front of all to see, and then dedicated it and himself to the service of the realm, to the people and to all of Britain.

"All Hail King Arthur! All Hail King Arthur! God save the King!!"

ixteen years aforetime, I had placed Arthur into Sir Ector's guardianship for King Uther. The lad had grown into a fine, strong man; the spitting image of his father, Uther. Albeit Arthur's eyes were kinder liken unto his mother Ygraine's eyes how'ere, there was no denying, that he was his father's son. Aye, he was heir apparent when he walked, talked, and e'en stood in the same manner.

Arthur had a big job to do, now that his father had passed on, and Arthur was slated to take the crown. Soon he would be burdened with considerable duties for the remainder of his days. There were many festivities and I was to guide him as his Mentor on his path. There was some darkness afoot though, and jealousy reared its ugly head in the form of a beautiful woman. It was she who plied her comely wiles to the inexperienced young man. Arthur was newly into the realm of court life and unaccustomed to being the man o' the hour. Morgause and Morgan le Fay had hatched a plan years before and were now launching it into action.

Word came to me that a fetching woman had seduced the young buck, Arthur, who was his father's son in the ways of passion as well. The false woman lured the would-be-King intently. When I did gaze into the ether, I saw that it was with a dark purpose she did so. In sooth, t'was his own half-sister Morgause, who bedded her own mother's son, with a willing heart and with evil intent.

It seems that Arthur had accepted the attentions of a slightly older comely and very experienced woman who seduced his vanity with flattery and fluttering eyelashes. In sooth, it was all very spontaneous from Arthur's point of view, a lusty buxom lady who needed some company, and he was all too willing to have his virginity be gone from him with her attention. E'en so, it was not a spontaneous event for Morgause (who never did tell Arthur her name, but was only coy and mysterious that fateful night). Nay, but for Morgause, this was a coupling long planned and charted. With her scouts and servants, she had discovered when the coronation was to be, and she placed herself in the path of Arthur, purposefully on the night before the Coronation.

The young Arthur was reeling with new knowledge, having servants himself for the first time, and fine garments and food. The world was his to command! Morgause knew all this, and when she stepped into his path, she did it with the calculating precision of a surgeon. The lad was swept off his feet with lust, mystery, power and the fineries of life and the new curiosities of passion! E'en as he willingly shed his virginity, Morgause cooed her pleasure back to him and taught him the ways of the flesh. She was sweet and beguiling to his face and to his body; she gave herself to her own brother, knowingly so.

They parted, sated and satisfied. He had learned carnal knowledge and could now be King knowing more of the world. The lady left his bed of tangled sheets with kisses and a fetching smile. "Anon" was all she said to him as she blew him a kiss farewell.

She was filled with him, and she had watched the moons until the day was right to do so. Quickly her womb did grow with his seed and, with that seed, a babe formed within. This was not the joyous occasion that should have been, nay, for instead, the bairn was to be raised to hate, and to grow into his father's demise. The babe was born in secret, and concealed from his father's knowledge. Arthur remained oblivious to the dark nature of a fleeting dalliance which would end up being his fateful end.

Morgause delivered the babe with hard labor, for aye, the Fates were not pleased with the manner of its conception. The boy was named Mordred and he, too, had the look of his father, Arthur, as he grew in stature. How'ere, his demeanor was not of Arthur's kind and noble heart, but was bred of a dark nature, jealousy and fed upon hatred for Uther and of the whole of the Pendragon name. Morgause and Morgan raised the boy to be strong, filled with vanity and hubris. He, after all, in their minds, would be *King* someday. All of this was hidden from Nivienne and myself by the cloaking spells that Morgan le Fay had put round the situation. We knew nothing of the storm brewing in Arthur's own house.

Arthur was crowned monarch of High Britain without any interference. I was there to place the crown upon his brow hailing him King Arthur Pendragon. All swore their fealty to this young King. Grand feasting parties and celebrations filled the land! Yet, e'en with every mouthful of celebratory food, whispers and talk quickly and wistfully turned to Arthur's need for a Queen.

In no time, likely batches of noble beauties were invited to a ball, and the King had the opportunity to meet them. Per contra, there was only one that caught his eye, and it was not the one I had hoped he would pick. The lady I thought would be a grand Queen for him was kind, stable, handsome in her way, and carried herself with decorum. Not the most exciting of lasses, surely, but one of solid trust, reason and a willingness to serve him and the nation. I had encouraged them to dance, sadly, there was no spark in Arthur's eye, nor his loins for her.

Albeit, for Arthur had other notions. He desired Gwenivere, who was indeed a fair beauty, and aptly named "The White Fay." Her hair was as white as cornsilk and just as tender. Arthur was smitten from the day he saw her, and liken unto his father's obsession with Ygraine, he had to have this woman, despite my counsel, despite his own reason.

Gwenivere was a sweet Lady with a good heart, but I felt that she lacked the true bearing of a Queen. She was too easily swayed by frivolity and sympathy and seemingly missing a strong backbone. She was liken unto a delicate flower that needed much care and patience and Arthur, in mine own opinion, had not the time to dedicate to coddling her so. It was not my counsel that he followed, but his own heart and loins that bade him make arrangements swiftly. Arthur married Gwenivere posthaste and with much grand ceremony. The people adored her as a Queen, and she quickly adapted to court life and busied herself with embroidery, frivolity and dancing. She felt that her purpose was to be an amusement to the King and nothing more than decoration to His crown, as His Majesty had bigger responsibilities in the Kingdom. The King was now rescuing a nation that had been slowly declining during the last years of Uther's illness and reign. Clan fighting and invaders had divided the country, filled it with skirmishes and wracked it with unrest.

It was during this worrisome, unruly time I then took to pondering the many faiths. It was for the unknown reason of which my mother converted to Christianity and entered the nunnery. Insomuch for I knew she too, was Druid afore, t'was sech a conundrume and curiousity to me. So I made it a point to learn all the information I could about faith in the hearts of men.

I knew that my mother had once believed in many Gods, and so her sudden embrace of this mono-theistic belief intruiged me. I found out many things. That the one they called Jesus seemed to me to be Druid by the leanings of his beliefs. He seemed a kind and goodly man. His followers started off meaning well, how'ere t'was only a matter of time, when Power reared its ugly head. This honest carpenter's son and his avowed pledge of poverty for the sake of others was uncharacteristically reinvented into lavish vestments of gold and rubies to the benefit and betterment of the ones who carried his story forward. It seemed the antithesis of his meanings and concerned me why so this had happened.

Nivienne and I decided to ask Spirit for direction by sitting together in a quiet place and asking our Spirit Guides (my wolf friend from old and her rocks) to show us the future in a vision. We wanted to know if the world would eventually join as one, or would division and animosities between all the faiths continue? It was not a comforting path that I saw laid before me when I traveled forward into the Mountain of Time. This pheonomenon of strife, particularly as it embodied faith, the frittering away of the earth, along with the lack of respect for nature concerned me greatly.

Nivienne and I had previously spent many happy hours of theological discussion together. I loved to hear her thoughts on the Universe, Gods and Goddesses, and of worshiping them through Nature. Since the time whence I had learned of my mother's path and her subsequent change of faith, my mate Nivienne and I had devoted ourselves to learning about many faiths and their beliefs. It worried us that the development of any single God, would ultimately foreshadow and seek the elimination of other cultures and their Gods and Goddesses. It seemed that the quest to conquer ownership of souls became the marker of large faiths.

In sooth, I had seen too much of this same story from Atlantis forward. Seemingly, once a thing unbalanced another thing the interdependant web of life suffered. When an unbalancing of Nature occurred in preference of man's greed, historians have noted that society implodes. Over and over again, throughout my studies, I had been privy to the knowledge of this frightening repeating pattern in history.

Nivienne and I researched and found that before each and every human calamity, similarities existed. The things that seemed to trigger social cataclysms were: blatant disregard for any other religion, culture or society (other than the accepted one at the time), disrespect of the Divine Feminine, lack of honor for the delicate balance of nature, the pursuit of greed and consumption over reason, and the obvious love of the fripperies of life. The earth then seemed to always respond to these harsh vibrations with harsh energies of its own with earthquake, violent storms and droughts. There seemed to be an opposite and equal reaction.

We observed that this was no small trend, as the past repeated itself over and over to the same conclusions, we saw that it would not bode well. If man's greed and domination was allowed to go forward unchecked into the ages it would be devastating for all of humanity. Druids, Pagans, Womankind, and any person who was weak, infirmed, helpless, would all suffer as well as the Earth herself.

We, as Druids, were bound by our vows to at all times, honor the earth. It made sense to us to try to save it and protect it. We had to get through to man via magick.

As Druid and Maven, Nivienne and I vowed to try and lessen the adversity and severity of politics and power of the singular religions over the Earth. We *must* protect nature from these conquoring zealots. Man would love war and gold and kill for it in the name of their God...(What'ere god that was popular at what'ere period of time, it mattered not.) It seemingly was merely a repeated pattern.

It made no sense to us, how'ere, I had learned that man was indeed, a giddy thing, easily swayed and sometimes easily herded. Change must come from within for a real change to be permanent. We were determined to intervene. Nivienne and I would do so, by adding a dimension of respect for nature, for women, and life itself, by protecting the theoloy of the Goddess and Mother Earth and keep it in the collective heart of mankind somehow.

Our calling was not only to preserve the Earth and all its creatures, but also to protect Womankind herself. Avalon knows that women are the keepers of the continuation of life. Druids are bound by our vows to offer information to protect the Earth. In my heart I knew that humans could succeed with love and grow with compassion o'er the years. E'en if it took many lifetimes to come and grow to fruition, mankind would, at least, be *offered* the opporutnity to Love and Nurture instead of Hate and Conquer. We were compelled to offer the idea that to succeed we should all support the Highest and Greatest Good of all. These are the Inner Truths to grow into, if not now, then o'er time. One of these truths was that life is Sacred, for we are all interconnected. For I had seen in my travels throughout the Mountain of Time, that without the Divine Feminine being included, man would spiral into wars of greed and posture for Power.

Without the Divine ways of the Mavens, the Druid way of life would fall from grace in favor of greed. Nature faiths were set to be obliterated with war, pollution and cruelty. The world *needed* to have a kinder way of life added to its resources if it was to survive into the future. Avalon's ways *needed* to have a place in the world alongside of the knowledge of Anglesey as well.

This was indeed new thinking and the world was not yet ready for what Nivienne and I planned to do. It had been assigned to us through Spirit to protect Nature and also the faiths of its believers. We were to guard and save the Earth from total annihilation. What could we do on this great mission?

Nivienne and I meditated and prayed and spoke much on this topic. We did spells of great importance for our Earth Mother. Finally, we received an epiphany! We were given inspiration in the guise of assimilation in the tenets of one of our Druid beliefs which states: "The power which can destroy a thing, can also be used to preserve it as well." Liken unto my lesson of the noble Nightjar with Taliesin so long ago, hiding in plain sight mayhaps is the safest camoflage.

So we prayed incessantly about all this, and we finally came up with a plan. We would bind the many conflicting faiths eventually into one, by blending it all into the Universal mind of Humankind through Spirit. In time, Love would eventually find its path, Nature would be honored and the Druid path would again find its footing right through the grass itself. Thusly, the Earth would be blessed and honored and we would have done our duty.

Our course of action was simple. We would start by planting seeds in the new apostolic priests' minds to knowingly absorb the Pagan culture. The priests would think they were doing their duty of destroying it and in doing so, would garner their followers in number. How'ere, in turn, the absoption of the Druid nature within the Church could actually safely preserve the Pagan faith until the time was right for it to bloom again. When people had forgotten about its meager beginnings, and that the building block of their holy days were actually our Pagan Sabbats and Solstices, our followers would be ripe to take heart. We would be more *like* one another than different. When the Earth

Mother was in need, humans would see that the Natural Path was also worthy, ancient and enduring. The new church would end up ensconcing our Earthen Solstices and Sabbats with gold, but they would *survive*. There would be a Christian focus, but Pagan Gods.

Brigit, Goddess of Hearth, would become St. Brigid. The Roman God, Mars, would become St. Martin. Demeter the Goddess of the harvest would live again as St. Demetrios, a warrior saint. The lusty Goddess Aphrodite would mischievously be called St. Aphrodite, the repentant "love peddler." Saint Peter the founder of the church would end up resembling the God Zeus. The Roman Goddess Venus would be St. Venera. The God Dionysius, and Orpheus- son of Apollo, and the God Jesus all had some similiar story elements, they too would be linked. For those of us who love the fruit of the vine, a Saint Dionysius as well as a Saint Bacchus would be more than welcome! The God Mercury was ofttimes depicted carrying sheep on his shoulders in the art of the ancient ones- soon the Good Shepherd would also be shown doing this as well. Mary, the God of Heaven is the ultimate Goddess and she is deserving of praise with offering her unconditional love, she is resplendant as Mother Earth, the greatest Mother Goddess, also deserving of our praise and care who doth offer her unconditional love as well. Mary also embodies the Divine Feminine of every religion. There are thousands of Pagan Gods, so there would be thousands of similar Saints!

Say what ye will, but I magickally constructed this ruse to protect our diverse religions in the face of total destruction of our culture. 'Tis true that the Earthen religion would be persecuted and fall dormant for a time, but then it will rise again and bloom when the soil was right in the future. This I had *Seen* in my time traveling.

In sooth, in the following countless counseling talks with the King, we set our plan slowly into motion. Nivienne and I suggested to His Majesty that it would benefit the nation if the King could rally and harness the devotion of his noblemen and encourage them to share ideas and to be kinder to the fairer sex as well. Worship of the Divine Feminine would have to begin subtley through the care of men. Noble men. It would be generous to invite distinguished warriors, and aristocrats of the land to be a part of this grand organization of a new era in which duties were to be delegated fairly amongst all. To be chosen for this group was to be a great honor, indeed.

Nivienne had meditated and counseled to use her position to influence the minds of men to change for the better toward women and children. It was Avalon speaking through her for all womankind, so she spoke to Arthur privately and counseled him about the state of affairs of gentlewomen, peasants and children in his land.

The King then included in his edict the premise that would seal the noble mind with charity for'ere. A council was to be established in sech a way that no one stood at the head, but all would be considered as equals. This was a first in our dark time that sech a manner of ruling had occurred. A special large round table was created to symbolize this equality, and the knights and King were all able to have a voice. Subsequently, a code of conduct was devised, and only the highest and greatest traits of manhood were honored as service in kind.

The manners celebrated and set forth in which a Knight of the Round Table were as follows: A Knight was ne'er to commit outrage or murder. He was to remain loyal to King and Country. A Knight was always to be merciful and shun cruelty. The Knights of the Round Table would always give aid and succor to gentlewomen, noble widows, and children. In sooth, they were to ne'er force nor harm a woman and to guard the weaker sex, for in them lie the future of our beloved Britain. Lastly, these Knights of the Round Table were ne'er to battle needlessly, nor for want of love nor worldly goods.

This code of conduct we called "Chivalry" and was implemented tout de suite. The King also renamed his family castle, "Camelot," at this time--which was less of a destination and more of a state of mind and heart. This new chivalous attitude was implemented swiftly and easily and Arthur made a solid statement which would ripple in everyone's minds for'ere.

Thusly, with these changes, a new mood came across the land and an era of good manners and love of humanity blanketed the whole of Britain. Positive energy swelled. The Knights showed mercy to a knave, who in turn started to pay for what he stole previously. Merchants and artists traded their wares and crafts and supported each other and promoted each other. The arts grew and excelled as did the countryside. Goodness and kindness enveloped the land and sprang up within the bosom of the peasantry who in turn were mild and compassionate to their children and livestock. The peasantry felt less threatened and were provided for by the King and his countrymen and so the farmers were kinder to their animals, who then were more rested and well fed. These animals then had more vim and vigor and the vibration of their health made a positive influence upon the land, the hearth and the home. Indeed, the world was becoming a better place. The land seemed to e'en respond with better crops and bigger herds, more children being born. It was becoming the fabled land of milk and honey. Knights and noblemen from other countries even came and pledged their allegience to King Arthur and joined the Knights of the Round Table and this new brotherhood. One Knight in particular was most celebrated to have joined into this brotherhood. He was

Lancelot du Lac from France, the greatest swordsman and jouster in all the land.

All was very well, all, except for one thing. Inasmuch as His Majesty still had no heir. Nay, Gwenivere did not conceive during her happy nuptials to the King. They had consummated their union fully and repeatedly, but she remained childless. She did not then become full with bairn neither after a full year of marriage to Arthur. No matter how much in love they seemed to be, it became apparent that t'was not in the cards that Gwenivere would be a mother.

O'er the years, her youthful body became more matronly, yet she was ne'er able to swell with child. At first, the Queen became distraught, and then she turned her sights on becoming useful in other ways. She hosted grand parties and wove linen cloaks for the poor. The Queen learned the ways of healing from Nivienne, who helped Gwenivere all that she could to adapt and go forward. But Gwenivere eventually descended into melancholy and took to her bed. No healer, jester nor potion could rouse her spirits. Her nickname, "The White Fay," paled in comparison to her ghostly look. The King worred more and more about her, so he took to having the Queen's litter carried outside to get some air as he felt some diurnal courses would enliven her with sunshine's healing qualities.

Nothing cheered her until Lancelot arrived and came to read poetry to her and to her ladies-in-waiting in the sweet tongue of the language of France. He would remain with her from morning into the shadows of late day at which time he would try to excuse himself to be of service elsewhere; the Queen would beg of him not to go, and to continue their discourse. She loved to speak French and was happy for the conversations with him in that tongue.

Gwenivere was so beautiful. Lancelot was so handsome. It did not take a scholar to see what would happen next. Aye, they were rapidly on course to being totally smitten with each other. Nivienne and I saw it bloom before our eyes. We also knew that whilst Arthur loved them both, he could deny his wife nothing. Surely if something was not done, scandal would soon fill the court.

T'was at this juncture that something wondrous happened. In the middle of a heated round-table discussion, I interrupted with an announcement: "There is an ethereal prescence here that wishes to enter!" Suddenly, a glowing light appeared. It was roughly in the shape of an hourglass, or mayhaps a goblet which shown brightly. I felt the need to channel this spirit which projected this curvy image to the men seated. Someone cried out that it looked to be in the shape of a vessel, and that indeed it was. I let them ponder and proclaim their suggestions until the vision faded into memory. Their in-fighting was forgotten and the ponderance of the mystical happening continue until Lancelot suggested that it must be the cup of the Lord Christ from the Last Supper.

The search for the Holy Grail had been offered up as an idea to appease the glowing strange-some Grail-shaped orb.

I posed a query to the King and to his Knights, that this may indeed be fortuitious and not a haunting at all, but a sign from the Heavens. That *if* a dedicated search of the land was undertaken for this ancient and reknown relic, namely the cup of the Last Supper of Jesus, verily the same which had caught his last blood, and *if* blessed with an Earthy Spell from me and Nivienne, that both the worlds of Christian and Pagan faiths would be entwined for'ere, in this land and the eons to come. That Britain would for'ere be noted for the Knights of the Round Table and their Quest and that Camelot would be a name on the lips of future generations for'ere. That this uniting of faiths and genders of God *and* Goddess would bless the country and his Knights for all eternity. A flurry of conversations filled the air, and it was decided. The Knights would take up this Grail Quest for King and Country. The search for the Holy Grail and its banner was taken up quickly and completely. Fealty to it and to King Arthur and Camelot were as One.

I also knew that this Quest would do e'en more. It would stop much of the bickering that had developed here at Camelot of late with the change of personalities that came from adapting to new ways. These men needed a cause and a

project to rally behind! The search for the Holy
Grail would also remove Lancelot from the
temptation of lying with the Queen behind his
liege's back. Lancelot was a gracious man, a
noble and devoted celibate by reputation. I also
knew that he was distraught in the possiblity of
failure to either the King (by the temptation of
adultery) or to the Queen (by lack of love's
physical proof of it to her). I knew that if
Lancelot were to deny either the King or the
Queen, he would surely fall, and with him, the
Knights of the Round Table. He was in a tight
spot and could not win without some outlet and
some guidance. Lancelot was the hinge piece to
the surety of the brotherhood. He would have to
remain faithful to the King and the Queen's
individual wishes in order to follow the Code of
Chivalry and be a beacon to the brotherhood. It
was his moral dilema.

The Quest for the Holy Grail was timely
and would be fortuitous in many ways. The
Knights swore that they would scour the land
and seek it everywhere, and it would return with
them posthaste (albeit it would be years, in
sooth, that they would quest far and wide for it,
which they knew not).

****

Camelot quieted down after this, what
with the noble Knights, and Lancelot away on
their crusades to find the grail. The King and
Queen would have time together to rule and to

find succor in each other's arms, and in doing so, without tribulation, mayhaps an heir to the throne would yet arrive.

With all this put into motion, Nivienne and I left Camelot and journeyed back to our home on Bardsey Isle to spin our webs of protection on the land. For we knew exactly where the Grail was. It was something we had been safeguarding for years. We also understood deeply that it was also something much more than a drinking vessel of the Christ. It was much liken unto the dragon lines that marked the spot where we origianlly were led to find the horn, itself. It was a way to unite people over miles. It was the Horn of Bran the Blessed, he who was called "The Grail Guardian." The legend was that long ago, Bran was son-in-law to Joseph of Arimethea. The cup had come to Bran in secrecy, and since then the Grail had been kept protected safe in the unknown realms for years. This magickal drinking vessel had been passed from one to another and had gifted those in whoever's care it remained. It could give healing drink to the sick, heal the dead because it held the secret to immortality.We had held onto this precious treasure of Britain since Bazaalth the Protector of the Sky had shown us where it lay. The vessel was safe in our keeping. We would release it in its own time.

The Knights were not warring but had embarked on a spiritual journey of each their own out to do Good to peasant and noble alike and to spread comraderie and humanitarian policy far and wide. The land was in the process of being united as One in faiths both Pagan and Christian and would eventually blend with joint holidays, customs, saints and angels, deities and ritual. In turn, also, Arthur was happy with his wife Gwenivere all to himself. Lancelot was safe and away and happily questing the land for the righteous cup. Gwenivere secretly pined for Lancelot, but devoted herself soley to Arthur. I was home with Nivienne on our blessed bardic island and she was with me. We were fulfilling our promise to unite male and female energies and bring the world into harmony with the earth and its conflicting religions. Peace would have the opportunity to reign. We were set to stay at Bardsey Isle and wait for the Gods to call us into leadership again.

****

Nivienne and I were blissfully happy together. In all the time we had spent together, nothing had dimmed our love for each other, or our passion for each other's hearts, minds or bodies. Nivienne had grown into a striking woman, beautiful, in her fourth decade of life. I was now a man of almost 60 years, an ancient one, albeit, my hair had only started to turn a bit salt and peppery with some grey hair of late. I was still fit as a fiddle with our wondrous diet and with no hardships to spake of. Magick was within me and could not be denied by my vim and vigor for my age. Nivienne and I gave our gifts of healing, spiritual and physical to the locals and we were paid in livestock and food and wine. We wanted for nothing...except more of our time together for'ere. There was so much to learn and to spake of together! Our conversations roamed free and large and nothing was off limits in our ways of projection.

****

Back at Camelot, King Arthur had bravely thwarted and pushed back invaders and the home front was secure. Queen Gwenivere had her husband all to herself, and yet, still no issue was given to the King in the form of a prince or princess. She pined greatly for a child, and a beneficiary to Arthur. She also still craved Lancelot with all her heart, notwithstanding she did show it not.

Seven years in all had passed with no Grail or child forthcoming. And so the brave Knights returned home to Camelot empty handed. Whilst journeying, Lancelot had stopped at Bardsey Isle and stayed with Nivienne and I for a fortnight. We spoke of many things and far into the early morning light. He told us that he was anxious to have pleased his master the King. Be that as it may, it was not in his hand to do so. For, without finding the Grail, he felt that he had failed the King in not returning with the vessel. Lancelot also confided to me, that he hoped beyond reason that his infatuation with the Queen had cooled and that he would be able to move on with his duties and his life once he returned home. He had some inner turmoil at seeing her again, but he was steadfast and resolved to overcome his lustful nature towards her and to see her with the heart of a brother and a friend instead. Nivienne gave him a large piece of Amethyst to help sooth his worries on his ride back to Camelot.

****

All was well in this world. That is, until chaos would have its way, as is the way of the world when greed reigns. Queen Morgause and her sister Queen Morgan Le Fay intervened and the tides turned once again. With their Dark Magick, they did a blood sacrifice of a trusting pet and read from the savaged entrails. They energetically detected through this dark divining that Nivienne and I protected the vessel of Bran the Blessed.

When this truth was revealed to the sisters, Morgause and Morgan through a crystal ball divination; all issues were laid on the table and a serious play was in motion. The King's undetected bastard, Mordred, son of Morgause (now a fully grown man raised on the bile of his mother's hatred, and his father Arthur's impetuous nature) began to make his move. They would seek a reason to raise an army against Arthur.

Together they would find a cause grievous enough to dethrone Arthur and

Gwenivere and then he would declare war on his father the King and Camelot itself. It would be done easily with only a little bit of treason and slander and with a lot of his mother and aunt's funding and emotional fueling. Mordred was prepared to take his father's crown by force, duplicity and scandal, what'ere it would take, in order to win victory and gain the throne.

The sisters saw that the chink in the chainmaille was Gwenivere. She was the weakest link and it would be easy to sway the delicate flower and the handsome dedicated Knight Sir Lancelot and increase their mutual desire. Morgan le Fay and Morgause fashioned poppets that resembled both Gwen and Lancelot and the sisters wove a spell of lust that would crush a kingdom.

And that is the precise moment when the Christians' hell broke loose.

226

VIII

T'was a fine spring day when the Knights of the Round Table happily came thither to Camelot to resume their places at the helm with King Arthur. Sadly, they did not succeed with their main quest to find the Holy Grail how'ere, there were many tales told of the great deeds that had been done by each and every Knight, and they in turn listened to each others' tales and applauded their efforts. Many a fair damsel had been rescued and many an evildoer pursued! Justice prevailed o'er all and the time that had been spent in quest was a noble accomplishment.

Sir Pellinore recanted the epic saga of his pursuit of one of the world's most unfathomable of beasts, one against which he held a bitter personal vendetta. He stood up and in the most solemn of voices said thusly, "My journey turned into a hunt for a creature unbeknownst to man. It be a questing beast, and one strangesome, indeed! It be a queer oddity with the head of a snake, the body of a lion and the feet of a deer! It be swift, cunning, savage and silent! I did spy it once and the sight of it was so fiercesome and so curious that I set my path to conquer it. Hence I tracked it o'er hill and dale, seen it many times, came close to slaying it in its sleep once but was foiled by its damnable instincts. Once the beast woke from its slumbers, it was savage indeed. I managed to fight it off with the help of Sir Palamedes the Saracen and my nephew. We were a courageous slaying team. We did extirpate it and I now, by your leave, present it to you, my Liege! 'Tis proof that the world is a grandsome place and that you reign o'er all!"

With this statement, the grand doorway was opened up, and a tumult of activity erupted with the King's men hauling into the courtyard a most bizarre and fiercesome beast. Aye, dead as a door nail, and slain through and through, but gargantuan, wonderfully queer and uncommon indeed! It had the upper part of its body the head and neck liken unto a snake, with its body bespeckled liken unto a leopard. Its haunches were liken unto a lion and the cloven feet of a deer. Never had we seen a beast such as this!

Sir Pellinore went on, "This fearsome beast I have sought for many a year. It did replace my Quest for the Holy Grail, in sooth, for I knew that it and I were linked in spirit and soul. I tracked it by following the sounds of its barking noise which was liken unto our hounds following close upon its heels." The King and all his Knights gathered 'round the creature and examined it closely. No one had e'er afore seen such a monstrosity!

After all this hullabaloo had somewhat subsided, Sir Pellinore thusly introduced his grand nephew to the King. "My Lord and King, I do present to you, my kith and kin, Galahad. He be one of the slayers of this Great Beast, a help to me in the Quest of it and its demise. We have helped to make the land safe again in that part of the Kingdom. It is known to many as 'The Questing Beast' but I should like to give unto it a newsome name, for it doth deserve one." Sir Pelinor put his boot up on the slain spotted deer-footed beastie and stated, 'I name thee, 'The Most Fiercesome Jeroef!'"

A murmur went round and all in attendance did not seemingly object, thusly, the notion was carried. And in sooth, he did go on: "By your leave, Your Highness, I beg a boon that the kinship I share with Galahad be honored with his admittance to this fine group of Knights for his bravery and courage shown to all in the killing of this most savage of beasts." For emphasis, Pellinore stroked the long furry neck of the slain creature. "'Tis a shame to annihilate something so unusual, how'ere, we canna have it destroying villages and ravaging towns!"

"Hear! Hear!" said the Knights and they toasted to Pellinore and his kin's bravery! The King was pleased indeed, and Galahad, Pellinore's nephew was swiftly knighted "Sir Galahad" and admitted to the realm of the Knights of the Round Table.

A day of feasting commenced with camaraderie, news, gossip, drinking, laughter and boisterous bouts of acclaim. Hobnobbing went far into the night as the men reveled in their friendships and the security of Camelot and the feeling of Oneness.

All during this grand and joyous time of festivity, how'ere, there seemed to be a mood of unsettled emotions lying within Camelot. I did gaze into my scrying glass and determined that this mood came from the heart of Lancelot. Whilst he outwardly smiled and nodded to others, deep within he was neither merry, nor joyful. T'was so, for he had not seen the Queen yet. Nay, she was not hither. She was off visiting her relatives when the Knights had finally come home after their years of absence. Lancelot had secretly longed to see her, but, aye, t'was too much to wish that she'd be waiting there, just to receive *him* when he returned. He resigned himself that he lived in folly to e'en think sech a thought. T'was obvious to him that she hath indeed moved on and in sooth had forgotten him, and verily, no longer cared for him. T'was just as well, he reasoned. And so, amidst laughter and jocularity, a sullen Lancelot remained present merely in shape alone. For his heart was elsewhere.

The next week overflowed with reunions, accolades and more of the same. Arthur had sent word to me and Nivienne reporting of the joy he felt that his men had finally returned home! Aye, sans the Holy Grail, be that as it may, they were indeed safe and had done many goodly deeds in their time spent questing!

Nivienne and I postulated what would now become of the land. While the news of their homecoming was grand indeed, an uncommon and unbidden feeling of dread filled us both. We decided to journey together into a trance to find out why we had such worrisome premonitions. We left our home on the top of Bardsey Isle and walked out into the night on this upcoming full moon. Bathing in moon-wash, we committed ourselves once more to each other. Nivienne was beautiful as 'ere, and the years had been kind indeed to her. I ne'er took her for granted, nor once regretted having taken her into my heart. She had given me new ways of thinking, seeing, feeling. There was goodness and wisdom in her of which I had found in no other. We had ne'er had any children and that was what we had wanted. We only had eyes for each other, and our mission to bring the world together in peace and its turmoil to an end was our progeny, if you will.

We felt led to heal mankind's heart and give it a sense of belonging and faith and solidarity amidst its divisions. We were compelled to try to keep our Mother Earth safe at all costs. We had long meditated and looked into the future and saw that there would come a time when the trees and animals would speak to man, and man would be forced to listen or else lose their entwined lives together.

T'was our sincere mission to bring about healing and for magick to root itself in the soul of man. The earth needed man and woman kind to carry on and to use their intuition freely. The current church and ways of politics coming would impose no free thought. Druids always need to be free thinkers. We would protect it the best way we knew how. We would disguise it for these days were dark and becoming darker. While it would sound mad to think sech a thought, I knew that what was to come was much persecution. *"Goodness revolves around the preservation of knowledge and culture."* This was always a pondrance to me…for inherent in every man, woman and child is a

Soul of Wonder. How could humans just turn off this curiosity? Standing looking at the stars and the sciences to come would show them how little they knew, and how great the Universe is. Our part in it is to persevere, to protect, to ponder and to honor. To preserve.

So Nivienne and I then did sit cross-legged facing one another and held our hands, palm to palm for the energy to connect. I looked into her eyes and felt the same longing in the pit of my spine that I had felt all those years before when I first laid sight upon her. Her long chestnut hair was starting to gray a bit and a few laugh lines framed her eyes and her mouth. I wanted to kiss her again and did so at this moment of joined spirit and energy. It only made me love her more, for I was growing through time with my beloved. I wanted to be with her always, and she spoke the same to me. We were ONE.

It was at moonrise whence we began our meditation together. After we stated our focus, and prayed together, we both held our mutual thought of Camelot. We then tapped the Great Unconscious Mind and did connect forthwith into that energy. Sparks did swirl and manifest around us. What we saw amazed us and we were caught up into the vision:

Morgan le Fay and Morgause were

concocting a strong love potion and we saw this draught being added to the goblet of Queen Gwenivere where she feasted with her clan. This drink was thusly added to the mug of Lancelot whence he drank whilst in Camelot. It was an intoxicating dram of magick that would seal for'ere their lusty fate. E'en though miles apart, deep within each of them something shifted. They each began to crave one another liken unto one who had an enslavement to poppies. The Queen hastily removed herself from her attendants without any cause and left her family quietly, and rode swiftly in an easterly direction. She did not know why. She was compelled without logic or reason.

Lancelot likewise slipped out of the feasting hall whence he swallowed the liquid in question and saddled up his horse silently and rode out into the night directly in a westerly direction. He too, had no reason nor cause, but was compelled by some urgent desire within. They both rode all night, without stopping, until they each arrived at a clearing by a placid lake. They had magickally arrived within moments of each other to the very same place!

So powerful was this libation that it had directed them to view one another at the exact time and locale where they were to join connubially. She dismounted and ran to him. He leapt from his steed. It was as if time stopped as they were drawn to each other with immeasurable force. Their embrace enfolded their bodies as well as their Souls and their kiss was enough to bring down a kingdom. They fell to the flowers beneath them and momentously consummated their enduring love and lust for each other many times o'er. Their Joy was complete. Here was Bliss. Here was completion. This was a match meant to be. E'en the Gods had foretold it. The potion was merely the device meant to o'ercome proprieties' restraint. In another culture or time, they would've been together from the beginning. How'ere, the decorum of the rigors of nobility staid their hands...and hearts. Thusly, they fell asleep entwined in blossoms, and the seed of Lancelot was within Gwenivere. And the love of Gwenivere was in his heart. Together they embodied undying love, and happiness finally filled their souls as it had ne'er done at any point before in this life.

Nivienne and I continued to hold our hands and pulse to each other and went on to see this:

Yet there was one who witnessed the fated lovers all this time. There stood a man in dark armor who watched it all commence. For hours he took in the lovemaking of the Queen to

*Lancelot, her Knight in Shining Armor. It was
Mordred, who stood and smiled a twisted grin.
When Lancelot and Gwenivere had finally slaked
their thirst, (which would awaken again when
they would awaken again and for'ere more), and
had fallen into the exhausted sleep after
lovemaking, Mordred had arranced for
Excalibur to be stolen away from his father's
house and then came and placed Arthur's sword
between the skyclad lovers. It was the sword of
Arthur, Excalibur. Mordred had stolen it away
from his father house for this very purpose. It
was a message to the wayward lovers that the
King knew of their indiscretion (or that he would
know whence Mordred delivered the news).The
dark knight then mounted his steed and rode
swiftly to Camelot.*

*When the loving couple awoke it was by feeling
cold steel lying between their bodies. "It is a
sign! What have we done?" Lancelot was the
first to awaken with the shameful knowledge of
betraying Arthur, one they both loved. "Aye. It is
Excalibur. It is his sword. I know not how it
came to be hither, but we must flee!" said the
now weeping Gwenivere. "Nay, we must return
and tell our truths, Gwenivere. It is the only
way." Lancelot held his beloved and she
whispered, "Nay, if we do so, we shall surely die
for it. Let us away. Surely there is somewhere in*

this world where true love is honored and we can live in peace?" Her eyes pleaded with his until his knightly resolve melted into the realization that they could be One. "Come with me, my beloved. Come live with me in my homeland. We will be safe and protected there, for'ere."

Whilst they were ashamed and somewhat regretted their actions, and e'en though they both loved Arthur, they loved each other MORE. They made a crucial decision with each breath and statement. Whilst they wanted to do the "right thing" for society's sake, as they had tried all their lives before to do so, it was folly to think that they could socially recover from this disgrace. They knew without a shadow of doubt that only dire circumstances remained for them in the future, should they go back. In sooth, they desired each other so much so that they turned their backs on their former lives, and, in sooth, they fled to France. Lancelot's family would hide them thither. There they would be able to live in love and lust for the rest of their days, in obscurity, aye, but in completion. She told Lancelot that she would live with him and love him all her days and would die in his arms, yet she would bequeath her body, as Queen, to lie next to her husband, Arthur, in Glastonbury for propriety's sake. For indeed, she did love the

King as well, although moreso as a brother and friend, and she did not mean to cuckold him, but could not, in sooth, go live her lie of a life e'er again.

The moon was high into the night and coming on into dawn when next Nivienne and I witnessed this vision:

The sword of Excalibur was magickally returned to its former keeping place in the King's castle, without anyone knowing its momentary disappearance.

Queen Morgause then arrived at Camelot with much pomp and circumstance as his Majesty's half-sister, and to the shock of the company gathered, in front of the King, she then presented Mordred to them all gathered as his child, by her. She boldly told of the e'en when he was conceived, and the King denied it not. There were those there who also had to agree, whence they saw the face of Mordred and realized the resemblance to his father, Arthur.

The King reluctantly acknowledged Mordred as his Son, Prince of the land, for he had no other heir. Mordred took his accolades without much resistance and with full ado and then with his next words sealed the fate of the land:

"Your Highness, I bring you grave tidings. Queen Gwenivere and Sir Lancelot have

betrayed you and the kingdom. I saw them with mine own eyes fornicating in the open air just this last e'en. The Kingdom has been abandoned by the Queen and forsaken by the noblest of Knights. Surely, justice must be done! I know that I am newly come to thee, but I shall be here for thee as your support in this, your hour of need. Aye, be she a Queen or a peasant, the sentence for treason is death, m'lord...and I cry your mercy for her soul." And Mordred knelt before his father whilst a roar of disbelief rose up from the court.

Arthur was visibly shaken and turned pale. The Knights of the Round Table rallied, shouts of disbelief went up and a search for the Queen at her family home and for Lancelot at Camelot proceeded henceforth. When no Queen, nor Sir Lancelot could be found, the Knights of the Round Table supported the King as he prepared to lead select troops out to arrest the errant lovers.

The King put out a decree to the town criers which stated: "Tis with a heavy and grievous heart I must follow the Laws of our Land. For the treasonous act against their King and Country, Gwenivere and Lancelot shalt both be pursued for their crimes, captured and thusly put to death by fire. So be it written."

E'en as he dictated this proclamation,

Arthur's voice clearly failed to resonate from his heart but only from his crown. Away they sped to search for two lovers who would not 'ere be found.

As a half-sister to the King, Queen Morgause and the rest of the Knights remained behind to keep the peace in the absence of both monarchs, whilst the King sought his missing Queen.

How'ere, peace was not in the mindset of neither Morgause nor Mordred. Unbeknownst to the King, Morgause and Mordred proceeded to poison the Kingdom with slander against Arthur, his Queen and his most favorite of Knights, Lancelot. Many a lascivious invented tale was told on the sly of the three of them fornicating and yet, still no heir apparent to the throne had come forth. Thusly, the gentry and the peasantry were swayed to remove their former loyalties to Arthur in favor of an unknown, yet virile, and seemingly honorable Prince, yet to be King, and they lay their hopes upon Mordred.

And with this last bit of vision, swirling the energy round, and with the moon's last setting rays dimmed, the sun starting to break o'er the watery horizon, we returned to our senses. Nivienne and I dissipated the energy, and we found ourselves still holding our hands, palm-to-palm, at sunrise. But now tears ran down both our faces. It seemed that Camelot had begun its demise.

"We must do something!" said my lovely Nivienne. "It is dark magick that has forced two lovely and loyal people against their King! Against their true and loving hearts and bent their strong wills! The sisters hath used their weaknesses against these two lovers as pawns in their chess match! 'Tis not honorable to be manipulated so and hath it used to their destruction! By the Gods! Love MUST reign! Lancelot and Gwenivere *must* be together. The King must not find them. They had no choice but to love each other, and so they shall!"
My dear wife was beside herself and nearly shaking with indignant fury. I was glad I had such a spitfire to call my own. I treasured her wisdom, her sense of fairness, her loyalty to Love. I was blessed indeed to have her as my mate.

I brushed the lock of crimson hair back out of her bright eyes, eyes so full of passion, and I said, "Aye, harm none and do what ye will' is a creed that we, and all people of magick *should* live by! But, my darling lady, there be some who will for'ere engage in selfishness for power's sake. Morgause and Morgan have twisted certain situations to suit themselves." I shook my head. "Let us pray and ponder together what our collective Powers can manage for the sake of Love and Britain and the state of Magick. I have no doubt that we can provide a healing balm of some sort."

And so Nivienne and I spent time roaming our beloved Bardsey Isle with purpose and watching omens. It occurred to us forthwith that it was time for the Grail to return. It may be just the saving grace if it were to come forward now.

In sooth, I sent a vibration message to Sir Galahad to sway his mind to quest once more to seek the Holy Grail. He set out posthaste. I led his mind and horse to a spot where he easily found the Grail there where I had lightly veiled it for only himself to find. It was, indeed, this same vessel which I had kept hidden under our express magickal shields of protection for so many preceding years. The vessel of Bran the Blessed was handed down from times past and with a history all its own. It was a magic cup, one which brought health, could be a tonic, a healing and, to some, immortality itself.

Thusly, the Holy Grail did come to Galahad the Pure to save our Kingdom which was swiftly being led astray and mayhaps lost for'ere to lust and slander.

Much damage how'ere, had already been done. Morgause had planted enough proclamations to the peasantry to sway the people against the Queen, and thusly to openly question the King and to preclude a faithful following. The Knights had rallied behind the King at first; but when he did not find Queen Gwenivere nor Lancelot (who by now had safely embarked to a life of privacy and anonymity far across the sea), some of the Knights lost faith in their longtime leader. For when Arthur returned to Camelot, he found that the mood of the kingdom was not in his favor. He then banished both Morgause and Mordred from all his holdings. He put a firm grip on what power he had left.

Morgause's plan for her son to rise to the crown and for herself to be High Queen Mother o'er all Britain was proceeding quickly and without reservation. The sisters Morgause and Morgan, had their revenge upon the House of Pendragon and it was payment for the death of their father, Gorlois. All was falling into precision placement.

In a ray of hope, how'ere, there is a converse magickal Law which states that "For every action, there be an equal and opposite reaction."
This too was true in the case of the sisters and their dealings with Lancelot and Gwenivere.

For e'en though Morgause and Morgan le

Fay had tried their might to ruin the Queen and her Knight in shining armor by forcing them against their wills to consummate their physical bond and to ruin the Kingdom…by this very same act, *great good* in the shape of Magick was also being done, unbeknownst to the dark magickal sisters.

For in this act of spellbinding which had manipulated the lovers, who would then unfortunately betray their loving husband, friend and King, the sisters did something else that they could not foresee.

This magick entwining the Knight and the Lady would for'ere make Camelot's tale one etched into history. For in this tale of Lancelot and Gwenivere (and their resulting acts of loving choice o'er forced sexuality) there did lay a great kernel of Truth.

Ultimately it be the beauteous fact which would always remain and it is this: that Love *can* triumph o'er duty. For in their love story, this simple truth of freedom to choose love o'er duty and function would always exist as a hopeful option to lovers eternally.

So whilst Lancelot and Gwenivere swiftly escaped to their new life of love together, they would also (thankfully) avoid the collision course that Arthur and Mordred were on, as father and son and as King and Prince.

E'en as Lancelot and Gwenivere had found safety in each other's hearts and beds.... Mordred officially declared war on his father and vowed to kill him and have his head, along with the crown. In efforts to decide the matter and still have a kingdom not ravaged by civil war, the King and his son agreed to a skirmish betwixt them and fourteen of their best men at an undisclosed location to decide the fate of the crown.

The Battle of Camlann was to commence at dawn on a pre-arranged day, if mediation had not been arranged. None was scheduled and so both men, father and son, went to their separate camps and prepared for an epic battle betwixt them.

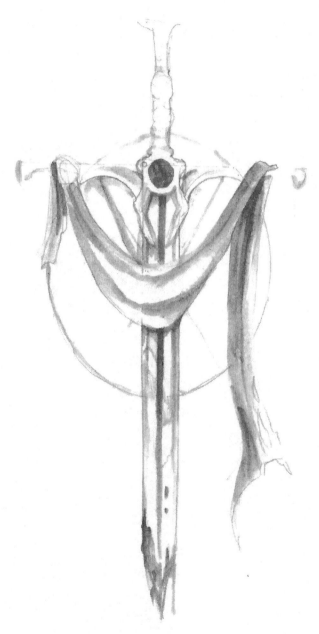

IX

"When all choices are taken away, a perfect path remains." And so it was to Arthur with the road to his next journey and the path to the beyond was beckoning. If a battle was warranted, then one would be given by the Powers.

I saw all this, and yet, I remained at Bardsey Isle until I was to be called by Arthur. This Great War between Arthur and Mordred was not of my doing, but of theirs. It was the consequence of action, which is the consequence of following thought. It is of mine own opinion that a person fails because they limit their own thinking. A man can be his own worst enemy, by creating his own limitations, and listening to the demons of doubt. For Peace is not the absence of strife, but the adapting to it.

And so it was with the King as he mused to himself, e'en whilst donning armor for battle. Arthur had long known in his own heart that Gwenivere would ne'er mother a child for him. They were more liken unto brother and sister though these last many years. There was no passion betwixt them. Aye, there was love, but it was placid and familial. Whilst Arthur had longed for a child of his own, he did not trust his own parenting skills, for he had nothing with which to base it upon.

Once years before, late in the e'en, Arthur had confided to me that although Sir Ector had been liken unto a fatherly guide to him, Ector was *not* his father. Ector was merely a mentor and mayhap, more liken unto an uncle to him, if he were to define him. Arthur then went on to say that I, his cousin, had more closely resembled a father to him that had 'ere had.

In sooth, I knew I had much to be desired in that way as well. I was not much of a father figure to this man who needed one so badly all his life, for I did come and go on whims and whimsy. As a Druid, and a sometimes teacher and friend, I was not the father he needed….nor did I have one to copy. Taliesin had been mine own mentor. Arthur had needed a King for a father, and it had been denied him, e'en as it had been denied to me, and to our fathers before us. This missing parentage was a piece of the puzzle that I have always felt in my life, and now I understood, that Arthur missed it as well as any other boy who did not have a good father to pattern himself after.

And now there was more. E'en as it had been denied to Ambrosius, to Uther, to myself, to Arthur, now Mordred, this child now a grown man that the King had recently discovered had also suffered the same fate. Thinking back, Arthur could remember the moment that Mordred had been conceived. He remembered the woman, comely and somewhat familiar. He cringed when he thought now t'was his own sister! This vile deception should have rung bells in his mind, but his own lust had silenced his intuition, and he went along with the dalliance to his own demise. This was his misdeed and his shortcoming. Surely, not listening to his reason nor noting the red flags were his sins. *"Thou shalt not disfigure the Soul."* Truly this was what had happened. And yet, now what to do? To do battle and kill the thing that you made? Aye, if it was to be, it would be for "The seeds of our fate are nurtured by the roots of our past."

It had been decided that Arthur and Mordred would rally a fighting force of fourteen men each. They would meet upon the battlefield at dawn and would fight until either the King or the Prince had secured a solid victory.

The night before, Arthur gathered his men about him in his tent and thanked each and every one for being brave and loyal kinsmen. "We are taken into deep water, not to drown us, but to cleanse us. One goes to knowledge, as one goes to war. And with this battle upon the new dawn's utterance, my prayer and hope is that I may be cleansed of my failings. I am a warrior and with you at my side, I shall redeem myself or die trying. This tragic sin of mine, of bringing my sister's child into the world, has devastated me and my kingdom. Mordred, he who has been suckled at the teat of malice and contrivance in order to bring doom to me and to mine own family. With my sin of randy impetuousness, I did not act like the King and leader I was to become. This man Mordred came to test mine own house -which found me wanting. I was weighed and measured for it. Because of it and the consequences it brought, my dear bride, Gwenivere, was taken from me. I am grateful that she did not have the knowledge of this awful joining that made Mordred. Whilst I did command the deaths of Gwenivere and Lancelot, I shall admit to you, my noble friends, that I did grieve those commands. I am glad they were ne'er found, and should she ever be found, she is STILL my wife and I wish to be lain next to her for all eternity, as she was a good wife, a sweet spirited woman to me, e'en though I was not the man she thought I was. Aye, and Lancelot, he who was my dearest of friends and the bravest Knight in the land. If anyone was to e'er make her happy and could protect and provide for her, t'would be he, for he carried a kind and stout heart. It is just and fair that my lack of fortitude with Morgause has caused all this ruin to come to me and to my beloved Camelot. By your witness, and to the Gods above, I vow to fight to eradicate my transgressions of the past. I will fight sincerely and honorably or die trying to be the man I had longed wished to be. I shall overcome my past with this my sword, Excalibur, and with this deed of honor to fight like the King I AM."All the men present did swear their fealty to him and promised to follow him to the end.

Mordred had a bit of a different night afore the battle. His was spent not in prayer and in humility, but in dallying with the camp's doxies and draining a hogshead of ale. His battle e'en was taken up in revelry, wenching, drinking, carousing and laughingly pissing on the tents of his own men. He was coming into his own authority, dammit. He believed he would be *King* and whence it happened, more o' the same would be his pastimes! He had been raised to believe that the world owed him his living and, by God, he would have it. His men would follow him, but they were not the sort that would be trusted, and frankly, that is why he liked them. They were like he was. No one could pigeon-hole him in to certain behaviors…be they Kingly or Noble. Camelot be damned. The world was anew and it would be *his*. With the morning light, Mordred pulled the doxie from his bed by her hair and threw her screaming out into the street with a blackened eye. It was how the day was to follow, and he was glad for it. His men roused bleary-eyed and with ale-head to the sound of the trumpets. The soldiers felt as if the demons of hell had invaded their Souls, and they were not far from the truth.

As the morning sun started to wake the day, Arthur and his men stood facing westward, along the appointed ridge of Camlann with the light at their backs. Dressed for battle they had been standing there well before daylight, patiently a-waiting dawn.

Mordred and his men arrived to face a line of warriors, stalwart and ready, anticipating their coming. The older and experienced Arthur, a warrior among men, had already set the battle stage with the sun in their opponents' eyes. T'was no small thing to have to squint to see an adversary as they stood ripe for battle with their armored gloves resting calmly on their swords resting point down in the ground. An eerie tranquility pervaded the scene of Arthur's soldiers quietly biding their time whilst Mordred ordered about his rag-tag men into position.

Whence the young Prince's men were lined up to his contentment, Mordred called out to Arthur upon the hill, "As per our agreement, I have brought my numbered strong men with me, and by your leave, Sire, I see thou hast brought thy ancient, old men with thee! Prepare thee to meet thy Maker!"

To which Arthur answered with a placid voice, "I am willing yet to forgive thee, as thou art mine own flesh and blood. Put down your weapons and swear thy allegiance to me as King and to Camelot and to these men as brothers, and we shall go home, unscathed, as father and son yet this day."

Mordred merely glowered and bellowed back, "I have no father, only a little man who drizzled in my mother….I mean…your SISTER." To which Mordred laughed a conceited snicker, and his men in turned followed with guffaws and jeers.

"I shall not be moved by a yapping, flea-bitten, toothless pup and his mangy litter mates. If ye wish to move me, Sirrah, then have at ye," said Arthur, who stood firm to his spot. At this, the King's men tightened their grip on their long swords.

Mordred could be patient no longer for it was not his nature to endure this long. He gave a battle scream and charged up the ridge to the waiting line of seasoned soldiers and his men followed behind him. The young Prince made a bee line to his predecessor, and Arthur was still standing unwaveringly so. Mordred's men ran into the wall of Arthur's men, and the melee' began. It did not take long for half of Mordred's men to be cut down in their impudence, for gall is a motivator but not a sustainer when in battle against a wise warrior. Arthur's men took great relish in using their long swords and maces against the effrontery of these mercenaries. Mordred had paid for his men, not won their hearts. Several did make mincemeat of some Knights who supported Arthur, but all in all, many fled when bested.

Launching himself up the hill, Mordred threw himself with all his anger and tilted his spear at Arthur and threw his entire weight behind the point and lunged at his father. The King stood and watched the trajectory of this wild man coming for him and knew that anger that throws the first blow, may be powerful, but also, mayhap be unproductive. The glare of blood in the eyes does not see logic. Arthur stepped aside at the last moment and to a direction not anticipated by Mordred who went sailing past the King without striking him. As the prince passed by, how'ere, Arthur took Excalibur and sliced the back of Mordred's right leg, severing his tendon. Mordred cried out in anguish and fell and yet continued to hurl obscenities at Arthur. The skirmish all around them was fast becoming one-sided, as Camelot's men silenced the usurpers' force one by one. With the last fallen mercenary, and one more who ran off (after stealing the helmet off one of the slain Knights) a fight to the death would pit father against son.

Mordred used his spear as a crutch and then used its reach to get past Arthur's long sword to cut a gash in Arthur's arm. Blood flowing from the back of his leg, Mordred lunged spitefully forward, balanced on one foot and dragged his injured leg behind him e'en whilst he hurled himself towards Arthur. Excalibur was then directed into the center of Mordred's chest and e'en as the blade cut through his son's chest bone, Arthur grieved for it. Mordred stared in disbelief at the sword impaled in his chest, knowing full well the game was up and the battle lost. He looked at Arthur with eyes filled with confusion. He had been raised to win this fight. E'en now as he was swiftly losing consciousness, it made no sense to him how the table had been turned.

The King staggered backward, disbelieving that he sinned so vilely! To kill your only son and to have deftly dispatched him! This his only heir so judiciously and succinctly! Arthur took off his helm and with tears and broken hearted words Arthur said, "Mordred, I am so truly sorry. I wished only to have loved you and call you my son. You could've been Prince and King of the Realm had you patience enough to wait for it. Please forgive me. O son of mine, I beg of thee."

And whilst the blood ebbed and flowed out through the cavity of Mordred's chest, anger filled his heart for Arthur, his *so-called father* professing his *love* e'en whilst he had just run him through. A shout from the distance came clearly from a wench from Mordred's bed sounding a loud "Huzzah!!" whence she saw the fallen Mordred. It turned Arthur's head and distracted him in that brief moment, Mordred turned his spear in hand, reached out and slammed the butt of the spear into Arthur's helmless head and struck him deftly in the temple. Then with this last blow and exertion of will, Mordred fell forward, driving Excalibur deeper, running the blade up to the hilt through his body. With Mordred's dying breath he was only to gurgle through red bubbles of blood that he hated Arthur and cursed him to Everlasting Hell.

Arthur had fallen when struck, and his Knights rallied round him to carry his body back down the hill to care for him. Sir Bedivere looked 'round at the dead and dying all around him and walked over to Mordred lying and bleeding out a pool of blood. The prince was dying and heaving his last breaths. Bedivere put a booted foot on Mordred's chest and pulled hard against it to exit Excalibur from the dying man's body. He looked at Mordred and said, "Nay. Ye shall not see Arthur there, lad. The ninth circle of Hell be for betrayers and treason mongers to those who returned not the love given. That place is reserved for *Thee.* An icy eternal punishment awaits thee and thy cold heart" he said and turned and let Mordred cough out his last breath. Bedivere took Excalibur and wiped the blade and polished it before tucking it back into the litter that carried Arthur back to Camelot. The Knights carried their leader away upon their shoulders whilst the crows circled in for Mordred and his men upon the hill. In a few days there would be nothing left of him but his bad name to be forever remembered.

When Morgause had thrown her Rune, she had *seen* the ensuing battle and death of her son. She hastened away and fled afar to go to her sister, Morgan le Fay. There together they would lick their wounds and grieve their lost chances to rule the kingdom. They also would grieve Mordred, aye, but not nearly so much as they pined for Power.

I had received a most sincere and grievous feeling that some dread had befallen the King. Thusly I felt compelled to drop everything at Bardsey Isle and go posthaste in the Chariot of Morgan the Wealthy straightway to Camelot. T'was the very same carriage which I had traveled to Uther upon his deathbed. It was a magickal contrivance and one to be respected and used under extreme circumstances. I did so only that I may be of service to help others. I was awaiting the King's men there at the Castle whence His Majesty was delivered nearly on death's door. Arthur was still alive, barely breathing, in and out of consciousness. I immediately took charge and arranged to transport Arthur to Avalon. We left Sir Gawain in charge of the Knights of the Round Table, and set off with Arthur still holding tightly to Excalibur.

I sent word to Nivienne to meet me, along the way to help me magickally attend to the King and minister to him as I had to his father and brother before him. Mayhaps, Freya, the Lady of the Lake, could heal his fatal wound, it was my only hope, as his head wound was of sech a nature that I could foresee no mending it.

As the Chariot of Morgan the Wealthy rolled toward the magickal Isle of Avalon, I stayed by Arthur's side. When he was awake, I spoke soothingly to him, much as I used to when he was a child. I recanted tales of his boyhood memories at Sir Ector's Castle Coch and tried to help him hang on to this life whilst this journey progressed. He, indeed, was liken unto a son to me, and the most family that I had 'ere had, besides Nivienne and Aurelius to me. From these thoughts, I began to think of my father, his life and his death, now that it seemed that Arthur was also to be taken from me and going to the Otherworld to be with them as well.

My heart was sore, and I did grieve of lacking a child at this moment. I inwardly also bemoaned the fact that I had not behaved more liken unto a father to this man, this man that I loved like a son. A memory then suddenly occurred to me. It was a remembrance of when I introduced my father, King Ambrosius, to King Oberon so many long years ago. It gave me great pleasure to think of it and that I was so glad to have made this bond with the Pendragons and the Fairy Realm. With this thought, I brought out the vial I had carried with me since my Spirit Quest and on which I had gathered the dragon tear from Bazzalth the Protector of the Sky. I dripped the tears into Arthur's lips to help sustain him till we arrived in Avalon. Then I sent out a sincere request to King Oberon and asked him to send me aid in this important and mayhaps, final journey of King Ambrosius's nephew, King Arthur, at this his time of greatest need. I prayed to the Gods it would be enough.

I was answered by King Oberon in the form of Queen Titania and her fairy maidens arriving at the shore to greet me. She and her entourage, Nivienne and I were to accompany Arthur to Avalon to meet Freya. Queen Titania and her fairies bathed Arthur in a circular glow of gold energy and white light and through all this he progressed to Avalon, still yet breathing.

Freya met us there. She took Arthur into her own household and nursed him back to health, along with the aid of Queen Titania. He would live hither until the day when England needed him again, far off in future times. All those in Avalon did promise to keep him hither, by his wishes, until such time that Gwenivere passed into the Otherworld from her old age. When she was to finally lay down to rest and died in Lancelot's arms then, and only then, would the King and Queen be reunited in statuary of their joint tombs. I promised Arthur that the kingdom would honor their leadership and their love by placing their tombs together forever to be celebrated at Glastonbury. Here would be a place for the world to remember the look and feel of forgiveness and love.

Arthur would heal and remain here without longing for his Bride, and he would instead be comforted in heart and mind by the Peace that Avalon would bring. There was a catch, though. Excalibur must also stay with him in Avalon. It was a magickal sword, only for Arthur, and now that he was here in this place of Love and Light. He would ne'er have reason to make war any longer.

With this momentous addition to Avalon, Freya then said it would soon be the appropriate time for the Transition of herself and Nivienne as Lady of the Lake. It would shortly be Nivienne's duty to keep Avalon safe, to honor the Goddess with her life as Freya had always professed to do. The Crystal Woman was now gearing up to take the scepter. Nivienne would then promise to guard the Mavens and to give hope eternal to women everywhere. This had been Freya's life's work, and now, t'was to be Nivienne's reward and honor as well. Nivienne loved Avalon, yet she also loved me. We talked about it far into the night. We agreed we could make it work, and we made a plan to accommodate Fate.

All was being healed and made ready, and I gave my sincere thanks to Freya, Titania and her court, and to Nivienne for helping Arthur back to his vitality. I was truly grateful, as was he. We embraced and I told him all that I wished I had told him before. I accepted him more as my son and less of a nephew or as my King.

Arthur would be Immortal now. For his name would remain on the lips of generations to come! Whilst Arthur was wistful to see his Camelot again, and to be of service to Mankind, how'ere, he was also glad to be without the responsibility and that he could now live life again, and this time, for himself. There would be much for him to do here and he was rejoicing in the freedom to live without regard of how it would seem to others. Here was a place of security, creativity, health and love. He deserved to be here. We were glad of it, and that Peace had finally come to this battle-weary soldier. Arthur rested after his ordeal and began to mend, and with his express instructions, I took Excalibur to the water and threw it into the Lake. Freya reached up out of the water, caught the sword and took it to reside in Avalon for'ere.

I foresaw that the day would come when I would have to live some of my future life without my Nivienne. It would be for the entirety of her duties whence she started serving as Lady of the Lake, the time was yet to be revealed.

But that day was not this day. This day was good, for the Gods had made it so. I held Nivienne, and we reveled in Avalon's beauty and loved each other far into the night and into the next day. Avalon gave us back our vim and vigor, and we felt exceedingly happy. We were One, and no one could affect us.

This is what we believed, even whilst others plotted darkly against us, we felt it not.

X

ll was proceeding as designed
by the Duke of Cornwall's daughters, except
forthwith for their planned ruin of me. This last
cornerstone of evil sorcery was saved for last.
The crowning jewel in the sisters' caps would
complete their stratagem for their power to rule,
verily, though in darkness o'er the Kingdom. I
could not foresee, due to their shielding, but I,
too, would also pay for my part in the
shapeshifting trickery of Uther o'er Gorlois all
those many years ago. For there is no storm like
a woman disparaged, and I was bound to smart
for it, aye, and twicefold thanks to those two
women.

I must say that in this wondrous world,
therein is a Power of Magick, and a Three-Fold
Law of Nature which states "That what'ere
energy one delivers to the world, be it for good
or evil, shalt be returned unto them times three."
E'en so, I was karmically set to receive my
punishment for my part in deceiving the Duke of
Cornwall, and it would be rightly delivered to
me by those most affected by his death. Those

two small, unassuming, slighted and abandoned girl children had grown into to calculating, rancorous and adept sorceresses to wreak revenge.

I decided to fret not about what may come- and it would indeed come. This I had Seen and life would unfold to me in its own Divine Timing. I would simply shield myself and go about the wondrous life I had with my beloved Nivienne. I would not send out evil, nor malice towards them- but instead I would cloak my being by projecting a reflective image liken unto a mirrored looking glass over my skin and aura. Anyone who attempted harm, or radiated goodness to me, would have their own intention energetically reflected back unto them, each in turn unto their measure given.

One day, Nivienne presented me with a gift, and it would be a great one indeed. It was a Druid Egg. It was oft called a "Serpent's Egg." T'was not really an egg but a stone, a smallish stone about the size of an apple, smoothsome as glass. This particular Druid Egg was from my beloved Crystal Woman and Stone Whisperer, and so it carried extra charms.
As she placed it in my hand she said, "It will protect you, come what'ere. Merlin, I love you like no other, in sooth, I beg of you to keep this upon your person at all times." She leaned in

closely to whisper loving words and my beard felt the vibration of her voice. By the Gods, I still wanted her. After all this time, I lusted after her as we did when we first coupled.

It was because we felt so kindred, our childhoods so bereft of friendship, both in need of the feeling of family, we were now each other's everything. So many years we had been together and had felt the luxuriousness of our passionate bed, the comfort of the closeness of hearts. The years had crept by, and still I wanted this Maven with all my heart. She was brave, honest and loyal. Nivienne was still shapely and ravishing, even as she showed her age with lines from her frequent laughter appearing upon her face. The streaks of silver just starting to stripe her chestnut hair gave her an overall shine in the sunlight and she actually sparkled. Aye, we were getting older now, but it mattered not. There was nothing more I wanted than to ponder the starlight together and to wake in the morning light next to her. We spoke of curious topics on a myriad of subjects and were constantly learning of this fascinating earth and all that the Gods had made. We searched for herbs and plants together, we made our intricate medicines to heal the sick. She counseled the local folks with her bewitching ways, common sense mingled with hard earned knowledge. Her Powers shone through to give even the weakest of the women the strength to continue on in their bleak lives, in spite of all odds. She was my guiding light and my world. She continued to learn from the earth, and their wisdom was eons old. With her rocks and stones to help her, she had built an exquisite stone altar for the Goddess Brigid. It served as the entrance of our home.

"She is the Goddess of the Hearth and Home, Mistress of the Mantle, and she is my Patroness. As she is yours, Merlin, my bardic Mate! Brigid is also the Goddess of Storytellers, Singers and Poets. She will protect us. These rocks and stones will honor her even as they mark her shrine."

It was the most amazing feat of balancing magick that I had 'ere seen. There were large boulders that she had levitated as if they were the weight of a feather and had placed them to make an archway into our abode. The rocks framed the entrance, and I joked that it looked as if they would fall at any given moment. Indeed they were placed so perfectly that they would stand for eternity, if she chose them to stay that long. With a wink she said, "It will give the villagers pause to disturb us whilst we are in the throes of lovemaking, for we cannot hear them approaching." She laughed and I pulled her closer. She was all I ever wanted and needed.

And it seems that she loved and wanted me in the same manner for she ne'er let me feel unloved. Not a day went by that we did not show affection for one another. If I could've made her into a Goddess I would worship at her feet and any other part of her body for eternity. She felt the same for me, and I would lie looking at the heavens whilst she kissed every inch of my torso, legs and abdomen. She would coo to me that she adored every bit of me. She seemed to worship me as well...at least I felt so much as she kissed me as we lay together.

After doing our duty for years with the Kings, serving our lands, we wanted nothing more now than sharing times of adventure and nights of bliss. I sought her comfort and wanted to be with for the rest of my days. I tried to forget that she would soon be leaving me to be Lady of the Lake. I tried to forgo thinking about Ygraine's daughters and their broodings.

This is when Nivienne would sense my unfruitful ponderings and jolt me back to reality. "The Druid's Egg will help you stay in the moment, lovey. Rocks don't plan for the future. They just ARE. They live in the present." I held the stone out in my hand, and we closed our fingers around the Druid's Egg and blessed it together.

I, too, had a gift for Nivienne. It was the

Mantle of Caswallawn, one of the marvelous treasures of Britain that had come to me through Bazzalth the Protector of the Sky, to use and to protect. It was a magickal cloak which rendered invisibility to those who don it. I took it out from its magickal protected hiding place and I handed this treasure o'er to her, I said, "You will need this. I know not why, but I feel dread if I think of thee without it in thy keeping! Please, my love, hold onto this gift from the Elements. When sech time comes ye shall be glad to have it. You will know how and when to use it, I promise thee."

Nivienne wrapped her arms around me and kissed me deeply. Ne'er had I regretted meeting this person who had grown to sech a state of talent and wisdom. She so clearly carried the Divine within her. She was the Maven to my Druid ways and I, the Enchanter to her Enchantress. We were One.

****

We were to spend the entire night under the stars on this late September day. It was Mabon and a time for gratitude for the harvest. It was also the night of an eclipse of the blood moon. Soon alchemists and men would look to the heavens and know how to plot their courses. Until then, I who had traveled throughout the mountains of time, knew only of sech things and looked forward to using them in my magick. Peasants to Princes would wonder in amazement when I could predict sech happenings in the skies. They did not know yet but there were ways to predict these occurrences, and so the gentry and the peasantry were both constantly marveling at my sorcery. Surely, it was a sign of the heavens, and it did portend great things.

Nivienne set a table of plenty beneath this brilliant full moon. It was time to celebrate the season of the harvest, sharing and being grateful. And by the Powers, we were so very thankful to be here. As Druid and Maven we were to hold a ceremony this Mabon for our home and hearth, when the earth was in balance on the Autumnal Equinox. This time, how'ere, we were able to enjoy it at our own home for a change. We did not have to live anywhere else for quite some time. I was not on a battlefield, nor in some lord's castle, nor was Nivienne yet required to be in Avalon. We were content and at peace hither.

We filled a cornucopia with victuals from our harvest: squash, grapes, nuts, seeds, cheeses, herbs, apples, berries. A full decanter of new wine was on the table as well as a bowl of earth. When the moon started to rise, we prayed together and gave our thanks to the Earth and to all the Gods and Goddesses who keep us in their care. Most especially we honored the Goddess Brigid and this night we also toasted to Bacchus as well! We dug our hands into the bowl of dirt and felt the coolness of the earth. We walked deosil round our domicile and every few paces we would stop and drive an iron nail into the ground. We tapped nails into the earth with a stone till each was flush with the ground once more. Many times we did this round until we had encircled our home. We then energized this spell by activating a ring of intense protective energy round our living quarters. We transferred out energy to each of the nails and they, each in turn, glowed and sent energy round to the next nail and the next until all were connected. This energy then encircled the entire perimeter of our home with a ring of power. We sat within our connected energy and drank our wine and ate our fill. As the moon started to eclipse, we stripped off our clothes and were skyclad under the moon. We lay on our backs looking at the Earth's sister until the world's shadow completely darkened the moon and it turned a blood red. We then made love to each other as God and Goddess under a world with no light, on the darkest of nights. We gave all of our thankfulness to the Earth and the Universe and to the Deities we honored. After we finished our lovemaking, we looked up and saw that the moon was starting to become its complete self again, and she shone on us in all our glory. I wrapped my darling and myself up in a fur blanket and we fell asleep under the stars, her legs entwined with mine, and mine with hers. All our limbs wrapped round each other like an ivy twined in the roses till one could not figure out where I left off and she began. And it was as it should be. We had discovered Love was living it, breathing it and appreciating every moment of it. We were Love itself.

After our blessed Mabon, joys came to us in many shapes, and we spent the rest of the autumn together, harvesting, storing away and filling our pantry and medicine jars with herbal remedies. It was a busy time, and we were content. In the evenings, we would enjoy our leisure, reading ancient manuscripts that had miraculously been saved from the Alexandria Library. Here was what was left of the knowledge of Atlantis and many former civilizations 'round the world that had been lost. They were saved by a Druid so very long ago, and unfortunately only shards remained of this wonderment. We tried to piece together what we could and memorized it all.

We spoke about the missing information and tried to connect the mysteries left unsolved with our own acquired knowledge. Sometimes we spirit-traveled to the Akashic Records, where Universal Knowledge is kept, to find wisdom there. It was a time of great expansion, adventure, and all from our wondrous cushions in the cave right here on Bardsey Isle.

In time, the wind would blow cold. Winter would be upon us. It would soon be Samhain, the end of the seasons of the year and the beginning of the next. It is the time when the veil between the worlds is the thinnest and contact with those in the Otherworld is easily accomplished.

Most days here on Bardsey Isle, we would receive occasional guests. They would normally be seekers of healing and knowledge and would come from near and far to approach us for healing. In karmic payment, they provided many niceties to us consisting of: blankets, food, small livestock and drink for our larder. The villagers who were brave enough to visit the Enchanters on the Hill went away healed and with a good conscience for helping the magickal ones carry on their good works. All was as it should be.

The wheel did turn, how'ere, as it is wont to do. A voice of need arose and we received unsettling news that the Holy Grail had been stolen from Camelot! The blessed vessel was found missing after Mabon, for t'was stolen during the blood moon, right underneath the noses of the watchful eyes of Sir Galahad and Sir Gawain! The Knights had hesitated to contact me, but tried to find it o'er the last few weeks, to no avail.

This was the call I had been expecting, and my heart sank. I had been receiving nightmarish dreams and knew that this was the time of my leveling. Karma had come to me and found me out where I lived in peace. It was time for me to go back to help restore order and to retrieve the Holy Grail. Aye, but there was so much more to this story than what was apparent to most who heard it, for I knew the identities of the theft. It was a lure for me to emerge from my protected place of safety and to return to the wide world of open spaces where I would appear more vulnerable.

I started detaching from my darling with my oath to her of a swift return, if at all possible. Would that we could spend as much time left with each other if only the Gods decreed it. She would carry on with our research and the good works of healing hither, whilst I braved the affrontery of malice once again. Leaving each other to answer this call of distress nearly tore us apart, so entwined were we that our hearts behaved as though our souls had been rent assunder

I returned the crystal that she had gifted me so many years ago. Because I had carried it for years upon my person, it was now imbued with my essence. Should I have dire need of her, this stone would glow for her as a message as once it glowed for me. It would call for her to rush posthaste. Whilst I did not want to make her fret, she read my mind and all that was in it regarding my upcoming trepidations and the dealings with Morgause and Morgan le Fay. I was at risk, and we both knew it. We did not want to part and we clung to each other for a long while afore I was called to leave.

With a longing in my heart, the Druid's Egg in my pouch and wearing my shields of protection, I left Bardsey Isle and headed for Camelot.

'was a bleak October day when I arrived at Camelot, and the mood in the village matched the weather. There was the dreary feeling of exhaustion mingled with grief and resignation. The people moved from one task to the next in some sort of stupor, yet inside the castle the feeling was far worse. There was no King, no Grail and the Knights were discouraged indeed. The country was in flux. T'would only be a matter of time before invaders would sense the precariousness of the kingdom and come sweeping down to claim the country which lay in ruins. I spoke with Sir Gawain, Sir Bors and Sir Galahad and had learned of the theft of the Grail. In sooth, it had been stolen away during the darkest hour of the blood moon eclipse on Mabon. After speaking to many of those dismayed souls hither, I knew exactly what to do.

I saddled up one of Arthur's horses and rode like an arrow to Urien and Morgan's castle. It was sans Urien, of course. Morgan had arranged to become his widow as soon as she could align events to cooperate; and it had been nigh unto a decade hence since King Urien had drawn his last breath. Morgan had disposed of King Urien with as much pomp and grief that she could invent, and her performance was admirable. She had even added tears for the effect which had convinced Urien's subjects that his death was indeed tragic and not the murder for which it was. Morgan le Fay arranged for a funeral post haste, and then took up the reigns of the territory. The land and castle were now hers, and I was assured that both she and Morgause would be there and, most likely, waiting hither for me.

For my arrival, t'would be liken unto walking into a scorpion's nest, and I knew it. But face it I would. It was also a full Hunter's Moon on Samhain this night of my visit, and the thinning veils would help further mine own Powers and agenda. For although this was indeed a unpredictable predicament, I was a Mage in mine own right and had been Arch Druid of Albion many a year. With my shield of protective aura round me, my mirrored shield o'er that, Druid Egg upon my person, my faith and wits and my memory for conjuring, I was securely armed against scorpions indeed. I dismounted, walked right through the gate, which was, of course, wide open and waiting for me.

"Welcome, Merlin. We've been expecting you," said a woman's voice. I looked around and saw no one, which was queer, indeed. No servants, no soldiers, no one hither nor thither. So my exploration of the castle proceeded, and I wandered throughout the oddly empty fortress. I picked my way through the deserted courtyard, the recently vacated rooms, and queerly desolate barracks until I came to the Grand room where Urien had always held court. He was not hither, nor would he 'ere be again, but in his stead was Morgan, on Urien's throne, and her sister, Morgause seated next to her. I was faced with two Queens, two formidible storms circling as an impending tornado.

"How brave of you to come." Morgan laughed, and Morgause smiled in response.

"Your Majesties," I said and gave a most courteous bow. "You have grown more lovely and radiant than when last I saw your visages. Indeed, this is a most fortuitous meeting. I believe that you have in your possession a certain drinking vessel that has unfortunately wound up hither. I do not question its arrival, only its departure. I do ask that ye return it to me, so that I may, in turn, take it to a guarded place to keep it safe. Please return the Holy Grail to me."

The candles flickered and sputtered with an unexpected gust of wind. "Nay, Merlin, 'tis ours now, as are you. It was unprotected and thusly, t'was easy to remove it from its resting place of fools. 'Tis time you served your penance for using Magick for dark purposes, oh those many years ago, when you were King Uther's hound. You are here to be judged for your crime of counterfeiting King Uther as our father, Gorlois, Duke of Cornwall, in order to bed our mother. You stand accused and guilty in our eyes."

I placed my feet firmly on the ground and increased my shielding and said, "Tis the truth, that I did camouflage Uther by deception and magick, I replaced the King for the Duke for a few precious hours, aye. How'ere, by the Gods, it was not by Dark Magick. I swear that my guilt is assuaged for I did what any subject was trained to do. I obeyed my King.

I am also a traveler through the tunnels of time and foresaw that the child conceived of Uther and Ygraine would be a great King to come. There was no harm done to Ygraine the evening of the countenance change of Uther into Gorlois. Ygraine was true to the spirit of her husband as she saw no harm in the lovemaking between her and he, whom she thought *was* her husband. It was a beautiful thing in her mind.

She did not lie with another man, in sooth, it was her husband as far as she knew. It was Uther's deception, and not Ygraine's, and yet Uther did want to bed her out of love for her. The fact was that Gorlois was off in the midst of battle of his own making, and it was his love of war that killed him, not Uther. It was the Duke's choice to emblazon himself into the fray in which he was involved. The fact that the two coincided was merely a ripple of Power, in that a marker to the enormity of the child conceived. Arthur indeed, is a great King. I did no harm to your mother. She was faithful in heart, soul, mind and body. Uther loved this woman, his subject and by rights, his. He gave intense pleasure to her, who would unfortunately be grieving on the morrow due to events unknown to her, yet to come. All was well. You were to have a brother and a King in the family! I, for my part in turn, was commanded to my actions by my sovereign Lord. Yet thusly, on your behalf, and for your knowledge, may I submit for your consideration that I also did plead with His Majesty, King Uther, not to attempt this madness of deception. Also, know ye, afterwards I did also beseech him to let me take both of you to Avalon for training in magic. I did recognize you were gifted. It was, unfortunately, all to no avail. I did not foresee, how'ere, that Uther would turn his heart against both of Ygraine's daughters and have you raised separately from your mother. But e'en so, ye have been provided for and raised to be Queens in your own right. My dear ladies, if not for me then thou wouldst still only be Duke's daughters and thusly married to lesser wealthy nobility. This ripple of magick has gone through the eons to bring us to this place. It is where we need to be. You are not the women you would've been had Uther never taken your mother. Methinks it is all in a case of perspective that has delivered the veil of pain you feel. All is well if you would only believe it so. I understand your grief and how your hearts have hardened, but now, my beautiful ladies, unless you let in the light of forgiveness and turn o'er your wrath to the Universe, madness and negativity will bond with your soul and reign within thee for'ere. There shall be no more goodness in ye and you will be damned to spin webs of sadness, anger and deception the rest of your days. No good will come of anything you lay your hands to, regardless of what ye may believe. Prithee, as my cousins through marriage, I beg of thee to take this opportunity. Cry yer mercy and accept my apologies for the duties of my office at the time. We are family. 'Tis ne'er too late to change one's ways and to forgive. "

I bowed deeply and stepped back one

step in reverence to the words. I slipped my hand into my cloak and sought out the Druid Egg and held it firmly in my hand. I was using the Druid axiom that stated "The true test of knowledge is not what we know how to do, but rather how we act when we don't know what to do."

It was up to the ladies now to make their own life choices. Could they change? Habit is a tricky thing. Sometimes a person holds on to some way of being, though it suiteth him not, forthwith because 'tis what has always been. For thoughts become feelings, then feelings may become action, action then repeated becomes habit and, ultimately, habit becomes character.

Morgause had been listening to me all this while. Her hands had been resting upon the arm of the throne and with every word I spoke, her fingers grasped the chair more and more forcibly until her fingers were white as dry bones. When I finished my address to them, Morgause leapt to her feet and shouted, "Duties of my office? Accept your apology? Our mother was duped to believe that Uther was her own husband, Gorlois of Cornwall! Uther did abuse his office and did RAPE our dear mother, Gods rest her soul! It is by YOUR DOING, Merlin and our lives were ruined for it!" She was pointing at me now, and her face had flushed with rage. "I have lost my son because of it!"

I looked at her most sincerely and stated, "Nay, my dear lady you merely engineered your son unwisely. In sooth, bad deeds can ripple forth for a lifetime of consequence."

I remained calm and tightly held the Druid Egg in the closed fingers of my right hand. It was the masculine hand of Power. Truly, it gave me comfort and serenity in this time of unpredictable and wildly strong feminine emotion. My thoughts briefly switched to the opposite kind of feminine power I knew of so well in my darling, now apart from me. I held Nivienne in my heart briefly and thought of her so very far away. Briefly, I longed for her touch and for myself to be done with all of this for once and for all. For that fleeting moment, I unconsciously turned the Druid Egg over in my hand, and my thoughts were immediately returned to the present moment. I must keep my wits about me. There was a feeling of heady enchantment all around me. Upon feeling the rough stone in my palm, it grew heavy and warm with a surge of energy. I must stay in this moment and not become victim of their magick. I must keep my shields up and stay in the moment. I focused on the efflux of power and made my defenses stronger while directing any incoming energy into the stone in my hand. The stone was accepting the flow and absorbing its ebbing transmission. My energy shield was now as thick as a fortress wall. The Druid's Egg was being charged.

Morgan then took up the torch and calmly said, "We grew up away from our mother, our father killed in battle whilst the King ravaged her in her own bed! 'Tis an unforgiveable slight. 'Tis time that we had OUR justice, here in Our Court." Morgan took her sister's hand, and they both raised their opposite arms on high and stated: "We, sisters be, daughters of Gorlois, Duke of Cornwall. We shall avenge our father's death. We shall avenge the despoilment of our dear mother."

I responded, "If that is the reality of how you see this event, then it must be so."
I waited for what I knew would happen next. A low rumble sounding like a rolling thunderstorm became audible and clouds started gathering outside. Or was it outside? Mayhap t'was inside as well....

Morgan's eyes darkened, and her eyes became black as if she had no soul within her beating chest. She took out a knife and sliced a gash o'er both of their arms. This blood offering flowed down their arms and filled their clenched hands of will and nefarious determination. Their blood mingled together and Morgan went on, unflustered, "We curse you, Merlinus Ambrosius

Pendragon, by the Powers of Darkness and Evil that we adhere to. On this Samhain night of the dead, when the two worlds are the closest and the veils between them the thinnest, we call forth the spirit of Gorlois, the Duke of Cornwall, to come stand before us. We call to you, our father, for a swift and dire demise upon this man, this sorcerer who betrayed you. Merlin shall feel the sands of time. For every minute of our grief and for every moment of our mother's pain, he shall feel it in his bones. We shall watch as he doth grow old and age quickly afore us. We shall revel in watching you, Merlin, go from a man- to a cripple- to an invalid- and die before us, a withered, powerless heap of dust. No one shall love thee nor remember thy name! Death will become thee. It is the Greatest of Levelers. So be it."

There was a crack of lightening and the shutters blew open and a cold wind came into the room. There was someone who looked to be Gorlois. I knew it was actually his shade, a wraith of himself, drawn from the Otherworld, dressed still in his suit of armor. It was his last suit of clothing from the battlefield on whence he died. He walked toward me, and his eyes looked blank. I could see that he had died from a fatal wound to his abdomen. The mace laceration was apparent and he had died an agonizing death, indeed.

Looking into his eyes, it seemed to me that his gaze was liken unto looking into a mist. There was no recognition other than the focus for the mission that he was on. He was not alive. He was only commanded to be hither. The apparition reached out and tried to touch me, but the ghostly hand could not penetrate my shielding. It only touched the outer layer of my aura. Indeed, I did feel a ripple through the energy layers, which felt sharp and numbing cold. It was only the vibration of hate that Morgan and Morgause had transferred to this apparition. It took a moment but then a feeling seeped within my energy shield. T'was only a wee bit, but it did enter liken unto the drip of the poison of a venomous creature. And when the connection had been made, the ghost did fade before my eyes into nothingness. Now I would have to deal with this breach and fortify myself against the poison.

"It is not the emotion that is ever wrong, but only how we express it," I said. "Your venom hurts you, more than me."

After which I had a most curious sensation. T'was an odd sensation, liken unto feeling a slight stiffening of my bones, and I heard the cracking of joints. My hair and beard were growing longer and longer, minute by minute. I felt my right hand, holding the Druid Egg, become instantly warm once again. The magickal stone had started to glow, and the stone began to drain the curse away from me and into itself. I was compelled to look at the stone, and it had changed its appearance. There was now a blood-red spot forming in the center of the Druid Egg; darkening with the addition of the curse. By holding the stone during the curse, I was energetically transferring the negativity to the stone, and it would now pass through me and not kill me, this I knew.

The sisters were amused at my discomfort and started to laugh until something began to affect them as well. Aye, their hatred and malice had mirrored back upon them and, in turn, had been unleashed upon their own selves. They dropped their bloody palm holding and started looking at their own hands. Their fingers started to wither, crook, stiffen, gnarl and grow cold…as cold as ice…and their hands became as gnarled as old tree limbs and branches.

"What…what is happening to us?" They cried aloud as they gaped at each other in confusion.

"T'is the Power of Three Fold coming back upon thee! What'ere ye give blessing or a cursing to others, 'tis what is delivered back upon thee. Forsooth, be it known, I did warn thee." And I did pause to marvel at the irony.

They were strong, though, much stronger than I had envisioned. This would slow them, not stop them. I was feeling the effects of their Dark Magick, but it wasn't the immediate effect that they had tried to create. Bit by bit, though, I was growing weaker, older, slower. I held the Druid Egg in one hand and opened my other hand and let the curse come into me and flow right through me into the Druid Egg. The Power Transfer was intense. I felt as if I should sit down…nay, mayhaps I should lie down. I couldn't make it to the divan in time, so I managed to stumble and sit down onto the floor. This in turn compelled me to lay down right there and then on the stone floor. I was overcome with drowsiness and immediately a Druid voice and axiom was heard speaking inside my head. It was Taliesin's voice talking to me.

He said, "Peace is not the absence of conflict, but the ability to cope with it. He who submits, rules. To call forth the Elders of the Deep, we only need pass into sleep, resting both palms upon thy cheek."

I let go of the darkened Druid Egg, and immediately I went into a trance to work my magick. If my body was in need of rest in order to cope with this latest onslaught, so be it.

Instead, I would work from the dream realm. I would be able to see from there, the state of things- not as they appeared to the onlooker- but I would see how things were- in actuality. I gazed through the dimension and saw much differently.

I could now see that Morgan had *hooked* me when I felt the ripple of the curse begin with Gorlois's shades' touch. Her energy attack had thrown a bolt of hatred towards me, and had connected to me fastening on with a barb at the end of it. Her hatred found a crack in my defenses which had opened up with my momentary daydreaming of Nivienne. Morgan had found entrance enough to wedge within my shield to transfer the curse. There was now a direct line from Morgan's body to mine and it looked like an electric blue sparking transfer that I had seen from far off from the future. It was very real but not apparent to the naked, untrained eye.

My next thought was to bring Nivienne here to me. I called to her in my dream state and reached out with my arms to her. I saw her at home with the Mantle of Caswallan under her arm, embarking to leave Bardsey Isle. She said to me in my dream state: "My love! I am here. I will be with you in sooth, along with this cloak. I now understand what I am to do with this gift."

I relaxed and waited for her. There was not much I could do. So in my dream state I was liken unto a dead animal for the time being and rested. Morgan and Morgause were deep in their own troubles now, aging quickly while their bitter natures started turning on each other with malice, jealousy and an acrid nature of slurs towards one another.

Soon, thankfully, Nivienne magickally manifested with Caswallan's mantle drawn all round to hide her; the Queens saw no one attending me. To them, my body lay silent as the grave on the castle floor, seemingly dead to the world. Morgause and Morgan assumed that I was officially dead, and when that thought occurred to them they immediately started to congratulate themselves on the momentous event, each taking pride and ownership of the murder of Merlin.

How'ere, scorpions will be scorpions. There was now no revenge left to be had, nor to drive their lives. Indeed, they realized that life was now of the essence; for much of their life thus far had been spent in seeking the revenge so recently won with my 'slaying.' Now life was wide open before them, and, unfortunately, there was less time remaining of it than ever. It occurred to both of the Queens that one of them should wield the power over Britain and take up

Arthur's crown now with no heir nor regent in place.

This all I saw whilst in my dream trance that even as the women began to age before each other's eyes, they also realized that only ONE of them would be Queen. And it was every woman for herself.

It was well, for they were indeed fully distracted while Nivienne did an energy healing on me. She was a most adept Enchantress. She reached into my spirit and aura to detect the energy hook that had been secretly attached to my person. In looking at the tether between me and Morgan, Nivienne observed that it was a complicated, three-twined etheric cord. This would take a bit more time.

One part of the cord was a ribbon. This one was symbolic of our joint experience from Morgain's childhood from whence I had felt responsible for her and her sister.

The second was a jute twine which represented the family tie that connected us as cousins through Ygraine and Ambrosius.

The third was a heavy forged chain which represented the military service in which we were both raised as Nobility close to the throne. It was all connected to the hook that was –Arthur- he bound us to each other from his birth.

Nivienne then looked at me in the ether and asked my permission to disconnect this tri-woven arrangement and asked me if she had my permission to heal. I looked in her eyes and I nodded my solemn agreement.

Nivienne reached into my spirit with my permission and removed the hook from my soul. She cauterized it with holy fire and sealed it with the purest form of Love. She whispered to me, "I must get the Grail. You need to sip from it in order to be totally healed, my love. I must seek it out thither. Rest here. Stay subdued. HEAL. I shall return for thee."

She roamed in the shadows about the castle to seek the hiding place of the Grail, all the while Morgan and Morgause fought more and more heatedly. Thankfully, Morgan did not feel her prey escape from her hook when my soul was disconnected from her. She was being drawn into wrath moreso by her sister Morgause. Their arguing and hateful postering was rising in intensity like a dry brush fire. The air around us crackled and popped and grew in temperature.

Finally Morgause would bear no more bickering with her sister as she felt justified to be Queen of the land, as SHE was the first-born of Ygraine. She was consort to Arthur, (albeit a trick, but nevertheless, he had bed HER and not Morgan). Also she stated that SHE was mother of the heir to High Britain (e'en though he no longer existed within this realm), so she reasoned that it be SHE should have the throne.

T'was then that Morgause pulled a bodice dagger from her cleavage and plunged the sgian-dubh directly into her sister Morgan's velvet covered breast.

Morgan le Fay looked at her sister with a surprised look e'en whilst she crumpled to the ground but t'was not before one last emotional stabbing thrust given to her killer. Morgan spat, "Morgause, you raised *one* of your sons to greatness to have him murder his own father, so, ye shall see the same fate. Your sons by King Lot, your neglected boys are now men who hate thee for it. I promise them justice as well. They shall rise against thee, Morgause. They are coming now to finish what I cannot." And with these last words, Morgan le Fay summoned all her Powers to conjure one last spell and when its transmission was complete, Morgan le Fay was no more.

Morgause stood with the dripping blade and stared down at her sister and all was silent. The last living Queen then looked about the empty castle, complete with the bodies of her sister and her powerful cousin, Merlin, both laying lifeless around her. She alone was left standing.

"I will reign supreme! And no, my dear sister, I disagree with you on one point. My sons adore me. Aye, in sooth, I did favor one above the others. but now I am Queen and my sons will be my support and my long arms. They shall have to wait, how'ere, till I am dead before I let them have the crown! My sons, Gawain, Gareth, Agravain and Gaheris were more like their dim-witted father, King Lot, than inheriting my gift for strategy like Mordred did. Those boys were not the men that Mordred was, nor will they ever be. Poor Morgan…tsk, tsk, tsk. Proven false, once again. I do not believe that your power was ever stronger than MINE… my sister, you never did learn…"

Morgause then turned round and approached me. Her blade longed to stab my lifeless body one time for her own joy and to claim her power o'er me. How'ere, those last words that she had uttered would be her final say. For e'en as she came towards me, the next sound I heard, was of arrows whizzing through the court. They had been unleashed by a presence newly arrived in the doorway. Three arrows found their mark in Morgause's chest and when she fell, her bloody bodice dagger fell from her hand and skittered across the floor. Three armed men stood in the doorway and they relaxed their bows when she fell. All was again quiet in the room.

"A right and fitting mark for a backstabbing conniving bitch of a mother," said Gareth to his brothers, Agravain and Gaheris, who lowered their bows and nodded to each other in agreement. "We have avenged our father, King Lot. It took some time, but we have finally bested *thee,* dear Mother. Your days of discrediting us and favoring that bastard Mordred have now come to an end. At least these are worth the keeping." Gaheris muttered even as they each pulled their own arrows out of the slain Queen. "We shall inform Gawain at Camelot of these dealings" and then they returned their killing points back to their quiver. No more would they be passed o'er. The brothers said a prayer to the Gods and saluted their father and his memory.

When the sisters had ceased to breathe, the spell which kept the Grail hidden also dissolved and it was at this time that the Grail was revealed to Nivienne. She then revealed her presence to the men standing there. They bowed in surprise and reverence to her. She was as renowned for Good works as Morgause had been for Evil deeds.

Nivienne spoke kindly to them, "Sons of Lot! Ye have done a most courageous deed by dispatching this dark Enchantress who vexed thee and the Kingdom. I am sorry for the loss of your mother, but in sooth, she never was the mother that you needed or deserved. You are the true sons of the Kingdom. It is now imperative that we hie away and transport Merlin back to Camelot."

The men looked at my still form and said, "M'lady, he has passed to the OtherSide." She went on, "Nay, he is not murdered, but very ill indeed. Ye shall be rewarded well for your courage and your assistance in this matter. Prithee, let us go thither quickly so that I may fully remove this curse from him. Ye shall all be hailed as heroes! With your help, we shall bring the Holy Grail back to Britain's people!"

Nivienne held up the goblet on high for them to see, and all were amazed. The men knelt before the Grail and promised safe passage for us all. They were now committed to something for which they felt redeemed, and for which their dark mother and aunt had traded their lives. Because it was Samhain, Nivienne bade the men to honor the day and put the dead to rest. They built a pyre for their cold dead mother and aunt. The men had learned to hate these women over the course of their lives, but they did not want to displease Nivienne, the Enchantress. Nor did they wish to have the dead have any issues with the living to feel a need to come back to settle accounts.

So a final resting place was built. These women were Queens, and daughters of a King, and thusly they needed to be honored as such regardless of their chosen path of treachery. They, too, had suffered from their own choices and would no more walk the earth. As the building of the pyre commenced, the villagers of the town and the residents of the castle reappeared from their hiding places. For the last ten years, this realm had lived in seclusion and fear and as minimally as possible to not garner the wrath of Morgan nor her sister, Morgause. All the residents would now note their passing and celebrate this last right and be glad for their release, as if from a dungeon of doubt. They all came into the light of day and shouted and kissed and danced. Music was once more heard throughout the land, as well as laughter and the spirit of joy! The Grail would now return to Camelot.

We left Morgan's fortress, this time I was the one carried on a litter, my weight borne by Morgause's sons and Nivienne riding next to me. I could not walk, and I felt extremely old. Indeed, I was old, most verily, an ancient one still reeling from what was not purged from the curse. I was very weak, and my beard had turned white as snow and was now as long as I was tall.

I had aged greatly, but I yet lived.

As we left, we looked back at the pyre which the Sons of Lot had erected for their mother, Morgause and their Aunt Morgan le Fay.

On top of their bodies, Nivienne place the Druid Egg, which was now red with the objuration that had, in the end, been mirrored back and killed them with their own treachery. Their own curse was to be burned with them.

The torches were lit, black smoke and an acric stench filled the sky.

XII

When our company arrived at Camelot the people cheered to see us all return in victory over Morgause and Morgan le Fay and, amazingly enough, we were also holding the Holy Grail in our possession! The sons of Lot, Gareth, Agravain and Geheris were strong, sturdy noble warriors and they were readily welcomed to the Round Table as Protectors of the Realm. Their noble brother Gawain was there to hear the tale of his mother's treachery and demise whilst he reeled in the knowledge, he reveled in the relief of it as well.

The Knights of the Round Table had been in flux for quite some time as to how to proceed with leadership in the Kingdom. It was now up to them to decide how best to rule, to compromise, to choose, to lead. I was not their advisor any longer. Verily, I was alive but suffering with mine own issues.

Nivienne had the soldiers carry my litter to our former dwelling place hither at Camelot so that she would work her healing ways upon me. At this point, after my ordeal, I could barely stand. I was still feeling the effects of the curse. My fingers had spotted and gnarled with age, my legs were bent with crippling arthritis. My back was liken unto an ironwood tree bent by the winds of time. The clear vision of my youth had become blurred and dimmed with the advancement of the aging process. I could hear sounds, but only faintly so. Through all this swift aging sickness and crippling disease, my face had become weathered and worn, my beard and hair had grown long and white. Yet, my darling Nivienne never left my side, nor did her love dim towards me.

She helped me lie back on our plush embroidered bed covered with velvets and she tended to my ills. Once I was settled and relaxed, she revealed to me the goblet of Bran the Blessed, aye, the Holy Grail itself. In it she poured some wine. She held the vessel on high and asked the Powers of the Universe and all the Gods to work their magick upon me, their Servant of Good.

She was quiet for awhile as if being delivered unto some great wisdom. She then looked into my eyes and asked me, "Merlin, my love, what is your heart's desire?"

"That is the question all must ask of themselves, isn't it?" I pondered for a few moments and said, "As a Druid, I have always wished to be helpful to the Earth, and to deliver a means of authentic Spirituality and Hope to mankind. I continue to desire those things along now with my wish for health and vitality, but most importantly, my love, I wish for us to live in love for'ere, come what may."

She smiled at me kindly and said, "Drink from this cup and wish thy wishes with all thine heart and Spirit."

She helped me prop myself up enough to drink from this magick cup. I felt the wine warm my mouth and throat as I swallowed the enchanted liquid. At first, I felt a deep calm come over me. A feeling of Grace and Love filled my heart. Then physical feelings made themselves known to me. I did feel a great lessening measure of pain that had gripped my body. My joints started to feel limber again and they did not crack nor creak when I bent my elbows and knees and hands. My fading vision cleared, and I could see colors and images sharpening even as I gazed about the room. I easily pulled myself up into a sitting position and then I stood, strong and straight. I could now clearly hear the wind blowing outside and the words of a servant in the hallway outside speaking to the Steward!

It was the miracle of the Holy Grail indeed! My vim and vigor returned to me! My health was as if I was a young man again! My long white beard hair, how'ere, were still with me, as was my aged face and wrinkled body. A younger appearance did *not* return to me. My visage as an old man was still upon me, and I knew t'would always be so. For indeed, I had not asked for youth, only health. I *did* have the health of my younger days, how'ere, which was a great gift indeed!

I held Nivienne's hand and looked deeply into her eyes, and said, "I do thank thee for being my healer, companion and my love all these years. You have been sech a wonderful wife and mate to me. Now, I am so much older in appearance than thou art, I must ask thee a query. Prithee, be true to thyself in the answering of it. Couldst thou still love me, as I am now, thusly?"

Nivienne gazed at me, and her face softened with the answer. "Always. My heart has always been yours since the day I met you at the river. The stones told me you were my Hope and my new life. I joined my soul with you that day and for all days since we handfasted. So be it. I am Yours, as you are Mine, for'ere. You have sipped from the Grail and tasted everlasting life. People will remember you from this time forward. Your name will forever be in legends in years to come! You, too, are now Immortal."

Then she winked at me, and wickedly said with a grin, "In sooth, thou art now as old as thou art wise." We both did laugh and the relief of the laughter broke the spell of trauma, and we felt very blessed indeed. She kissed and held me close to her and, I knew that I would be a lover to her in all the ways of a man. Age be damned. Love lives on, no matter. So much had changed and yet, so much was as before. It was a great gift to be alive, present and still I had so much work yet to do.

When we had rested, loved and healed each other from our trying times, we emerged from our room. We were hailed by all the people there who marveled at this now aged old Wizard and his very much younger Enchantress. We stayed in Camelot for a time and helped those there who needed counseling, advice and healing. I gathered up our books and parchments and items that had served us here at Camelot, and we packed the Holy Grail in our safe keeping to go with us.

The following morning, we were saddling up our horses and mules when Nivienne said, "I have been summoned to Avalon and will be Lady of the Lake at Yuletime. We must hie away there, straightway. Merlin, I fear the time has come when I must take the Lady of the Lake's scepter. I do not want to leave you, yet, I will serve my time in honesty and in strength."

I too knew that the time had come. The dream I had the night before was indeed, prophetic, for in it was revealed to me, this very same news.

I took her in my arms and said, "My dearest, we shall travel this path together. Come what may."

We mounted our horses and rode for Avalon. We arrived to find Freya and Arthur waiting for us, along with the Mavens standing in honor as we dismounted.

Freya saluted us, "Welcome, Nivienne and Merlin! The time has come for the Lady of the Lake to change hands. Prithee, we bid you Peace." Freya and Nivienne withdrew to her chambers to discuss the roles and duties the new Lady of the Lake would be undertaking.

"Arthur, so good to see thee," said I as I hugged my long time friend and cousin, who hugged me steadfast and long right back.

He said, "Merlin, verily, I have missed thee! What news?" and we retired to speak of all that had transpired and been resolved hence. When I placed the blessed vessel in his hands, he wept. He was stunned and marveled at the Holy Grail now placed in his final care.

We stayed here for a time, catching up and making all in readiness for the transition in Avalon.

Before the ceremony was to take place, I met with Freya and Nivienne and offered them an idea that I had been contemplating this whole trip. I bade them sit down and to ponder with an open mind what I had to offer.

"My dear ladies thou art wise and just, and I would beg a boon of thee. I have served my whole life helping Britain and Mankind. I wish to continue to do so. Ever since I have drank from the Grail, I received a plan from the Universe. I wish to share it with thee at this time: Freya, you have also served your life for others. You deserve a time of rest and it is well that you have decided to do so. Nivienne will--as I have Seen the future--carry on the duties of Lady of the Lake for Thee in good stead. She will hold the Mavens and indeed all of Womankind and their Yin magick in her protective care, whilst humanity does travail through tumultuous times to come. There will be a heavy responsibility for her as humanity experiences its growing pangs of fear, hatred, distrust and war. Womankind will especially be attacked through the upcoming years of Inquisitions via the horrid Malleus

Maleficarum, which, unfortunately, is yet to come. This dire document will herald the degradations of women and the removal of her rights in favor of man becoming powerful over the earth. Nivienne will need all her Powers and Strength to guide women through this awful time to come. She will manifest inner strength within them and will offer them hope when there is none. She doth need to focus fully upon position and her duties. I understand the gravity of this position and why she, of all, was chosen for it. I am Immortal now, how'ere, as she will be when she accepts this scepter. My wish is to remain alert, learning, living and growing through the time that she is serving her purpose and her destiny hither. I would ask to be in contact with her, to give her my strength and knowledge that I learn along the way for her to use as she sees fit. The world will not be a safe place in some future years to come. Magickal people will not be honored for a time. So, I would ask to be securely and magickally sealed up safely into our abode on Bardsey Isle for the length and breadth of time that Nivienne serves as Lady of the Lake.

Whilst she is serving her term and until her replacement is found, I shall keep up with the times as the years proceed. I will remain the student of knowledge that I have always been, the Alchemist that strives for Enlightenment. If I must be apart from her then I shall live my life quietly acquiring the knowledge that man needs. I shall discover knowledge as man himself does, through all the years that lie ahead. I would only ask that before Nivienne starts her position as Lady of the Lake, that she travel home with me one last time to Bardsey Isle. I shall give her the Power with which to seal me within our abode. I shall wait for her thither until which time she has served her reign and has found the next perfect candidate who will replace her."

I went on, "Arthur is the perfect choice to be the Guardian of the Holy Grail here at Avalon until the world is ready for our joint return. May I have your permission and promise to do these things, as it is for the World's Greatest and Highest Good, in which I ask?"

Freya and Nivienne nodded in agreement, and Freya said,

"'T'is well, Merlin, Nivienne has told me that she can hardly bear to be apart from thee. I allow that she will connect with thee magickally whilst within your sabbatical time away from daily life. You will be able to see that which is outside of this magick spell. You will be able to feel the world's assets and liabilities. You will be able to grow with knowledge and machinery that is coming, for you will help the world in days to come by knowing its knowledge. You shall be safe within, and no one will find thee even if they dig for you. Our combined magick will conceal you for ages to come. When Nivienne has served her time and purpose and when women have come through the "trying time" and are starting to gain the social power which is theirs by rights, the next Lady of the

Lake will appear to take her place. Then Nivienne shall be released from her duties and promises here so that the new Lady can continue where she left off. The new Lady at that time, will bring her own gifts to the world. At the time of your completion of your promises, vows and enchantments, you will both be free to sail away on the Crystal Sea. Ye shall have a joining, adventurous, loving time as your due rewards, until man is ready to live without hatred, without borders and with each other and the Earth as One. So I have spoken." And a flash of energy went out in waves to seal her words into reality.

For this I was tremendously grateful and felt relieved. I was now willing to return to Bardsey with my darling, one last time before her transition.

It was at the time of Yule, when the Winter Solstice brings the Power of the darkest night to the shortest day, Freya transferred her title of Lady of the Lake to Nivienne. Freya was now able to go and to live a dream life of her own making having served her purpose. Health and Good Fortune were hers and she handed the scepter and garland of lights to Nivienne. The new Lady of the Lake drank from the Light and Power and took her vows to protect, nurture and keep the Divine Feminine safe.

Nivienne would serve well through the coming ages and Womankind would need her. She glowed her radiant aura that I first saw when I met her balancing stones in the river all those years ago. She had grown and her spirit shown with a luminous quality of the full moon luster. Celebrations and congratulations were given to both of these amazing women on this festival day of lights and plenty!

I stayed with Nivienne for her acceptance of duties and we celebrated as did all of Avalon. Yet with her new beginning, meant that my time had come now to leave.

I said farewell to Arthur for what would be ages to come, but I gave him the promise that he may rule again one day in unity for humanity's sake. He held the elusive Holy Grail in his hands and felt joy for the finding of it in his life. He was also honored with a promise that a tomb for he and Gwenivere would be placed and revered in Glastonbury for the world to remember them in the future.

Nivienne and I traveled one last time and arrived at our cave home dwelling at Bardsey Isle on the day of Imbolc. February 2nd which was my natal day as well.

We entered under the stone entrance she had made for Brigid so long ago. The stones were still balanced perfectly, yet unrealistically so. We made love to each other one last time in our bed, with tenderness, with hope, and our hearts and souls entwined with our shared Powers. The light was brilliant with the energy we manifested, and we were complete. We were Male and Female and we were One. Never had we felt so pure, so intensely connected and so hopeful for our futures. And all was as we envisioned, and all was as we made it to be. I went into my 'hibernation' on the historic day of my birth. Nivienne then called the stones above our entrance to lay themselves down upon my current dwelling, ever so carefully. If a bypasser were to look on, they would only see a mountain of rocks and not our home as before. People in the land would say that Nivienne, the Enchantress, Lady of the Lake, did spellbind me and bury me within it alive for'ere. They would not be far from the truth for the fact that she *did* use her Power, she *did* seal me up and I *am* buried underneath. It matters not what the uninformed may say, as their slanders will keep me safe for it. Let them think what they will, that this, my current resting place, is a-cursed.

As I gaze out my window of glass and see the world floating by--my heart, like my cave--is filled with light. All is dark outside, how'ere, it must be so, for now. The world needs to go through Dark Ages without us so that they may learn to seek the Light. I remember the vision from my youthful Spirit Quest when I saw the world pass me by, and I realize that my world now is how I saw it then. Surely this was always my destiny and I now revel in it. I am where I should be. All is in Divine Order.

In sooth, I now have finished my tale of what was and how I came to be hither, underground. I have not been damned, nor cursed, nor tricked. T'was mine own design to be set here and to wait for my Beloved. For now I shall live whilst watching what will be.

Mankind will create his events and I will learn and grow along with knowledge of man's creations. When he and his religions become less motivated by greed and more concerned with what is Good for all…Then, and only then, will be the time of our return. The Once and Future King, Arthur, my beloved Nivienne and I shall all return to be a part of this wondrous earth and all her glories. We shall help Mankind on to its next step up for the Greatest and Highest Good for all. Until that occurrence, I shall remain hither until Nivienne and I are reunited again.

At that time, we shall embark on our Quest to sail the wonders and joys of the Crystal Sea together. We will unite humankind with the knowledge of its own goodly magick powers; powers which have always been theirs to wield, but they believed it not. Then people shall learn to manifest Goodness and Kindness! They will keep the Earth and all its creatures in honor. They will worship the wonder of the Universe. The Old Ways shall become New Ways again. The circle shall be complete, and what an amazing adventure that shall be.

Faithfully submitted for your learning and your loving growth,

Prince Merlinus Ambrosius,
The Blessed Bairn of Beltane,
The Wild Man, Myrddin Wylit,
Or as most know me,
Merlin, Friend to All.

All One Under The Sun

by Ron VanNostrand   (an excerpt of his song)

The butcher, the baker, the candlestick maker,

doctor, lawyer, heroin taker,

Rich man, poor man, beggar man, thief,

farmer, soldier and Indian chief.

There's Jesus and Buddha, Krishna and Moses,

Mohammed, Confucius, Zoraster, Peacemaker,

Now wouldn't it be so fine,

if they were all in one big chorus line,

Arm in arm on Broadway in an extended run,

singin' when everything is said and done,

We should've been one, under the sun.

Because we're all one under the sun

And we're all born under the sun

Where we live each day in work and fun,

Til the day we pass on..... under the sun

We come in all different colors, notions and desires,

Sizes with surprises, all uniquely wired,

Beliefs and fears and ways to have fun

But undeniably, If you look, you'll see

We're all one under the sun.

Well you got two choices, sorrow or fun,

if I have to choose, I know which one.

So let's celebrate 'til the day is done,

'cause we're all one under the sun

Because we're all one under the sun

And we're all born under the sun

Where we live each day in work and fun,

Til the day we pass on..... under the sun

Afterword

When I was 14 years old, I stumbled upon the writings of Mary Stewart and her tales of Arthur and Merlin. So smitten was I with these works, that I immersed myself within the novels desperately craving to be in the stories! So much so, that after school I would go home, cast off my schoolbooks and caring not for telephone conversations with peers, instead I would crawl into the stories of Merlin. I even went so far as to have my afternoon snack of cheese cut into chunks and served in a wooden bowl and my "wine" (grape soda at my age) was poured into a goblet so that I could more fully enjoy the moment lost back in time. I am sure that my love for the Medieval and Renaissance Faires that I have performed in as a minstrel for nigh unto 20 years hence has came from this former time in my life. My nickname of "Merlyn" was given to me by friends, resulting from my love of Arthurian legend, and because frankly, I lived, breathed and exuded it to the point that I *became* it.

I found that in many of the former famous legends I studied and researched since those days, however, there were a few unsettling things to me. I felt that Merlin got the wrong end of the stick with the way his love life and ultimate end was portrayed. It felt so unfair to me that he worked so diligently helping everyone all his life, using his gifts, his connections, his Powers, only to get infatuated with some duplicitous conniving girl who ended up stealing from him and incarcerating him with his own magick!

Merlin's "crime" of using his imagination, talents, powers, gifts and influence, meant that he was puritanically doomed to be sealed up forever without a whimper and without his Powers. I have always hated the moralistic insinuations and endings on this story which seemed to imply the unsaid reasoning that, "If you do magick, you should be punished" sort of deal.

Well, that's not very fair, in my own opinion. Why should a person be punished for their helpful gifts? As a writer, I wanted to change it up for people's Greatest & Highest Good! I wanted to make right a terrible injustice!

I felt there was one other tragic flaw in this legend and that was one that I, as a female and advocate for women's rights, wanted to also make right. For in reading these wonderful stories, there was also a palpable tearing down of women as a whole throughout many tales. It was the culture and the way of the times then. Yet, in reading the Athurian Legends, it always felt to me that women, in general, usually got a bad portrayal.

For instance, Gwenivere is almost always portrayed as being nothing more than adulterous, daft, pretty "Queen," surely not aware of her position, repercussions, or political surroundings -sort of woman.

Contrast her character with that of other strong major female characters in Arthurian legend (Morgan le Fay, Morgause, Nimue, Lady of the Lake) who are always portrayed to be distant, (and sometimes interchangeable) with each their own self-serving agenda!

More often than not, these strong female characters were shown to be conniving, deceitful and selfish, or at the very least, unmotherly (God forbid).

Aye, there can be that element in life out there , found in women- as well as in men- and a bit of it is understandable …and… true.

How'ere, what I object to is the overall negative portrayal of females within these legends. It was not the actual picture of womanhood, for they were the comforters, the healers, the midwives. This is especially true when women were doing their level best- while being hunted down, demonized and then terrorized by such literature as the Malleus Maleficarum touted in history. I very much resented this part of the tales greatly for it. Women received a bad reputation and have been killed by it!

Well, what to do?

What could I do about it as a woman?

As a writer?

As far as Merlin goes, well, after all, let's face it…legend *IS* legend. Which simply means: that if the main points remain the same, some of the contrivances, details and circumstances can all change and yet the story can remain the same! It can go forward embellished with these wondrous new additional adventures. It is a folk tale and I am merely taking part in the oral tradition.

The man, Merlin, wasn't born "old." Yet most of the images conjured up by literary contrivance of the name "Merlin," always feature him as an elderly man. He was a child once (which is what I always loved about Mary Stewart's writings), and he had fun too (thank you T.H.White). There was also some real respect given to the Divine Feminine (Goddess Bless Marion Zimmer Bradley).

I felt compelled to join their wonderful ideas with some thoughts of my own, and add ideas given via new breakthroughs in religion, science, geology and literature that are coming forth now. You will see as you proceed with my story, that I will "give a nod" to these great writers and some other stories you may recognize. This is my humble attempt at gratitude and respect for all that they gave to me. For "imitation is the greatest form of flattery."

I needed and wanted to continue "bringing forward" the legends to those not familiar with it.

So now I present to you my "Merlin for Today and the Future." He is here to give us HOPE. We need to protect the Earth! We need the Divine Feminine to be noted and revered in the hearts of mankind! Like Maiden, Mother and Crone, She will link us together with love and nurturance and get us to care and to stop our divisive warring! Women don't need to posture for position. We need to honor what we already have.

For the main female role, I made a new character for Merlin's love interest with Nivienne. She is part Vivienne, Nimue, Niniane, and Lady of the Lake (who are all named at points throughout different legends as sometimes the same character!).

Yet my Nivienne is a lady with heart and soul and a true love for Merlin. If true Soul Mates exist – this is what they look and feel like in my world.

Merlin is a magickal, outgoing, open

minded, time traveling kind of guy and he deserves a smart, magickal babe who is awesome in her own right! She comes with her stand-alone gifts, virtues and backbone. It's the whole God/Goddess, Enchanter/Enchantress, Yin/Yang, Male/Female completeness concept. Hey, I like my Deities, Heroes and Heroines to embody both male and female strengths. It seems right to me. Complete.

For those of you out there that are historically pure in your literature out there, I offer you this disclaimer:

Yes, I know that I have mingled up time frames. Yes, I know that this isn't "historically correct" with language of an era and with the matching documented historical facts. Yes, I know I presented some Pre-Roman conquest with courtly Renaissance feelies, language and culture.

But let me ask you, do you *really* want to read Beowulf in its original form now with its original language? Or do you want to enjoy the legend for its story, now in terms familiar? I mean, do you *really* want to go back to the Renaissance times now without the gifts of antibiotics and flush toilets? Probably not. So please, suspend your disbelief! Just enjoy it all for what it is. Historical Fantasy Entertainment.

The same goes for the swirling up of

many religions and cultures here in my legend.

Yes, I know I've muddied up the waters and included other legends, philosophies and factoids from other timeframes, cultures and beliefs. *That's the point, dude!* I want us all to get along. Stop freaking out about the differences, and let's start celebrating the unity and commonalities!

As a dear friend of mine, Ron VanNostrand, likes to sing, "We are All One under the Sun."

Maybe it's time we started learning from other religions, cultures and folktales and start behaving like the awesome folks we *can* be, and leave our bloody, prejudiced past behind us! Even though we may all be of different beliefs and culturues, surely there are things within each that are complementary and kindred! Let's find those things we have in common and link up and build a great world together and find out how we can learn from each other! This is way better than decimating what we don't understand, carpet bombing antiquity into dust and killing whole populations because one side doesn't pray the same way as the other side. The whole Earth and all the creatures suffer for it! We lose much more than just a way of praying when we destroy.

We may lose our very human existence!

So, I now present to you, my dear Merlin-Freaks and Fans, the weavings of many Merlin tales together in this tapestry fable-fabric of mine.

I offer to you, a kinder, wiser, more inclusive and lusty Merlin! He is a man of Power, intellect, open mind and loyalty. For all his efforts and for the worlds' benefit, I also give him *(finally!)* his "Eve," in the spirit of Nivienne, whom he very much connects with.

She is a woman of the New Age, with nurturance, guidance and good old fashioned kitchen witchery, yet with her own personal Power and a libido all her own. You go, girlfriend!

And finally, Merlin gets an ending that I can live with! My soul is at rest now with this story!

My wish for you and for this book is to have conjured some original ideas and to connect them with the many legends already existing. There are so many stories out there concerning this same, single, enigma of an archetypical character named Merlin. Yet, I want his story to make sense for you, NOW.

Why? Because we very much need a Merlin in our world; someone who is kind, wise and flexible enough to guide us to our own hearts, back to Nature , who needs us to be Good

Stewards of this Earth. We need role models and leaders that we can trust to not screw us over. So much media out there these days wants us to believe in charlatans who profess grand things but with ulterior motives.

I believe that Merlin's motives are for our Greater Good as well as for his own. This is how I project goodness to you, and want us all to be! So, Slainte' and three Cheers! Here's to Merlin and Nivienne! We beg Thee to come hither soon! We await you and all the positive, healthy and grand times to come! Show us how to build a world in tune with Nature and human Beings! You are just what we need to find and be within our own selves! We shall try to be like you, until you get here!

So, my dear reader, until then…go fetch thyself some cheese, fruit and nuts, place them thusly into a wooden trencher to feast upon! Pour thyself a goblet of aged wine (or grape soda, if ye prefer) and drink hither to thy fill!

Prithee, please spread this word to your friends on the towpath and get them read it.

Start a wondrous ripple for the Greatest & Highest Good for ALL of us.

Magically Yours,

Merlyn Fuller

Acknowledgements

My most sincere thanks go out to:

Dharma Lefevre – Thank you for agreeing to be the talented illustrator in this book! She, like me, *is* a serious Merlin-freak, so it was bliss to participate with her on this project! I wanted a "hot" Merlin and I gave her some parameters and she took them, absorbed them and rocked him. I drooled when I saw his visage. He is perfect as he should be. You rocked the art within and without!

Russ Tarby--Thank you for being a patient copy editor who slogged through reams of habitual comma errors, run on sentences, and my liberal use and heavy leaning on the vernacular. You help me write books. With your style, grace, and an accurate "red pen," your simple scrawled words on my manuscript, "Keep on writing, Mer!" has always push me forward when I was tired and didn't want to continue.

Susan Wolstenholm- What a wonderful help you have been! Thank you for your input on wordage, grammar and story line! You helped to make this a better read! You ROCK! Your support means the world to me.

Linda Nestor- Thank you for your friendship, help, writing prompts, compliments and for your technical assistance on getting this all configured into book form! Couldn't do it without you! Great job on formatting the genealogy! Awesome!

Debbie Cleveland- Thank you for helping us capture the artwork of Dharma's artwork for the cover in all its gilded glory! You are a great photographer! If you need a great photographer email her at: **wabisabiarts.us**

Ron Wilbur-Thank you for helping me format all the high resolution photos, illstrations and the cover. I need computer wizards in my life.

Valerie Chism, Heidi Nightengale, Sean Polen and Thank you for being Guest Readers of my preliminary work. Your support and feedback was good to have. Writing can be a solitary experience. It was less lonely to have company here aboard this journey with you here to keep me company.

Ron VanNostrand- Your music and friendship and outward thinking has always inspired me, as has your song "We are All One Under the Sun." Thank you for doing all you do.

Bill Berry, Jr- thanks for kicking this book off

with a sneak peek by pre-publishing a preview in your online publication! Surf to:

www.aaduna.org to read Volume 6, No.1!

To my husband, Wayne- Thank you for your daily patience while I write, rewrite and edit far into the night and for listening to my many tales over and over again. Thank you also for your input on the glossary term offerings .

And last but not least~

I thank you, my dearie-darling reader, for your open mind and your support. I hope you enjoyed the tales. If you did, please be so kind to tell your friends nice things about this book, have them read it. Maybe it will help open many other minds too. This is how good ripples start. Let's change the world for the better!

Glossary

Akashic Records-" In theosophy and anthroposophy, the Akashic records (a term coined in the late 19th century from *akasha* or *ākāśa*, the Sanskrit word for "sky", "space", "luminous", or "aether") are a compendium of thoughts, events, and emotions believed by theosophists to be encoded in a non-physical plane of existence known as the astral plane. There are anecdotal accounts but no scientific evidence for existence of the Akashic records." Edgar Cayce and many other psychics have used these records through trance to give healings to others.

Alexandria Library- "One of the largest and most significant libraries of the ancient world. It was dedicated to the Muses, the nine goddesses of the arts. It flourished under the patronage of the Ptolemaic dynasty and functioned as a major center of scholarship from its construction in the 3rd century BCE until the Roman conquest of Egypt in 30 BCE, with collections of works, lecture halls, meeting rooms, and gardens. The library was part of a larger research institution called the Musaeum of Alexandria, where many of the most famous thinkers of the ancient world studied. The library is famous for having been burned down, resulting in the loss of many scrolls and books; its destruction has become a symbol for the loss of cultural knowledge."

Anglesey- "island NW Wales."

Amulet- "a small object worn to protect the person wearing it against bad things (illness, bad luck, etc.)"

Avalon- "a paradise to which Arthur is carried after his death."

Bedlamite- "madman, lunatic."

Belladonna-"a poisonous plant of the nightshade family that has reddish bell-shaped flowers. A drug is made from it. Sometimes the berries were called "murderer's berries, sorcerer's berries and even devil's berries." They are thought to be the poison that caused Juliet to appear dead in Shakespeare's "Romeo & Juliet."

Beltane- "the Celtic May Day festival."

Brigid- "was a goddess of pre-Christian Ireland. She appears in Irish mythology as a member of the Tuatha Dé Danann. Saint Brigid shares many of the goddess's attributes and her feast day was originally a pagan festival (Imbolc) marking the beginning of spring. It has thus been argued that the saint is a Christianization of the goddess."

Cairns- "a heap of stones set up as a landmark, monument, tombstone, etc."

Candlemas Day- "February 2 observed as a church festival in commemoration of the presentation of Christ in the temple and the purification of the Virgin Mary."

Cast a circle- A magic circle is a circle (or sphere, field) of space marked out by practitioners of many branches of ritual magic, which they generally believe will contain energy and form a sacred space, or will provide them a form of magical protection, or both. It may be marked physically, drawn in salt or chalk, for example, or merely visualized. Its spiritual significance is similar to that of mandala in some Eastern religions."

Datura- "and herb of the nightshade family sued in folk rites or illicitly for its poisonous, narcotic or hallucinogenic properties.

Divining Rods- "also called a dowsing rod. A stick that is used to detect water."

Deosil-"Used by Wiccans/Pagans to describe a clockwise motion."

Diurnal-"daily cycle related to the sun."

Evil Eye- "an eye or glance held capable of inflicting harm; *also*: a person believed to have such an eye or glance."

Freya's Day- "The English name Friday is derived from Old English and literally means "day of Frigg", the Norse goddess of fertility and love, who is often perceived as the same deity as Freya."

Gibbous-*"of the moon or a planet*: seen with more than half but not all of the apparent disk illuminated."

Gossamer- "a very light or delicate material."

Hausfrau- "housewife"

Imbolc- "February 2nd. A Gaelic festival marking the beginning of spring."

Malleus Maleficarum- "(commonly rendered into English as "Hammer of [the] Witches"; is a treatise on the prosecution of witches, written in 1486 by Heinrich Kramer, a German Catholic clergyman." It made very real the threat of one being branded a heretic, *simply by virtue of one's questioning of the existence of witches* and, thus, the validity of the Inquisition. It set into the general Christian consciousness, for all time, a belief in the existence of witches as a real and valid threat to the Christian world. It must be noted that during the Inquisition, few, if any, real, verifiable, witches were ever discovered or tried. Often the very accusation was enough to see one branded a witch, tried by the Inquisitors' Court, and burned alive at the stake. Estimates of the death toll during the Inquisition worldwide range from 600,000 to as high as 9,000,000 (over its 250 year long course); either is a chilling number when one realizes that nearly all of the accused were women, and consisted primarily of outcasts and other suspicious persons. (Old women, Midwives, Jews, Poets, Gypsies, anyone who did not fit within the contemporary view of pious *Christians* were suspect, and easily branded "Witch".) Usually to devastating effect. It must also be noted that the crime of Witchcraft was not the only crime of which one could be accused during the Inquisition. By merely questioning any part of Catholic belief, one could be branded a heretic.

Magickal- "In Wicca and certain other belief systems, action or effort undertaken to effect personal transformation or external change." Distinguishes the difference between "sleight of hand magic tricks" with that of spiritual or emotional transformation.

Maidenhead-"the quality or state of being a maiden: virginity."

Mandrake- a Mediterranean herb of the nightshade family with large ovate leaves, greenish-yellow or purple flowers and a large usually forked rook resembling human form and formerly credited with magical properties. The root of a mandrake formerly was used to promote conception, as a cathartic or as a narcotic."

Maven- "one who is experienced or knowledgeable."

May Day- "May 1 celebrated in many countries as a spring festival and in some countries as a holiday in honor of working people."

Night Terrors- "a sudden awakening in dazed terror that occurs in children during slow-wave sleep, is often preceded by a sudden shrill cry uttered in sleep, and is not remembered when the child awakes."

Novitiate- "the time when a person is a religious novice. A beginner who will begin training in a religious or spiritual pursuit."

Objuration- "a binding or charging by or as if by oath."

Pendulum-"one of the simplest and easiest forms of divination. It is a crystal or a stone suspended by a length of string, chain or wire. Used best with "yes", "no" questions."

Per Contra-"On the contrary. However."

Runes-"rune stones are used as tools of divination- a way to predict one's future. A small alphabet of symbols each had a name that hinted at the philosophical and magical significance of its visual form and sound for which it stands. From the Norse culture."

Sabbat-"any of eight neo-pagan religious festivals commemorating phases of the changing seasons."

Salmon of Knowledge- "Irish mythology and recounts the tale that nine hazelnuts fell into the Well of Wisdom. The first person to eat of its flesh would in turn gain this knowledge. In Welsh mythology, the story of how the poet Taliesin received his wisdom follows this pattern."

Samhain- "Samhain is a festival of the Dead. Meaning "Summer's End" and pronounced *saah-win*. Samhain is a celebration of the end of the harvest and the start of the coldest half of the year."

Sgian-dubh- (pronounced "Skeen-DO") "a small, single-edged knife (Gaelic *sgian*) worn as part of traditional Scottish Highland dress along with the kilt. Originally used for eating and preparing fruit, meat, and cutting bread and cheese – as well as serving for other more general day-to-day uses such as cutting material and protection."

Sidhe-"Sidhe is pronounced "Shee". Its origin is Celtic and it means "Faerie" or "Fairy."

Skyclad- being unclothed and naked under the sky.

So Mote It Be-"equivalent to "Amen," "So Be It" or "The Truth has been spoken" and "As God wills it to be." Used by modern Wiccans as well as Masons and Freemasons."

Somnolent-"tired, inclined to or heavy with sleep."

Tussie Mussie- "a quaint, endearing term from the early 1400s for small, round bouquets of herbs and flowers with symbolic meanings."

Widdershins-"anticlockwise."

Pronunciations

Ambrosisus- "am-BRO-zee-us"

Anglesey- "Angle-sea"

Aurelius- "uh-REAL-ee-us"

Castle Coch- "Cast-EL k-O-(back guttural sound)"

Freya- "Fray-yah"

Gorlois- "Gor-LOY"

Nivienne- "Niv-EE-an"

Taliesin- "Tally-ESS-in" or "Tally-YES-in"

Uther- "oo-THUR"

Any other Gaelic or Celtic name or term I've noted in this book not mentioned on this list...well, your guess is as good as guess as mine.

Works Cited

Ashe, Geoffrey. "Geoffrey of Monmouth." *The New Arthurian Encyclopedia.* Ed. by Norris J. Lacy. New York: Garland Pub., 1996.

Griscom, Acton and Robert Ellis Jones. *The Historia Regum Britanniae of Geoffrey of Monmouth.* New York: Longmans, Green and Co., 1929.

Malory, Sir Thomas. (2000) *Le Morte D'Arthur.* London, England: Cassell & Co.

Tennyson, Lord Alfred. (1983) *Idylls of the King.* London, England: Penguin Books.

The Book of Taliesin VIII from The Four Ancient Books of Wales.

Websites searched:

http://www.ancient-origins.net/myths-legends-europe/legendary-origins-merlin-magician-002627

http://www.timelessmyths.com/arthurian/merlin.html

http://www.maryjones.us/jce/night.html

http://www.timetravel-britain.com/articles/stones/stonehenge1.shtml

http://www.earlybritishkingdoms.com/bios/ector.html

http://medieval.stormthecastle.com/essays/a-typical-day-in-a-medieval-castle.htm

http://paranormal.lovetoknow.com/Aura_Colors_and_Their_Meaning

http://www.angelfire.com/sc/majick/axioms.html

http://druidnetwork.org/what-is-druidry/beliefs-and-definitions/articles/common-practice-and-beliefs-within-druidry/

http://www.nairaland.com/1238665/patron-saints-christendom-pagan-saints

http://www.summitpost.org/pumlumon-fawr/339694   Lewys Glyn Cothi (c. 1420 - 1490)

http://philipcoppens.com/anglesey.html

http://www.mythiccrossroads.com/13.htm

http://www.spellsandmagic.com/protection.html

http://www.readakashicrecords.com/articles/edgar-cayce-akashic-records.html

http://people.opposingviews.com/catholic-saints-pagan-gods-3012.html

http://www.nairaland.com/1238665/patron-saints-christendom-pagan-saints

http://www.badnewsaboutchristianity.com/bd0_ideas.htm

Dictionary References Noted

www.dictionary.com

http://www.merriam-webster.com/

www.urbandictionary.com

http://www.healthline.com/health/belladonna-dark-past#3

http://www.motherearthliving.com/garden-projects/tussie-mussie.aspx

http://www.timeanddate.com/calendar/days/friday.html

https://en.wikipedia.org/wiki/Magic_circle

https://en.wikipedia.org/wiki/Imbolc

http://paganwiccan.about.com/od/divination/qt/Pendulum.htm

https://en.wikipedia.org/wiki/Salmon_of_Knowledge

http://norse-mythology.org/runes/

http://www.britannica.com/topic/Library-of-Alexandria

http://www.bibliotecapleyades.net/cienciareal/cienciareal12.htm

About the Artist

Dharma Lefevre is a southwest Florida based Fine artist that participates in Festivals street art, murals, and commissioned pieces.

Her background in art inspiration is Mythology, Art Noveaux , Impressionism and Surrealism, Live Street Art and Fantasy.

Dharma is self taught, besides a few art classes when she was younger. She is always doing art, sketching, referencing, looking at others art to keep herself transforming, motivated and terribly inspired.

She is available for Commissions in watercolor and acrylics, gallery, show or exhibition. Dharma is also a dancer and fire performer!

If you are interested in a fine artist or Live painter, please contact her:

jennatlefevre@gmail.com

https://www.etsy.com/shop/RaveTheSaneforest

About the Author

Merlyn Fuller is a Central New York writer, musician and seeker of wisdom and knowledge.

She has been writing since she found pencils; along the way she stumbled onto pens and then keyboards and hasn't stopped since.

Merlyn wants to document life, love, fantasy, spirituality, and make a difference for good in this world. It has been said that as a writer, she is a cross between Erma Bombeck and Flannery O' Connor. She says, "Thank you for the compliment," but she feels her writing is 'somewhere in between Beatrix Potter and Janis Joplin!'

You never know what she will expound upon, blog or pen, but there is always some new twist that emerges: entertaining, funny, profound, frightening or spiritual!

Her memoir *Fairy Tales & Horror Stories* was nominated for the Central New York Book Awards right out of the gate and it was her first book. Her stories come from real life experiences and happenings. Merlyn's fantasy tales are from her intricate imagination which is still brewing in her fantasy mind. Her poetry comes from her Bardic spirit and all are blended with a Crone's experience and a Healer's touch.

She is a Minister in the Universal Life Church and a Unitarian Universalist who runs lay services at several churches.

Merlyn is also a professional musician in the 20 year duo "Merry Mischief" with her mate "Harry." Together they perform in many venues from Renaissance faires, schools, churches, libraries and festivals throughout the eastern seaboard from NYS to FL.

You can find out more about her at their website: www.MerryMischief.net.

**"Introduction: The Blessed Bairn of Beltane"
was initially published**

www.aaduna.org

aaduna Volume 6, No. 1

Other books by Merlyn Fuller:

"Fairy Tales & Horror Stories"

CDs featuring the music of Merlyn together with her husband, Wayne "Harry" Fuller in the duo of Merry Mischief are:

<u>Kismet</u>
<u>Cakes & Ale</u>
<u>Panacea</u>
<u>Evening on the Erie</u>
<u>Lusty Ditties</u>
<u>Just Love Songs</u>
<u>Scallywags</u>
<u>Up Close & Personal</u>
<u>Heroes and Rogues</u>
<u>Christmas Presence</u>
<u>Kids at Heart</u>

All these products are available at:
<u>www.MerryMischief.net</u>

Made in the USA
Charleston, SC
21 August 2016